The 🌿 Lady of Situations

Also by Louis Auchincloss

The Lady of Situations

Louis Auchincloss

Houghton Mifflin Company ⨍ Boston

1990

Library of Congress Cataloging-in-Publication Data

Auchincloss, Louis.
The lady of situations / Louis Auchincloss.
p.   cm.
ISBN 0–395–54411–4
I. Title.
PS3501.U25L34   1990
813'.54 — dc20   89–26883
                                    CIP

Printed in the United States of America

WAK 10 9 8 7 6 5 4 3 2 1

Here is Belladonna, the Lady of the Rocks,
The lady of situations.

T. S. Eliot, "The Waste Land"

Part One

1 1 1 1 1

Ruth's Memoir · · ·

MOST OF my contemporaries, those of seventy summers or more, would find me absurdly oversimplifying the situation in dating the origin of my niece Natica's troubles to the day her family decamped from the large florid red-brick Georgian mansion in Smithport, Long Island, which my brother-in-law Harry had so rashly built in a palmy year before 1929, to the modest superintendent's cottage huddled at its gate. Harry did not, it was true, have to open and close the iron portals for the new owners, the DeVoes, when their big green Cadillac and the smaller sports cars of their offspring whizzed in and out, but he had to pay a rent that, alas, in four more years he found himself unable to afford and was obliged to move my sister, his two sons and Natica to a simple white clapboard house in the village where, to the eye of all but their oldest friends, they began the rapid and ineluctable process of merging with the "natives" and losing their identity with the summer and commuting colonies.

To young people today, however, in these troubled 1960s, the artificial class distinctions of that earlier time will be only too readily accepted as the origin of every kind of spiritual woe. I like to think that I can steer a balanced course between their generation and my own, having led the unprejudiced life of a spinster school teacher, and I can perfectly concede that if Natica suffered from the virus of snobbishness and social aspiration, her two brothers were seemingly immune to both, so that background cannot be the sole factor unless it affects the sexes differently. At any rate, for all her shortcomings Natica is the one whom I have always most dearly loved.

My most vivid picture of my niece, though I have known her at all ages up to her present one of nearly fifty, is at fourteen. I was then living in Manhattan and teaching English at Miss Clinton's Classes to upper school girls, one of whom, a singularly gifted student, Mary DeVoe, was the eldest daughter of the family who had bought my brother-in-law's house in Smithport. Shortly before her graduation Mary very kindly asked her parents to invite me down for a weekend there. When I told my hostess at Saturday lunch that I would be visiting the gatehouse that afternoon and explained why, she immediately called down the table to Mary:

"Darling, did you know that Miss Felton was Mrs. Chauncey's sister? What a small world it is! And of course that makes her an aunt of that pretty little Natica. Edith," she continued, now addressing Mary's younger sister, "why don't you go down with Miss Felton after lunch and ask Natica to your party tonight? Or better still, telephone her. No, come to think of it, I'll call Mrs. Chauncey myself. Oh, what a happy idea!"

When my eyes took in Edith's long, pouting countenance, I knew that it wasn't a happy idea at all. Edith, though fourteen and just Natica's age, had obviously no wish to add her to her little party. But Mrs. DeVoe, a large woman, a sort of a Roman matron, though somehow a touch messy, perhaps because of her uncontrolled if magnificent auburn hair, was not one to allow a child to stand in the way of a plan.

"What tosh!" she exclaimed to Edith's protest that Natica would make an extra girl at her evenly balanced table. "You talk like a dowager of sixty. This is a *children's* party, for goodness' sake. Why should Natica Chauncey sit home all evening because of your silly ideas?"

I knew quite enough about girls to envision the kind of cruelty of which the frustrated Edith would be capable once her mother's broad back was turned, but there was nothing I could do. A natural force had been unleashed that would have to spend itself.

What happened that night it still pains me to recall. Poor Natica spent the whole afternoon getting ready for the party. She borrowed the long gold-mesh clinging dress of the diminutive mother of a friend of hers in the village (without the mother's permission) and put on powder and lipstick in the car when her father, who drove her up the hill to the party, wasn't looking. Actually, Harry never looked at anything but a fish or a fish hook. It had been arranged that the DeVoes and Mary and I should have our dinner in the library, but we were to remain in the parlor with Edith and her young guests until they went into the dining room. I was therefore a reluctant witness to my niece's rather stagey entrance.

She was certainly pretty enough. She had lovely pale skin, an adorable little turned-up nose and smooth brown lustrous hair. She was too thin, it is true, at that time, but she moved with astonishing grace and maturity. Her great feature, however, was her eyes. They were large and brown and seemed to envelop you in a worried and at times quizzical look. It was quizzical, anyway, that evening. She took in the room to find out if by any remote stroke of luck she had succeeded in pleasing. It did not take her long to see she had not. Even Mrs. DeVoe's too hearty greeting: "Well, if you're not a perfect stunner!" lacked conviction and seemed almost a reproach to the girl's simperingly articulated: "It's such a privilege to be here, Mrs. DeVoe" and the extension of her hand with fingers tapering downward.

Had there been some boys present of even seventeen years of age she might have been a hit. But the callow youths at that gathering took their lead from the girls, who, all in short dresses, not only scorned Natica's attempt to seem older and more sophisticated than she obviously was, but unerringly spotted the cheap quality of the gown she had borrowed. She received the coldest of stares, the briefest of nods, and when the group disappeared into the dining room I had a horrid fantasy that I should soon be hearing, as in the second act of *Tosca,* the cries from the offstage torture chamber.

There were in fact no such demonstrations, but the DeVoes'

butler, who had been placed in charge of the youthful feast, came in to interrupt our card table repast in the library to inform me gravely that "Miss Chauncey" was ill and had gone upstairs. I hurried to the indicated guest chamber and heard from behind the locked bathroom door the sounds of the unfortunate child's vomiting. I called in to assure her that I was there and then waited for some twenty minutes after the sounds had ceased for her to emerge. She buried herself at once in my outstretched arms.

"Oh, Aunt Ruth, I'm a disgrace! To Mummie and Daddy, to you, to everyone. I can't go downstairs. I wish I were dead!"

"My poor darling, you mustn't take it so hard. We all have to go through these things. You were the prettiest girl in the party and by far the brightest. Oh, I know they don't know that now, but they will. Mark your old aunt's words. They will!"

She refused to return to the party, nor did I seek to persuade her. When she seemed to have pulled herself together, I called my brother-in-law to drive up the hill to fetch her. We waited in the guest room until we heard the sound of his wheels on the driveway below and then descended to the hall where we found Mrs. DeVoe waiting for us. Natica was splendid. At the landing she drew herself up and extended an arm to her hostess in farewell. She might have been eighteen or more.

"Good night, dear Mrs. DeVoe. It's been a lovely evening, and I do so appreciate your asking me."

I was almost sorry that her hostess, kind and big-hearted though she was, mitigated the dignity of the scene by throwing her arms around the girl's neck and exclaiming: "Oh, my poor child, you don't have to say that."

✒ ✒ ✒

On Sunday morning I walked down to the gatehouse to have a talk with my sister. Natica was still in bed; she had been excused from going to church, for which event her mother was rather pointedly dressed and ready.

"I think the less said about last night the better, Ruth."

"I haven't come to talk about last night."

My elder sister and I were both plain women, but I used to flatter myself that I had converted my plainness to the austere dignity that befits a school teacher by keeping my body lean, my hair neat and my dress simple. Kitty on the other hand seemed to exult in her roundness and bustling manner. Her hair, like Mrs. DeVoe's, was untidy, but if the latter had probably forgotten to go to her hairdresser, Kitty's abstinence was intentional, the result of a theory that permanents spoiled her "natural sheen." Smug, I regret to say, was the word that evokes my sister. She would tell you that a "really nice" person could get away with almost anything. It never crossed her mind, for example, that other "nice people" would even notice what she was up to in economizing when she tore off the picture pages of last year's Christmas cards, scribbled her own Yuletide greeting on their back and mailed them out for the current season, some no doubt to the original senders.

"I'm afraid, Kitty, that I'm still of the opinion that Natica should go to a private school."

"But you know we can't afford it! Why must we go into all that again? A private school wouldn't have prevented what happened last night."

"I'm sure I could get her a partial scholarship at Miss Clinton's," I persisted. "And I'd make up the balance. I still have a bond or two I could sell."

"And how would you propose to get her in and out of the city?"

"She could stay in my place. There's a day bed in the study."

"It's very kind of you, I'm sure, but Harry and I are not yet ready for charity. Besides, difficult as it may be for a teacher at the exalted Miss Clinton's Classes to realize, Smithport High is one of the finest schools in the state."

"I don't dispute that. My reasons are not educational. They're psychological. Children shouldn't be wrenched too violently from a background they may have come to regard as their natural heritage."

"And who is wrenching Natica from her background? I thought we were talking about schools."

"A school today just about is that."

"And anyway, her brothers seem perfectly happy in public school."

"They're boys. The world was made for them."

But here I had made a mistake. Kitty could now cross me off as a nutty female rights buff. Wasn't I to her a sour old maid who hadn't been able to catch a man? And mightn't I even want to make the same of Natica? She rose and straightened her dress. "Well, I'm off to church. I assume you're too advanced for anything like that. I'm afraid there are a number of matters over which you and I must agree to disagree. But there is one thing you seem to forget."

"And that is?"

"That Natica, after all, is a Chauncey. I hate to sound as snobbish as you've been sounding, but let's face it. Her grandmother wouldn't have received half the parents of the girls at Miss Clinton's Classes today. We may have had our trials, but we have faced them with our heads high. I think my children have been inspired by the example of their father's courage and endurance."

With this she strode off, leaving me, as she no doubt conceived, with the image of her husband as a man who had sacrificed his inherited fortune in some gallant losing cause rather than to his idiotically held stock market theories. But I was only too sadly sure that the bright eyes of my all-observing niece had long seen through her father with his foolish faith in his own quaint concept of economics and his more valid one of the techniques of fly-fishing. It was needless to say that she had also seen through her mother's brave theories to the actualities that lay so close behind.

1 ...

Natica's nostalgia, as she approached the end of her high school years, was more for the gatehouse of Amberley, which her family had had to give up in favor of the plainer little cottage in the Village of Smithport, than for the stately residence the gatehouse had guarded. She remembered, of course, her family's proud occupation of the latter and the still earlier time when even this mansion had been merely the summer alternative to the wide brownstone in Manhattan. But the little red gatehouse, square and flat-roofed, the first stage of her family's social descent, and actually attached to one of the stone pillars which supported the grilled portals of the entrance to the long blue driveway, had yet a squat, uncompromising and memorable dignity of its own. If it belonged to a lower order than the big house up the hill, whose handsome façade could be glimpsed through the stripped trees in winter, it was still an integral part of the special world whose visitors it announced and whose trespassers it barred. And it obviously fitted in better with the Victorian fiction in which Natica reveled than did the village with its Elks Club and Masonic Lodge and the corner drugstore where her classmates were prone to gather.

She made no apologies to herself for her preoccupation with the world of Thackeray and Trollope. She privately (for she had

learned not to air such opinions) considered herself the only cultivated member of a family who never read at all, unless one counted,
as she decidedly did not, her father's fishing periodicals or her
mother's mysteries. Her two younger brothers, Leroy and Fred,
stolid and unimaginative, though not unattractive in a briefly youthful, muscular way, were concerned with sports and mechanics and
rarely looked beyond the athletic fields and laboratory of Smithport
High. But as Aunt Ruth said of them, on one of the Saturdays that
she spent with her in the city, they were happily classless, essentially American, and might even look forward to recovering some
part of the Chauncey fortune as engineers.

Natica was too much of a realist to identify with the aristocrats
of the fiction in which she immersed herself. She chose instead the
humble but dauntless governesses of the Brontë sisters whose patient merit was always rewarded in the end. No one, not even Aunt
Ruth, could understand the value of her fantasies, for no one could
dare to hope, as she did, that they might prove the raw material for
the creative genius of a Natica Chauncey who would one day make
use of both Amberley and Smithport in a great novel, which would
exist long after the mansion, gatehouse and village cottage had
crumbled into deserved dust. Had not Flaubert exclaimed: "Madame Bovary, c'est moi"? Might not Natica Chauncey make a simi-
lar claim?

Aunt Ruth tried to interest her in the fiction of living writers:
Virginia Woolf, Willa Cather, Ellen Glasgow. "There ought to be
more relation between the world you live in and the one you read
about," she warned her.

"Oh, but I find all kinds of relations. Even family ones. Take
The Mill on the Floss, for example, that I'm reading now."

"You see yourself, no doubt, in Maggie Tulliver."

"Somewhat, perhaps. But I see more Mummie in Mrs. Tulliver.
'Healthy, fair, plump and dull-witted.' Don't you love it? With her
milk of human kindness turning the least bit sour?"

Aunt Ruth frowned. "Your mother has had her trials, my child.
And she has never lacked courage to face them. You should always
remember how much she loves you."

II

"Should I be grateful for that? Then she should be grateful to me. For I love *her*."

"I hope you do, Natica."

"That's all we care about today, isn't it? People seem terrified of not loving or being loved. Even Saint Paul isn't allowed to speak of charity anymore. It has to be love. If they'd only change the fifth commandment the same way, I might be able to obey it."

"You mean you don't honor your parents?"

"How can I, Aunt Ruth? You know they're perfect fools."

"Natica! I can't let you talk to me that way."

"Then what's the use of our talking? The moment we touch on a serious topic you get cold feet."

It was only another proof, if proof were needed, that there was no true communication. But should an artist, a true artist, need it? Natica could enjoy casual, gossiping, even giggling friendships with girls in her class at school because of their very unimportance to her. If every now and then one of them resented her failure to convert such an attachment into intimacy, whose was the loss? Her parents and brothers usually accepted her undemonstrative conformity to their plans and habits as an appropriate family response, but this was not always the case. There were some sharp fallings out. If Natica felt her "secret garden" intruded on, if her mother interfered with her constant reading in favor of outdoor exercise, if one of her brothers tried to peek at what she was so furiously scribbling, if her father sought an hour of her valuable time to teach her his stock market theories, her passive resistance could erupt in bursts of appalling temper.

"Cat!" a brother would mutter, while her father gladly quit the room and her mother broke into a useless crying fit.

There was only one serious threat: boys. These were less easily disposed of. Natica found herself all too readily and strongly attracted to male classmates of the athletic type, and as early as sixteen she was known as a "hot neck." But as she never went further, scratching and biting if need be to ward off aggressors, and as such tactics soon tired her boy friends, she never became seriously involved. Also, her basic boredom with the kind of male who most aroused her helped her soon enough to regain her detachment. But what most contributed to her oft threatened but fiercely cherished emotional independence was her sense of the general expectation, encompassing not only her classmates but her family, that sooner or later Natica Chauncey, for all her intellectual airs and "fancy pants" notions of her proper niche in the universe, would yield to the basic female need of a brawny male to knock the silly ideas out of her snooty head and turn her into a clucking wife and mother. It sometimes seemed to her that the gray slatey sky over what seemed to her the eternal autumn of Smithport contracted in a vulgar damp wink at the inevitability of sexual intercourse and the futility of a girl's settling for anything else.

Her parents seemed to sink, with a slow, an almost contented acceptance, into what she deemed the turbid ooze of their village life, seeing some of their older friends, when the latter chose to remember them, but gradually coming to social terms with the more prominent of the tradesmen whom they had once called "locals" or "natives." Harry Chauncey had aroused his daughter's futile resentment by keeping his less expensive individual, as opposed to family, membership in the Smithport Beach and Sailing Club, so that he could use its fishing camp in the Catskills, with the result that his children had no privileges. It was this, more than anything else, that convinced Natica that anything done for her socially would have to be done by herself, that her parents, well meaning but ignorant, had simply no conception of the things they had deprived her of.

She made a point now of being at home whenever one of the old "summer" friends called, in the hope that she might be asked to a party for one of their children, and this sometimes happened, although she usually found herself sitting silently and awkwardly by her hostess while the latter's daughter and a clique of friends, excluding her with the ruthlessness of youth, chattered on about their own affairs. At home in the evenings, when she had finished her school work, and her brothers were at friends' houses or bowling, and her mother was listening to one of her idiotic radio programs, she would draw her father out about his past and the careers of long-dead distinguished Chaunceys. Harry, an utterly unsnobbish man, hardly even aware of the hierarchical classifications so definite to his daughter, had little interest in family history as such, but he liked to tell what to him were affectionate and funny stories about dear old aunts and uncles and grandparents, and as these were of a deadly dullness to his wife and sons, he much appreciated Natica's flattering interest. She would carefully note the rare detail that slipped into an anecdote, unbeknownst to its teller, to betray the social status of the characters: the casual reference to a coachman, or even once to a footman; the use of a proper name ("As old Mrs. Astor used to put it"); the changing of the *mise en scene* to Bar Harbor or Newport.

In the summer before her senior year at high school, however, an opportunity came to Natica for a more extended visit behind the barrier guarded by the gatehouse at Amberley. Mr. DeVoe was to be kept in town all summer by a business crisis, and his loyal wife, refusing to go without him to their seaside villa in Maine, chose, to the disgust of her daughter Edith, to pass the "dead season" of July and August in Smithport, to which her husband could comfortably commute. And Aunt Ruth, Edith's English teacher at Miss Clinton's Classes in the city, had a project for her pupil's use of this slack time which she imparted sarcastically to Natica.

"The future is always full of surprises. Who would have thought that a girl like Edith DeVoe would ever want to soil the golden glory of her approaching debutante year with anything as sordid as college? Yet such is the case. Vassar and Smith have become the 'thing.' Or perhaps some 'radical' beau of Edith's has accused her of being a kind of a social dinosaur. At any rate the poor girl has seen the light and has asked me about her qualifications. I've told her she'd better start filling in her educational gaps if she wants to get into a decent college, even a year from now. She says she'll have nothing to do all summer, and I hinted that I had a clever niece in Smithport who might fill the bill as an English tutor. How about it, Natica? It should pay well for very little work. She asked if you were the girl who used to live in the gatehouse, and I told her you were also the girl who used to live in the big house."

Natica knew better than to allow her eyes to express the spurt of her sudden joy. Even Aunt Ruth, she had learned, could be dishearteningly puritanical where "joys" were concerned.

"Well, I suppose I can try. Though remembering Edith, I doubt we'll get through *Adam Bede* before Labor Day."

Natica was very nervous on the day she bicycled up the blue drive to Amberley, but she found Mrs. DeVoe friendly and Edith tolerant, and she soon settled into an easy routine of morning lessons and family lunch. Edith had matured into a tall, dark, handsome girl with a sometimes attractive indolence of manner and a never attractive conceit. She had read almost nothing and had no use for any of the arts except as necessary preliminaries to the now fashionable world of college. But she was pleasantly pleased with her new tutor's way of abbreviating her tasks. Natica neatly summarized the plots of the novels that Edith was supposed to read and never suggested that there was anything of real importance to be gained by a study of literature. In her desire to make a friend of her pupil she even went so far as to imply that Edith needed only to add to her natural embellishments by absorbing a few capsules of classics, which might be expected, by some process of painless digestion, to make a minor contribution to the sprightliness of her social conversation.

Edith's regular companions being largely abroad or in New England, Natica had little difficulty in making herself indispensable. She knew better than to talk about herself or her own affairs and demonstrated an insatiable appetite for details of Edith's boy friends, Edith's dresses and Edith's anticipated social triumphs. In one respect she was lucky enough to be particularly helpful, for it turned out that Edith's special beau, Roy Somers, though a son of the richest resident of Smithport, was something of a rebel.

"Roy doesn't think like other people," Edith complained. "Everyone knows that Roosevelt's a horror and a traitor to his class, but he refuses to see it. He makes Daddy furious by touting the New Deal."

Natica was able to educate Edith in a few of the fundamentals of what the Roosevelt administration was trying to accomplish, so that her pupil could impress the radical Roy.

Her success with Edith's brother was even greater. Grant DeVoe was two years older than his sister, but her equal academically, as he had been dropped a form at Averhill School in Massachusetts and was, like her, now facing his senior year (or, as it was known at Averhill, his sixth form). He too felt the ennui of a Smithport summer, and his conversation was full of the visits he would make, if invited, to more socially active summer communities on the New England coast. He was pleasant looking rather than handsome, with a round, cheerful, rather thoughtless face and large brown eyes that seemed to promise a better temper and a more affectionate disposition than he had, and his dark curly hair and small tight figure, usually wrapped in bright blazers, completed this impression of amiability. Natica saw that, as with Edith, his interest in her sprang entirely from the summer vacuum. But it was also an interest that could be worked.

She met Grant at first only at the family luncheons where she was careful to make a not too pointed note of smiling at his jokes. His immediate appreciation of this revealed the man who was quite accustomed to taking a second, even a third, place among his peers. Soon he was directing his smarter remarks in her direction, and at last he invited her to go sailing with him. It was a hot and almost windless afternoon and the small boat required a minimum of handling. Grant was free to talk uninterruptedly about himself: how difficult it was to be the only boy in a family of four girls; how much his father preferred his older sister, Mary, to him; how constantly and articulately disappointed both his parents were at everything he did and didn't do.

"They think I should be more like Daddy," he complained. "Daddy was senior monitor at Averhill and I'm not even a house prefect. Daddy was Phi Beta Kappa and Bones at Yale. Daddy's the great banker . . . Well, you see, there's no end of it."

They were in the middle of the little bay now, and Natica, looking back, could make out one of the gables of Amberley, high on the hill. For a moment her yearning for such a home and such a father was so acute as to be actually painful.

"Your old man's a tycoon, of course. He can't help that. And everyone respects and admires him. But perhaps being a tycoon isn't the only thing in the world. Your father has to pay for his success with the awe that surrounds him. He can't expect to be popular and easy the way you are."

"Oh, do you really find me that?"

"Well, aren't you?"

She let him kiss her, but then drew firmly back.

"What's wrong? Do I offend?"

"Not at all," she replied in a definite tone. "But I don't think I want to get involved with you."

"Even a wee bit? Even for a summer afternoon?"

"Not even that. Because, if you must know, you're just a wee bit too attractive."

And she proceeded to show that she meant it by sitting farther away and continuing the conversation pleasantly but on more neutral grounds. It was thus that she intended to show him that, however much attracted she might be by his charm, she had no idea of constituting any sort of a social threat. It was not difficult; he did *not* attract her.

He was evidently pleased, for in the ensuing days he did not renew his amatory gesture. He continued to devote his attention to her at family meals, and he took her sailing once again, but it seemed enough now to be able to tell her of his troubles, to joke with her, and sometimes, at the family board, to wink across the table in recognition of their special link. Perhaps he was relieved not to have to do more. Perhaps it was less challenging to be a god on a pedestal.

"You seem to have made a convert of my brother," Edith drawled one morning at their lesson. "I've never seen him take such trouble to be agreeable. If he keeps this up, he may become almost endurable."

But then came a lunch when Edith's mother nearly rang down the curtain on the little drama of Natica's fantasy of living with the rich. She did not mean to. She had a generous nature, but

Natica was always aware that it was limited by the lazy impatience of a woman habituated over a lifetime to the devotion of family and the servility of staff.

Edith, as was her wont, had been talking of the approaching revelry of her debutante year, now only ten months away (she would "come out" in June), and her mother made no effort to conceal her impatience.

"I thought one of the advantages we might hope to derive from your going to college was that it would put a stop to all this silly talk. You won't have time for more than a handful of dances, will you?"

"Of course I will. All the best parties are now given in the summer or on weekends. People realize how many of us will be in college, so they make better use of the holidays. It's not like your day, Ma, when a girl had nothing to do but dress up and dance."

"Dress up and dance! I like that! The year I came out I had to take both German and Italian lessons and practice at the piano an hour a day. And your grandfather used to drill me in the evening to see what I'd learned. I didn't have a smart little Natica Chauncey to drill things into my thick head."

It always made Natica nervous when Mrs. DeVoe used her as a weapon against her daughter. She knew who could only be the loser. But Mrs. DeVoe now gained momentum.

"I wonder, Edith, if you and your friends have any conception of how many people on relief could live on what your father will have to pay for your coming out party."

"Now, Ma, don't try to persuade us you're a socialist."

"Well, maybe we need a bit of socialism where debutante parties are concerned! I think it would be a very good idea if every debutante was required to share her party with another girl who couldn't afford one." Mrs. DeVoe's eye now fell on Natica and at once lit up. "Exactly! Take Natica here. By all rights she should have a party of her own. If the depression hadn't so hit her family, she would be having a lovely one, I'm sure. And that tells me just what

I'm going to do. Our invitations will read: 'In honor of Miss Edith DeVoe *and* Miss Natica Chauncey.' There! I think that's a splendid idea. What do you say, Natica, my dear?"

Natica hardly needed to take in the glaze of Edith's dark eyes to understand how odious was the idea of sharing her glory with anyone, let alone a girl who went to high school in Smithport and knew none of her friends.

"Oh, Mrs. DeVoe, if that isn't the sweetest, kindest thing I've ever heard! And I can't imagine a greater honor than sharing the least part of Edith's ball. But my aunt Ruth Felton has set her heart on giving me a little party in the city, and I'm afraid she might feel her thunder sadly stolen if I accepted your kind offer."

"Well I'm sure that does you great credit, my dear. And no doubt you know best what your aunt must feel. Please give her all my best wishes when you next see her. I have no doubt she will give you a lovely party. And I hope she will ask Edith to it."

The invented excuse was accepted, and Natica almost smiled at Edith's transparent relief. But the danger was not yet over. Edith, in a sudden desire to make up to the humble tutor for the ball that the latter's welcome sense of propriety had induced her to decline, turned to her brother.

"Why don't you ask Natica up to Averhill in my place for the Halloween party? I know you only asked me because Daddy suggested it. But I've decided I don't want to go as a brother's guest. It looks as if no one else would ask me."

Grant's stare at his sister hardly expressed gratitude for her suggestion, but Natica spared him the embarrassment of an ungracious answer.

"I think Grant should be free to make his own choice," she insisted, smiling. "And anyway, my parents don't like me to go away for weekends during school term."

That might have been the end of it except for the fact that Grant, on his return to Averhill in September, happened to ask the senior prefect, Leverett Chauncey, if he was by any chance related to his sister's summer tutor. He was informed that they were indeed second cousins.

"Lev says he's never met you and would love to," Grant wrote to Natica in an epistle imbued with a new respect. "He's got a girl named Jessie Ives coming up for Halloween, and he suggested, if I asked you, that the four of us might have a table together at the dinner dance. How about it? Do you think your parents would make an exception? Tell them my mother says she's coming up for that weekend and will take you in the car and deliver you safely home Sunday night."

Mrs. DeVoe did more than that. She telephoned to Natica's mother, who made no objection to this infringement of a supposed domestic rule, and then asked if there would be any obstacle to her making Natica the present of a new evening dress. Mrs. Chauncey agreed to this as well. Turning to her daughter after the call she said:

"I don't know why people say that Madeleine DeVoe gives herself airs. She seems to me just as nice and dear as she can be. And arrogant? Why, she's as simple as an old shoe!"

Natica smiled to herself. The world was not so hard to put together. Certainly Grant DeVoe was as obvious as his sister. She had already learned about Leverett Chauncey from Aunt Ruth, who gleaned much from the girls at Miss Clinton's. He was not only the senior prefect at Averhill; he was one of the cleverest and most popular boys in the school, and the principal heir to his maternal grandfather's oil fortune.

2 ....

Natica would have many occasions to alter her first impressions of Averhill School, but she would never altogether lose her sense of the bright idealism in which she had initially chosen to see it bathed. On that clear October day it had struck her as a vision of rosy red brick and gleaming white columns around a broad green campus, with here and there a stately elm, and presided over by a serene gray Gothic chapel which seemed to bring a domesticated medievalism into harmony with a restrained transcendentalism. Natica had read about the school and about New England; she had heard Aunt Ruth, who had some prejudice about boys' schools, describe Averhill as "a mixture of Emerson and Wall Street, sugared over with a glossy sermon by Phillips Brooks." But she had not been prepared for the red and yellow glory of the countryside beyond the school gates, for the rich smell of varnish in the polished corridors and classrooms, for the unexpected Palladian splendor of the gymnasium, for the hurrying, laughing, jostling boys, so seemingly scrubbed and clean for the festivities, yet so muscular, so agile, so noisily good-natured. And when Grant, on their initial tour of the grounds, took her into the chapel and showed her the great Daniel French statue of a wounded doughboy, a memorial to the war dead, she murmured to herself the lines:

This is the chapel; here my son,
Your father thought the thoughts of youth
And heard the words that one by one
The touch of life has turned to truth.

Not that she thought that Grant had such dreams. But surely there had been, or were now, those who did. Or if not, anyway, this was the place for them. There was no such place for Natica Chauncey.

For the moment the sadness of this reflection, tempered with the silver sweetness of a conscious self-pity, was not unpleasant.

The weekend proved a good deal easier than she had anticipated. She and Jessie Ives, chaperoned by Mrs. DeVoe, stayed at a small white inn, owned by the school and used for visiting parents. Grant's mother, as the wife of a prominent graduate and trustee, was received by all from the headmaster down with a demonstrative warmth and respect. Jessie Ives, small, tritely pretty and rather aggressively blond, with an air of faint malice in her pale tan eyes and slight snub nose, was adequately polite to Natica, who had heard all about her from Edith. Her father had also been ruined in the crash, but her mother had faced that plight very differently from Kitty Chauncey. Mrs. Ives, haggardly but stylishly thin, and always elegant in the last year's dresses of her rich friends, supported her family by giving bridge lessons to, and playing the game for high stakes with, the donors of her wardrobe. She clung passionately to every link with her old world, fiercely determined that Jessie should "get it all back." And indeed the girl showed every aptitude and inclination to do just that.

Natica sighed to think how cheerfully she would have labored in that vineyard had her own mother adopted the course. She wondered if she could not read, behind Jessie's thin cordiality, the distrust of another girl in the same boat. Her wonder became assurance the moment Lev Chauncey showed an interest in her. Was this common creature from a mere high school, Jessie's instant glare demanded, trying to elbow into *her* territory?

It was not that Lev's interest was more than cousinly, even second cousinly. He showed a genial concern in getting to know "this long-hidden blossom" of his family tree. He was a restless squirrel of a young man, with bright blue eyes and black hair, who dominated his schoolmates by his cheerful, strong-willed vigor and an irresistible good will. It had been a feat for one so diminutive to be elected to so high a school office, and Natica guessed that Jessie's principal attraction was that she, too, was small.

Lev was good to his promise to Grant that they would constitute a foursome, and Natica's escort was obviously pleased that his guest was proving (as he had no doubt planned) a wedge into the senior prefect's more intimate circle.

At the dinner dance in the big hall of the gymnasium, whose Palladian elegance had been garishly disguised with pumpkins, lanterns and streamers, Lev and Grant and their girls sat at a table with two other couples. Lev introduced the topic of careers for women. He favored them.

"The women in my family have more brains than the men," he observed. "And I'm sure that Natica here is no exception. What about the DeVoes, Grant? Doesn't Edith have more bean than you? Not that that's saying much."

"I doubt Edith has much bean," Grant retorted. "But that shouldn't hold her back, should it? When my sister wants something, she wants it with a terrible force. It's awesome to watch Edith wanting something."

"Is that the way to get things?" Jessie asked. "I thought it was important to hide your wants."

"If you can. But Edith couldn't possibly hide hers. You'd see them sticking out under her dress."

"But does Edith want a career?" Lev inquired.

"Edith wants whatever the going thing is. She picks the box office with the longest line. And then claws her way to the front of it."

Natica reflected that sibling rivalry had made Grant almost intelligent.

Lev turned to Jessie. "How about you, Jess?"

"I might like to do some designing. Or decorating. I think I may have a bit of a flare for that. But my family would always come first."

Natica noted the conventional qualification, designed, no doubt, to improve her grade in the matrimonial market.

"And you, Natica?"

Natica resolved suddenly to sparkle. Or try to, anyway. It had to be worth a gamble. When would the chance come again?

"Oh, I want a career! By all manner of means a career."

Her tone caused a slight stir of interest around the table.

"What kind of a career?" one of the men asked.

"Oh, the very squarest, the least feminine. One where I'd wear mannish suits and be taken very seriously indeed."

Jessie squinted at her as if trying to divine her game.

"Would you wear those awful three-cornered black hats, like Madame Secretary of Labor?"

"Or even something uglier!" Natica clasped her hands in affected enthusiasm. "I adore Madame Perkins's hats. I adore everything about Madame Perkins!"

"But surely a woman can have a career and still be attractive and well dressed," one of the girls observed.

"No, no," Natica protested. "The men would associate her with dolls and put her in a little house to be played with. A butterfly that wants to be esteemed by moths must shed its bright colors."

"So we men are moths, is that it?" Lev demanded.

"Well, look around this hall. All those gray and dark blue suits. But the girls are like the lilies of the field, quite unsuited for toiling or spinning. Even my humble gown would hardly be the uniform for the floor of the Exchange or for Grant's father's bank." She glanced at Grant, who had been watching her apprehensively, and saw that the reference was mollifying.

"Then I take it," Lev pursued, "that you've liberated yourself from the onerous labor of having to attract the moths. You can all ravage the linen closet together."

"Is that how you see Wall Street? No doubt you know. But yes, I suppose, a girl must make a choice. An ambitious girl, that is. She can marry her way up or work her way up. Of course, it might come to the same thing."

The four men at the table laughed; the girls did not. Natica's sharp ear took in Jessie's murmured remark to her neighbor: "They say there's a lot of feminist agitation in the public schools. At Foxcroft we learn to be ladies before we're men."

"You wouldn't want a family and children?" another girl asked Natica.

"Well, when I consider the brand of joy I've brought to my own darling mama, I wonder if I might spare myself that."

"Haven't plenty of wives and mothers become famous?" Lev put to her.

"Of course! But don't they owe at least their start to wedlock? Not the movie stars, of course. That's another dimension. But who would have heard of Eleanor Roosevelt if she hadn't made effective use of her feminine charms to catch the wandering eye of our president?"

Both sexes at the table indulged in crude guffaws. It was a stoutly Republican group.

"It's rather shaming, really," Natica mused. "Fortunately not many charms are needed."

"Fortunately? Aren't you downgrading your sex?"

"No, yours."

"*Touché!*"

With Lev's exclamation the conversation changed, but Natica felt suddenly elated. She had had her moment in the spotlight, and she felt she had brought it off. Dancing with Grant between the courses, she wondered if she didn't love everyone in the great chamber except Jessie Ives.

"Could we go outside a moment?" she asked him. "It's such a lovely warm evening. Oh, I know we're not supposed to leave the party alone, but others are sure to follow."

He led her, albeit reluctantly, to a door which opened on a wide terrace used for gymnastics in the spring. It was empty and they strolled about. Natica's spirits were so high that she felt she had to do something to give them expression.

"You know what I'd really like? I hardly ever smoke, but I'd love a puff. You don't have a cigarette, do you?"

"Of course not!" He was shocked. "It's absolutely *verboten*. Dr. Lockwood told us that if any of our girls just *had* to smoke, she could do so in his study. But of course he was being sarcastic."

She laughed. "It would be fun to test him. Shall we try?"

"Natica! Are you crazy tonight?"

"Well then, you can give me a kiss instead."

He drew back. "There's not supposed to be any smooching either. Certainly not at the party. It's a strict rule."

"I don't want to smooch. Ugh! What a disgusting idea. I want just one kiss. A chaste one, planted lightly on my lips. Come, sir. A gentleman can't refuse a lady that."

He glanced nervously about and then gave her just what she asked, no more. But she wanted no more, and she would have been quite satisfied had not fate intervened.

"Ooops!" came a voice from the doorway. "Let's not go out there. I thought we were at Averhill. But it seems we've stumbled into Smithport High."

Jessie Ives turned around in the doorway and pushed Lev back to the dance floor.

"It'll be all over the place now," Grant said sourly. "She'll tell everyone we've been necking in the bushes. Let's go in."

"Necking in the bushes! When I've had one tiny kiss! And when I *think* what we've spied going on in corners and behind stairways this weekend!"

"That wasn't the party," he said stubbornly.

It was the end of her exhilaration; there would be no more of that now. She felt only disgust with the whole visit and with herself for having accepted Grant's invitation in the first place. On the dance floor he was sullenly silent, hoping that someone would cut in, but not sanguine about it. She looked up to see his mother sitting on the balcony with the other chaperones. Mrs. DeVoe waived to her gaily.

"I'm going up to sit with your mother for a bit. You can dance with some of these lovelies. But be sure they don't lure you out on the terrace!"

Mrs. DeVoe remonstrated volubly at the idea of Natica's leaving the dance floor to talk with "an old woman like me," but when Natica insisted, she was happy to tell her how she had been employing her time on the balcony.

"I'm keeping count of the number of times the more popular girls are cut in on. Of course, my dear, you're subjecting yourself to a severe handicap by being up here."

"Oh me. I wouldn't have a chance anyway." She marveled at this manifestation of Mrs. DeVoe's relentless competitiveness and wondered if it mightn't explain some things about Edith and even Grant. "I don't know anybody but Grant and Lev."

"Pish! A pretty face and a good figure are what they're after. Oh, look!" Her eye had not left the dance floor. "The Sargent girl has been cut in on again. I wonder what she's got that's so alluring."

"Mrs. DeVoe?"

"Yes, dear?" The brown, oddly noble face under the high crown of loosely gathered auburn hair, too noble, really, for her present occupation, perhaps for any of her occupations, was turned now to Natica.

"I want you to know how deeply I appreciate all your kindness to me."

"Don't be a goose. It's been my pleasure. And now you should go down to that dance floor and wow all those nice young men."

Mrs. DeVoe turned resolutely back to her game, and Natica was left to sit silently by her side. She was overcome with a sense of dry desolation. She wanted to love and be loved by Mrs. DeVoe. She wanted to throw her arms around her, to hug and be hugged. But that could never be. If the older woman should catch even a glimpse of how passionately she coveted all the things that Mrs. DeVoe, having them, could afford to regard as the mere externals, the mere decorating externals, of the essentially good inner life, she would turn her back with scorn on her as a climber, a schemer, a sinister watcher from the dark street of the lighted festival within.

Gazing down at the agitation of a rumba on the floor below, Natica knew with an ache in her heart that her trouble was that she saw herself just as she was and at the same time saw the different image that she managed at times to create in the eyes of others. She saw herself as doomed to wear a mask, and were not masks in the end almost invariably detected? Life's trophies went to the self-deceived or to those who were capable of deceiving with relish. Armed with a fatuous complacency or a fuzzy emotionalism, she might make her way into the society that so dazzled her imagination without in any way impressing her intellect. But the girl who saw her own story unfolding chapters ahead of where she was placed in it was headed for an unhappy ending. Why? Because she saw the ending, and, seeing it, had already composed it.

What could she do but write? Ah, yes! She clung to the old salvation, pressed it to herself. Hadn't Jessie Ives in her spitefulness offered her a character for a story as good as the snooty Blanche Ingram, who had made life so miserable for Jane Eyre?

Grant unexpectedly appeared behind her. Was she ready to go back to the floor? Of course, he could hardly abandon the girl he had invited and who had been brought up to school by his mother.

"I'll be keeping score," Mrs. DeVoe said cheerfully.

It turned out that Natica had enough partners not too much to disappoint the scorekeeper. The senior prefect had passed the word that his cousin was to be looked after.

✟ ✟ ✟

But the next day, before her departure with Mrs. DeVoe, she had a ritual which she had promised herself during her largely sleepless night to perform. She had slipped a cigarette out of Mrs. DeVoe's purse in the Parents' House, and after lunch, holding it between her fingers, she asked Grant to show her where the

headmaster's study was. He glanced in horror at the cigarette and
demanded what the hell she thought she was going to do.

"I'm not asking you to take me there. I'm asking you where
it is."

He refused point-blank to have anything to do with her insane
project, so she left him, and having been informed by a small boy
on the campus that the headmaster's study was in the vast red-
brick cube of a residence that formed the end of the largest school
building, she made her way there. She was ushered by a maid
into a dark room in the center of which Dr. Lockwood was reading
a book at a table desk under a green lamp. Of course, she had seen
him when he greeted the Halloween guests, but she had not been
close, and now she made out the curious red stare in the rocky
square face that looked up to the doorway. He was about to rise
from his desk when she said:

"Is it all right, sir, if I smoke in here?"

He sat back at once in his chair, waving her to a seat opposite
him. Without uttering a word he resumed his reading.

Natica, puffing at her weed, gazing at the long tiers and rows
of framed photographs on the walls — of teams and crews, of stalwart athletes expressionlessly holding oars or bats or footballs, of
suited figures in chairs clasping copies of the school paper or maga-
zine, of classes arrayed on steps after commencement, of gathered
faculty, all male — felt like Kipling's jungle boy who had come,
hidden, to see the mystery of the elephants' dance. When she crept
away silently at last and cast a furtive glance back at her companion, it was to note that he remained as motionless as a Buddha.

3 ✦ ✦ ✦

NATICA HAD so prepared herself for the letdown that would inevitably follow her Halloween weekend that she found it not too hard to cope with. Besides, she was busy preparing for college entrance examinations in the spring, for Aunt Ruth had arranged for a partial scholarship at Barnard if she got in, and she was to live the following winter in her aunt's apartment. So liberation, at least from home and Smithport, was in sight. Edith DeVoe was at school in the city, and Grant, after one perfunctory letter, had ceased to write, so she had no further relations with the family at Amberley, even on weekends, when they presumably were there. No doubt it was just as well. She had evidently served her purpose in giving Grant an access to the senior prefect's crowd, and the cigarette episode with the headmaster had no doubt scared him away for good.

There was, however, to be one more meeting with him. Kitty Chauncey, seemingly assured of pleasing her daughter, announced one evening in the Christmas vacation:

"I saw your friend, Grant DeVoe, in the drugstore this morning. The family are here for the holidays. I asked him for Sunday lunch."

"And he's coming?" Natica asked with unconcealed dismay.

"Of course he's coming. Why shouldn't he come? Do you think he's too grand to sit at our humble board? I thought I had to do something about him, seeing that he asked you up to his school and his mother paid for your trip and a new evening dress. Really, Natica, one never knows how to please you."

Natica could picture the little scene at the drugstore. She knew how persistent her mother could be and what a poor actor Grant was. He would have stammered out a lame excuse which she would have promptly punctured, and he would have been left with no alternative but to accept.

It was all quite as awkward as she had anticipated. Grant arrived so late that they repaired at once to the dining room. This, at least, was the best room in the house. The Duncan Phyfe chairs, rare surviving Chauncey heirlooms, with their simple but vaguely offended dignity, like marquises in a Jacobin prison, distracted some attention from the dreary backyard and the frame houses beyond and from the flapping pantry door through which the black cook, hired for the day and not even in uniform, slammed in and out with the dishes. And on the sideboard, raised on a stand, was a fine George III silver platter which her father had refused to sell because the coat of arms of its original owner, an English earl, was supported by two large fish. But nothing could make up for the way her father used a toothpick behind his napkin. As a host in his former glory at Amberley this might have passed for an "old New York" eccentricity, an amusing reminder of high life in the 1840s, but in their cottage it was simply vulgar. And would her mother never cease with her odious comparisons?

"I know you're used to better things up the hill, Grant, and I'm sure it's very good of you to take potluck with us. We're not as fancy as we used to be, but I don't think we do too badly, either. Some people like to talk of the good old days before the depression, but do you know something? I'm not sure they were all so very good. What I've learned about human decency and good, old-fashioned simple kindness since we moved into this village I couldn't begin to tell you. When you come here just for the summer or weekends you don't get to know the real Smithporters. And they're great people, they really are!"

"I don't doubt it, Mrs. Chauncey."

"One of the reasons I'm glad that Natica has gone to public school here is that she'll feel more at home with many of the girls at Barnard when she goes there next fall. But I suppose in Harvard you'll find so many men from schools like Averhill and Groton and Saint Paul's that it won't matter."

"What won't matter, Mrs. Chauncey?" Grant asked in some bewilderment.

"Why, that you've not been to public school! Have you never thought that it sets you apart just a bit?"

"Isn't that what it's supposed to do? If you're already in heaven, how can you improve yourself?"

But there was no point trying to joke with Kitty. She took immediate umbrage. "Well, I still maintain — and I shall continue to do so no matter what all the smart young gentlemen may say — that there's no such great advantage in setting yourself above your fellow men."

Harry Chauncey at this point started one of his endless fishing stories, which was almost worse. Natica decided that the only way to endure the meal was to try to see it as a scene in a play and store it in her literary memory for some kind of future use. Watching poor bored Grant out of the corner of an eye she assessed him with dispassion. It was plain to her now that even possessed of the charm of a Marlene Dietrich, she could never really attract him. In him snobbishness was a virus so virulent as to cause something like panic at the prospect of being trapped even temporarily in a milieu not acceptable to the arbiters of his tiny world. Where had he caught it? His parents were persons of stalwart independence; his background fairly bristled with security. But the way he never looked at her, the way he took his leave immediately after the meal, with no word as to a future meeting, was ample evidence that he wanted to flee the house as an infected area.

"I daresay he's a nice enough young man," Kitty observed after his departure. "Though a bit spoiled, of course. I hope you won't mind my saying, dear, that I don't think he's ever going to set the world on fire."

"No, Mother, I shan't dispute you there. We must look elsewhere if we want an arsonist."

"I thought he was rather snooty about private schools. Who does he think he is, anyway?"

"I think he thinks he's someone who's never going to have another Sunday lunch with the Chaunceys."

4 ✦ ✦ ✦

NATICA WAS admitted to Barnard without difficulty, and she occupied the unused maid's room in Aunt Ruth's small apartment on Lexington Avenue. Her freshman and sophomore years were not eventful, marked principally by her consistent industry. She elected courses in French and English literature and in art, music and European history, reading exhaustively from the suggested lists and earning high grades.

She took pleasure in her work, but it seemed to her that the pleasure was largely in her sense of equipping herself with undoubted competence for the achievement of goals that were for the most part hazy. Her motive for reading fiction, of course, was clear enough. She wanted to learn the elements of style. But what of her courses in art and music? Was she seeking the pleasure of perceived beauty or was she aiming to be a finished lady of the world, commenting at a dinner party with wit and precision on Picasso, Braque and Satie? And was history itself anything more than a series of dramatic scenes involving colorful personalities where she could enjoy the titillation of imagining herself as the young Victoria stretching out her hand to kneeling ministers on the dark early morn of her accession or as Marie Antoinette proudly facing a howling mob in the Tuileries? Did she ever get out of herself enough to read even a sonnet just for the loveliness of its fourteen lines?

When she put her problem to Aunt Ruth the latter pointed out that at least she knew what she was missing.

"If you know *that*, you're ready to make a start, and that must be what education is all about. For once you start, you never stop. Most of the girls in my school never make any start at all. I work my fingers to the bone to instil in them some tiny sense of the shimmering beauty, not just of art and books and music, but of the cityscape and landscape around them. But too many of them are simply obsessed with the idea of boys and parties and marrying and leading exactly the same lives as their parents."

"Why should any girl who's lucky enough to come of a family that can send her to Miss Clinton's want anything different? Edith DeVoe, I'm sure, wants to duplicate her mother's life. In her shoes I'd feel the same way."

"Natica Chauncey, you're just pulling my leg!"

"All right, Auntie, that's it. I'm just pulling your leg."

There was no use repeating to Aunt Ruth that in her opinion any girl at Miss Clinton's who was not content with the hand stuffed with trump cards that fate had dealt her was not worth worrying about. Natica had read in the memoirs of Edith Wharton, just published, that New York society ladies in the author's early years had considered writing too inky an occupation for the well bred. Natica thought she could perfectly understand such an attitude. If one had a great house to manage and a great position to maintain, what need was there to scribble? Scribbling was for those who didn't have the big things, for the Natica Chaunceys, if they were lucky enough to have a style, and what did they usually scribble about but the big things themselves?

She knew that Aunt Ruth's failure to understand these things, her sharing of the common fallacy that people actually lived by their professed moral principles, had ruined her own life. For she could have married a man who was now president of one of the largest banks in the city, a man, too, of unblemished character and widely acknowledged charm, who had waited a whole year for Ruth to make up her mind before turning to one of her less attractive classmates and making *her* his wife and the mother of his children. But did Aunt Ruth have any regrets?

"None, dear. You see, I wasn't in love with Alfred. I admired and liked him immensely; we always were and still are the best of friends. But that is not love."

"But you didn't have to tell him that! You could have been a perfectly good and faithful wife to him."

"A faithful one, I certainly hope. But not a good one, at least by my standards. For my idea of a marriage is something more than a contract, even faithfully performed. It's a union of two souls."

Natica could only sigh. She had read in the society columns that Alfred's wife was president of the Colony Club and had her own box at the opera.

She made some friends at Barnard but no close ones. She worked as a salesgirl at a bookstore in the afternoons to help pay for the part of her tuition not covered by her scholarship, and in the evenings she prepared her courses or listened with Aunt Ruth to the latter's large collection of classical records. She had a few dates but did not find a man who really interested her. Work became gradually a habit and at last something of a drug.

She began to live increasingly in a world of fantasies. When she was not actually engaged in study, as when she was walking around the reservoir in Central Park — her sole exercise — or riding the long bus route to school or listening to music, she would let her mind be the theatre of acted plays. The basic plot was always the same: the heroine would be born to a family who did not understand or appreciate her. Her parents would be bigoted Boston puritans or narrow-minded British burghers or anachronistically snobbish and impoverished French nobles, and she would escape their stifling but retentive milieu to a distant metropolis to write or act or sing or even marry a great man and return in triumph to confront her stupid but now dazzled kin and treat them with a generosity they did not deserve. The details of these constructed adventures were worked out with meticulous detail. But she had too much sense ever to write them down. She had learned enough about writing to know that good fiction was not made of daydreams. For that a clear head and an unencumbered day were required. In one whole year she wrote but a single short story.

In the spring of sophomore year she suffered a mild but prolonged depression. She supposed that it could have been the result of her solitary and passive existence; she preferred anyway not to admit that its real cause might have been Aunt Ruth's reaction to the short story she had been rash enough to show her. It dealt with a couple, obviously modeled on her parents, who had survived a precipitous tumble down the social ladder by the simple expedient of not recognizing what had happened.

"I suppose you meant to show there's a strength in sticking to one's guns or standards or whatever. But I'm afraid you've only shown there may be a kind of salvation in stupidity."

"But does the story come off at all?"

"I don't really think it does. There's too much of you in it. And I'm sorry to say it's not the best of you, my dear. There's a note of unkindness in your tale."

"Oh, I know your theories about compassion," Natica retorted, scarcely trying to hide the sharp hurt of not being instantly praised. "But must you have compassion in *everything* you read? Must you have compassion in a short story? Next, you'll be looking for it in a sonnet."

"I don't see why not. Compassion is essential to all great literature."

"Where do you find it in *Madame Bovary*?"

"Why, all through it, but particularly at the end. In that pathetic description of what happens to Emma's little daughter."

"You mean the aunt sending her to work in a textile factory?"

"Yes. I always find that passage almost unbearably moving."

"But, Aunt Ruth, it's simply the bleak statement of a fact! The compassion you bring to it is all your own. Why can't you bring it to my poor story?"

"I don't know, my dear."

Natica had been surprised at the depth of her own disappointment. She could only explain it by its suggestion that Aunt Ruth's confusion of compassion with sentimentality might be one shared by the greater portion of the reading public. And if that were so, how was a writer as clear-headed as herself ever to be accepted by the fuzzy-minded? Had she invested all her pennies in a salvation that might not be available?

As she brooded over this in the days that followed a grimmer doubt assailed her: that perhaps Aunt Ruth was not guilty of the confusion she had attributed to her, that, on the contrary, what Natica had deemed sentimentality could indeed be compassion, and that her own lack of it might disqualify her from the ascent of Parnassus before she had even reached its base.

Looking about her classrooms now she began to see in those earnestly listening young women not the dull housewives or toiling teachers or thermometer-shaking nurses whose drab future lives she had imagined as lightened by the reading of Natica Chauncey's fiction, but persons who would be actively and usefully engaged in existences that repudiated her own passivity.

Aunt Ruth, concerned with her moodiness, suggested that she might have a low blood count and urged her to have a physical check-up. Natica at length agreed and went to Dr. Sanford, the old family physician, in his Victorian office at the rear of his brownstone in Murray Hill. He was a small round bald Dickensian gentleman with a bustling air and a glinting eye who appeared to believe there was hardly a malady that couldn't be cured by common sense, or that at least would not be incurred by a person possessed of it. When he had pronounced her fit and she was about to take her leave, he offered this suggestion:

"Ruth tells me you've been depressed, my dear. Maybe it would help if we talked it out a bit. I don't set myself up as a Park Avenue Freudian, but who knows? I might be able to shed a small ray of light."

Natica, looking into those kindly eyes, thought suddenly: why not? She sat down again and for half an hour she answered questions about her daily routine, her particular interests, her boy friends if any, her relationship with her parents.

"Maybe that's part of it," she said about the latter. "I think I've always been rather horribly ashamed of being ashamed of them."

"Why are you ashamed of them?"

She sighed, preparing herself for the expected reproof. "I shouldn't be, of course. But I suppose I have to be truthful with you if we are to accomplish anything at all. And the truth of the matter is that I consider my father an ass and my mother a fool. So there!"

He said nothing for a moment, but he appeared to be thinking. "But doesn't everyone think that?"

"You mean, doesn't everyone think their parents idiots?"

"No. I mean, doesn't everyone think *your* parents idiots? Amiable ones, of course. Even lovable ones. But still fools."

Natica was later to consider that he had, with a single sentence, pulled her out of a dark tunnel. For her father and mother suddenly loomed in her mind as two crumpled, rather desperate and pathetic souls.

She called her mother that same night.

"What's on your mind, dear?" Kitty asked.

"Does something have to be on my mind? I just wanted to know how you and Dad were."

"If you'd ever come down to Smithport you could find out. But of course we know it's too dull for you here."

"I'm sorry you think that."

"But, my child, it's hardly anything new. You've always downgraded us. The difference between the way your brothers treat us and the way you do is . . . well, dramatic."

Natica thought how fiercely she would have once flung back her own cherished wrongs. But now she felt only a faint weariness at the prospect of combat.

"How have I downgraded you, Mother?"

"Do you realize that you have not come home once since Christmas? Unless you count that trip to pick up your summer clothes."

Natica had been planning to spend July and August in the city except for a short visit to Aunt Ruth's cabin by a lake in New Hampshire. Now she changed her mind.

"Suppose I come home for the whole summer. Would that help to make up?"

Had she expected her mother to be taken aback, even a bit disappointed by this quick cessation of hostilities? She was not sure, even as she was not sure of the motive for her abrupt resolution. At any rate there was no question as to the utter pleasure in her mother's tone. Perhaps parents, at least mothers, *were* different.

"Oh, my dear child, that would be simply divine!"

✦ ✦ ✦

Natica had expected the summer to be dull but tranquil. Its dullness, however, was interrupted by an event that doomed tranquillity, though not as decisively as such an event might have doomed it in a novel by Jane Austen or a Brontë sister. The minister of the Episcopal church in Smithport departed for a two-month leave of absence to visit the Holy Land, and his place was filled for the summer by a thirty-year-old bachelor priest, Thomas Barnes, assistant to the rector of Averhill School, who wanted the experience of administering a parish. Natica, who had now come to romanticize the school, having elected to see it as the shrine of the values of the great world and the training ground for its leaders, was curious to meet a member of its faculty and went with her parents to church on the first Sunday when Barnes was to preach.

He looked adequately handsome in the pulpit, with long wavy brown hair rising high over what seemed a noble forehead and large earnest eyes. He conveyed a pleasant, an even stimulating sense of masculine vigor not overly repressed by his black robe and shining white cassock. And his voice was rich and warm, his smile almost intimate.

He invited the congregation to share some of his biography, explaining that he was a pedagogue in a church school for boys. He even allowed himself a discreet joke at the nature of his institution, admitting that a journalist wag had described the stu-

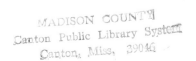

dent body as "overfed, overhoused and overclad." But he hastened
to emphasize the basic idealism of Averhill and then warmed to
his theme: how he had discovered, in seeking to make Jesus more
human to boys, in likening him to a friendly master who shared
the troubles of campus life with his charges, that this was much
the same Jesus that adults needed.

"There are those who claim that he has no merit for the patience
and courage with which he bore the agony of his trial and execu-
tion. He was God, so how could he have felt pain? Boys, I find, are
particularly prone to ask this. But isn't it evident from the Gospels
that Christ became so wholly Jesus, the man, that he must have
suffered pain even more keenly than we do? He actually subjected
himself to such minor human afflictions as irritability, of which we
catch a glimpse when he blasted the fig tree that yielded no fruit.
Does that not bring him to a level where we feel we can reach out
a hand, however timidly, to touch him? Ah, how he welcomes
us, how he spreads his arms!"

Kitty Chauncey, who was very active in parish work, had invited Barnes for lunch after the service, and he beamed at the
assembled family. Natica's two younger brothers, who had little
interest in church matters, were silently polite and took their leave
the moment the meal was over, but she and her mother sat and
talked with the voluble young minister on the verandah for an
hour afterwards.

Natica chose to take issue with him over the humanity of Christ.

"I wonder if it's not a mistake to make him too mortal. Aren't
you afraid that people will identify him with themselves? And that
you'll have as many Christs as there are worshipers?"

"Would that be such a bad thing?"

"Well, wouldn't it tend to proliferate the sects? The Catholics
stay united because they have one God figure who's too awesome
and distant to be identified with."

"Why shouldn't each man worship God in his own way?"

"Because it's not efficient. You get a lot of nutty groups. Look
at California. I like a splendid God. Majestic. Terrifying. Only

such a one could control the universe. It seems to me Jesus has
to be that or nothing."

"Nothing? Oh, Miss Chauncey, how can you say that?"

But now she had said it, she rather fancied the idea. "If he's too
human he may become all human. And then he becomes fallible.
When he talks about the last judgment coming in the lifetime of
some now living, you begin to suspect he's talking through his
hat. Or his halo."

"Natica!" exclaimed her mother. "Mr. Barnes, I apologize for
my daughter."

"Please don't, Mrs. Chauncey. I see just what she means. It's
very clever, really. Your daughter knows how to make her point.
But I shan't give up trying to persuade her of the beautiful lov-
ability of Jesus."

Natica could see that his technique as a priest was to disarm his
audience with candor, to insist that he was just an ordinary guy
who was nonetheless overwhelmed to the point of hyperbole (as
you, listening to him, would be too, if you'd only let yourself go)
by the simple overwhelmingness of Christ. But "you" were not to
be put off by that; he was still a regular fellow.

"When you spoke this morning about . . ." She paused.

"Yes?"

"Never mind. I'm sorry. I think you've already answered it."

She had been about to ask him about the blasted fig tree, but
now she thought better of it. How many men had tried to make
themselves as agreeable to her as he?

He had certainly succeeded in making himself agreeable to
Kitty, who remarked after his departure: "I don't see why you had
to be so disputatious with that perfectly charming man."

"Was I really so bad?"

"Well, you weren't good, my dear. But you'll have a chance to
make it up. He asked me when he could call on us, and I told him
he'd be welcome any day. He had his eye on you, Natica. Don't
think a mother can't tell!"

"But, Mother, he's a holy man."

"Enough of your sarcasm. He's as male as he's holy, and Mr. Eliot told me, before he went off to Jerusalem, that one of Barnes's reasons for taking this parish was that he never meets any marriageable girls up at Averhill. Nothing but faculty wives and cleaning women!"

"And the cleaning women are all over fifty. I've seen them! So Mr. Barnes has come to 'wive it wealthily' in Smithport. Well, he's come to the right place if not the right house."

"The summer girls are too snooty to look at a minister. And most of them are away now, anyway."

"So this is the poor girl's chance?"

"I know you want to cast me in the role of a matchmaking old busybody, but I won't have it. I don't care what you do about Mr. Barnes. But I think it's only intelligent at least to recognize that he's a man of integrity and character who may well be a headmaster one day."

"Or even a bishop. There's not much competition in the church these days, one hears."

"All right, dear. Have it your way. I'm sure you'd be happier with some communist teacher at Columbia plotting to blow up Smithport."

"Oh, Mother!" In a rare gesture Natica rose to kiss her battered parent. "I promise I'll give you and Dad fair warning before we light the fuse. And thank you for asking Mr. Barnes for lunch. I definitely think I'm going to see him again."

He asked her to have dinner with him at a fish place in the village the very next day. Slipping into the seat opposite him in the booth where he was waiting, she ordered the fillet of sole, which she knew to be the cheapest item on the menu without glancing at it. She did so briskly, in the manner of a woman who knows her own mind and wants to get on to the serious business of conversation. She expressed an eagerness to know all about Averhill.

"When I was there, I couldn't help putting myself in the shoes of a boy whose family had been wiped out by the depression, like my own. There are such, I suppose?"

"Oh, my yes."

"Don't they find it hard, living with other boys who have so much more money to spend?"

"Not nearly as hard as you might think. Because being poor doesn't show much at school. We don't allow the boys to keep any cash. All they get is an allowance of twenty-five cents a week, and a nickel of that goes in the plate at chapel, leaving twenty cents to be spent in the village where they can only go on Saturday afternoon. Everything on the campus is theoretically available to everyone."

"I see. It's a kind of communism. But I remember the Parents' House. All those mothers in mink arriving in limousines."

"Oh, the world creeps in. You can't keep it out altogether. And some of the boys wear expensive suits and ties. Fortunately my sex doesn't go in for clothes the way yours does. In a girls' school they have to wear uniforms. It's a funny system, but it works. What outsiders find it almost impossible to believe is that there's no snobbishness *inside* Averhill."

"Because they're all from the same class?"

He preferred another term. "All from the same background. In the same way there's no anti-Semitism."

"Because there are no Jews?" There was a note of irony in her tone.

He didn't get it. "Exactly. It's a kind of ethnic vacuum."

"And what happens when they graduate? Do they carry these fine Christian principles with them through life?"

He smiled, but it was not a smile that conceded much. "We do our best, we really do. And you know what Browning wrote: 'But a man's reach must exceed his grasp, or what's a heaven for?' "

Natica's conception of Averhill had been as a symbol of power, glittering, even admirable in its aloofness and pride. She had not understood that its board of trustees had deemed it politic or maybe necessary to cover it with wrappings quite so idealistic. And now she saw that this earnest man was precisely what they needed. He believed it all. He really did!

Well, why not? she asked herself, as she drank her wine and leaned back in her seat. What had her life really taught her but that cynicism got one nowhere?

He went on to talk at considerable length about the school, which was obviously his passionate, perhaps his only real interest. It did not seem to occur to him that their conversation was one-sided, though he did ask her some questions about her courses at Barnard which he found a bit deficient in American literature. She felt an immediate conviction that *Moby-Dick* and *Huckleberry Finn* were his favorite novels and decided it was not the moment to express her own preference for Henry James. Her mother had probably been right that he was looking for a wife, one who would fit in with faculty at Averhill. Of course, he would have to fall in love — his sincerity would require no less a state — but he would have no trouble with that once he had found the girl who qualified.

By the time he had driven her home he had become very friendly indeed, and she wondered if he would kiss her. She hoped he would. But instead he said:

"Will you go out with me again, Natica? I mean real soon? I think I should warn you that I'm beginning to like you very much."

"And I like you, Tom," she replied in a firm, no-nonsense tone and walked to her front door without turning back.

Two nights later they went out again to the same restaurant, and he told her about his life. His background was modest. His father was an Episcopal minister in Burlington, Vermont, where Tom and his only sibling, a brother, had gone to school and college. Both had graduated from the seminary in Cambridge and the brother was now a missionary in Nigeria. Tom had gone straight to Averhill where he had been teaching sacred studies and history and assisting the headmaster in chapel for five years. He admired Dr. Lockwood immensely and, of course, did not say anything about the possibility of succeeding him, but Natica knew that the post required a clergyman and Tom did mention that the rector would probably not retire for another decade. At forty, with fifteen

years' experience at the school, would he not be just the man to
whom the trustees would naturally turn?

He told her nothing about other girls in his life, but this time,
when he took her home, he parked down the road and they necked
vigorously for half an hour. Yet he was evidently a very disciplined
man, for he made no move to go further, and she was very hot and
flushed and unsatisfied when she went to bed.

Tom was handsomer, it seemed to her, when she wasn't looking
at him. Absent, or viewed from a distance in the pulpit, he could
suggest an English poet of the Georgian or pre–World War era, a
kind of Rupert Brooke, whose love of beautiful words in no way
implied a bohemian point of view or precluded a passionate pa-
triotism. But close to him, she couldn't but note that his large
brown eyes were too close together, his lips too thick, his oblong
chin somehow suggestive more of stubbornness than of strength
of character, though it didn't necessarily deny the latter. He seemed
all sincerity and openness; his frank friendly stare and self-deprecating smile or chuckle appeared to be telling her, apropos of his
particular enthusiasms, that if he liked grand opera he had no
objection to her preferring chamber music, if he believed in private church schools it was not to knock public education, or if he
believed in God, he was sure that the Almighty would forgive her
agnosticism. Tom, in short, seemed anxious to assure her that his
world was only one of many, but did he really believe it?

But, more importantly, did she really care whether he did? Her
languid mood in that slow hot summer seemed not to change.
There was something easy and comfortable, in their steady dating
of the following days, about the assured flow of his respectable
opinions. She allowed herself lazily and rather luxuriously to bask
on the sunny beach of an existence where nothing was expected
of her but to let this positive and gentle man take the lead in
everything.

One Sunday morning, listening to his sermon in church and
glancing from his spotless surplice to the gray harbor and seagulls
through the open pane of the stained glass window by her pew, she

found herself envisioning a visit to the rectory after the service to discuss the day's homily which would draw them into a deeper relation. She imagined him pausing in his too prosy explication, suddenly inarticulate, half choked; she felt his hands around her and then under her skirt; she heard his desperate, mumbled apology, and then suddenly it was too much for both of them. They were on the couch amid a flurry of skirt and panties and black robe and surplice and nakednesses, and she experienced with a sigh of relief, echoed by his own, the hard rhythm of his thrusts.

"What were you thinking about during the sermon?" her mother asked as they came out of church. "You seemed a million miles away."

"I was thinking I'd better marry Tom," Natica replied flatly.

5 ‚ ‚ ‚

WHEN NATICA came to Averhill the following September as the wife of the assistant chaplain, she found herself a smaller cog in its academic wheelworks than she had anticipated. This was not because of her exiguous living quarters. At such short notice the school could not be expected to provide a cottage for a new faculty bride, and she rather liked the little apartment improvised in the abandoned "Pest House," a one-story bungalow just off campus where boys with contagious illnesses had been confined before the erection of the new infirmary, although the windows of the latter were so close to her own that she had to keep the shades drawn. Nor was it because her husband cut a lesser figure at school than might have been expected from his confident talk. Tom was indubitably popular with masters and boys alike, and there was no mistaking the warmth of the welcome extended to his spouse. Nor was it even in the lowly position of wives in an institution dedicated to the proposition that the female of the species was at best a nonentity, at worst a dangerous threat, in the educational process of the young male.

No, Natica, having made the initial discovery of her own insignificance, soon made a second: that this insignificance was shared by all. Or all but one. The headmaster was everything at Averhill.

The Reverend Rufus Lockwood had come there four decades before, at a time when the school was smaller and poorer, not only in endowment but in qualified teachers, and he had brought to the solution of its problems an ambition as great and a mind as tough as his birth had been humble and his looks unprepossessing. He had managed to persuade a desperate but prescient chairman of the trustees to sweep away an incompetent administration and give him a free hand, and he had proceeded to turn Averhill into one of the finest and best-endowed preparatory schools in New England. Now he reigned supreme over board, faculty, parents and student body. His all-encompassing vision took in everything, from the Almighty and his angels brooding in the sky over that favored campus to the condition of the tin wash basins hanging over the green soapstone sinks in the long lavatories where the boys had to take cold showers every morning at 6:45.

Natica at her first interview with him felt as if she were being examined for a job. He was a short square man of craggy features, with a bulbous, blue-veined nose and small staring reddish eyes, who wore his thick gray hair in a Teutonic crew cut.

"Your father, Thomas tells me, is a graduate of Saint Paul's, so you presumably have some acquaintance with our church schools?"

"Only through his reminiscences, sir."

"Your brothers did not attend?"

"No, they went to public school in Smithport on Long Island. My parents couldn't afford the tuition."

"Ah, yes, that is hard. I wonder that scholarships could not have been arranged. But that is beside the point. Thomas tells me also that you once came here for a Halloween ball. With Grant DeVoe, I believe?"

"That is so, sir."

Those small eyes penetrated her. "Were you by any chance the young lady who smoked in my study?" The tone was mellifluous, but the air was tainted with danger.

Of course, she had a lie ready. The Lockwood memory was famous.

"It was I."

"And may I inquire if you are still addicted to the weed?"

"That was my last cigarette, sir."

"Oh? And dare I attribute to my (I trust silent) disapprobation so beneficent a result?"

"It was you who cured me."

His broad smile now welcomed her to Averhill. But after a brief reflection he sighed. "I'm afraid Grant is not doing very well at Harvard." The great brow darkened. "He is a most unsettled young man. A pity. A pity."

"I haven't seen him for the last two years."

The headmaster at this rose almost to gallantry. "No doubt he has suffered from the loss of a good influence. His loss, anyway, is Thomas's gain. I'm sure Thomas has told you that we expect our faculty wives to be present at lunch at the school and sit at their husbands' tables. And also, of course, to attend Sunday morning services at chapel. I like my masters to be on or near the campus at all times. Naturally I do not presume to control *your* comings and goings, but I expect each master to inform me when he plans to be away from school overnight and why."

"Oh, Tom has made those things very clear, sir." She decided that she might now venture a smile. "You'll have no trouble with me, I trust."

He came as close as she supposed he knew how to beaming. "Oh, I'm certain not, my dear. And let me assure you how happy I am that Thomas has picked so charming a bride. I shall call you Natica, if I may. I like to think of my faculty as one big and, I hope, happy family."

Natica learned a good deal about the headmaster in a very short time. The "family," particularly the faculty wives, discussed him almost compulsively, and it was soon evident that her husband's worshipful attitude was by no means shared by all. Dr. Lockwood was controversial in the strongest sense of that word. He excited fierce loyalty and equally fierce hostility.

All were agreed that he was a dictator. His harsh voice, rever-

berating down the long school corridors, exacted immediate obedi-
ence from boys and masters alike. Yet that same instrument, heard
from the pulpit, was capable of extraordinary modulations. It could
soar in almost musical notes of sweet piety; it could suggest a faith
as simple as it was deeply compelling. For the headmaster appeared
to see no inconsistency between the strict disciplinarian of the
campus and the loving comforter of the chapel. Heaven hovered
in the air over the buildings of Averhill; the school life was a plain
of laborious preparation for an ultimate blessed union with a divin-
ity who was supposed as well to be a living presence in the hearts
of the faculty and student body, particularly the latter, at every
minute of the day.

To the boys Rufus Lockwood was for the most part a headmaster: a thing to be obeyed, a presence to be avoided as much as
possible, a loud and usually disagreeable noise, part of the donnée
of Latin texts and parents and arbitrary rules of conduct that had
to be accepted. A few — a dedicated and devoted few, it was true —
were deeply impressed by his faith and brilliant sermons, but these
"converts" had little effect on the majority. Among the faculty and
graduates, Natica gathered, there was a split of opinion between
those whose admiration of Lockwood as an administrator and fund
raiser was unqualified and those who wished that his undoubted
virtues were less tarnished by snobbishness and autocracy.

For Lockwood, atypically among New England church school
headmasters, had been lowly born — his father had been a butcher
in Worcester — and his struggle up the social ladder, aided by his
cloth and ultimately crowned by his marriage to a Lowell, had not
inspired him with any lack of reverence for the goals attained.
Lockwood distressed many with his almost hand-rubbing appreciation of old names and large fortunes.

When Natica mentioned this to Tom, however, he spoke to her
sharply for the first time.

"Dr. Lockwood has had to raise immense sums for the school.
Where was he to get it but from rich graduates and parents? And
they don't open their checkbooks for people who don't know how

to talk to them. I hope you're not gossiping with faculty wives, Natica. That's a poor way to begin."

"I like to know what I'm getting into, that's all," she replied sulkily.

The penetration of the headmaster's personality, even into Natica's more private moments, was blunt. She and Tommy were frequently awakened by his early morning rings.

"Good morning, Natica. I want to talk to Thomas about changing the hymn for morning chapel."

And sometimes her day would end in the same way, the jangle of his call startling her out of the deep sleep into which she had just fallen or interrupting the climax of their lovemaking.

"I want to ask Thomas about his changes in the third form sacred studies schedule."

She and Tommy seemed never to be alone together, which gave an eerie intensification to her feeling that she had married a man who was essentially a stranger. This feeling was not diluted by her awareness that it was not shared by her loving but too satisfied spouse. Why was Tommy so sure he had got exactly what he had bargained for? And what, for that matter, *had* he bargained for?

He was off to chapel after an early breakfast and in classes all morning. Then she joined him at lunch in the dining hall and shared the perfunctory chatter of the fourteen-year-olds at his third form table. In the afternoon he coached lower school football, and three evenings a week he had to preside over a study period from eight to nine. On weekends attendance at the varsity football game and the headmaster's tea was virtually compulsory, and Sunday was taken up by midmorning and early evening chapel.

As the academic community had little affiliation with the village of Averhill or the local countryside, and as the school housekeepers, trained nurses and secretaries were not considered the equals of the faculty, social life for the latter was largely confined to themselves. Mrs. Lockwood, who as everyone knew had been born a Lowell, like Lady Macbeth, tended to "keep her state," allowing the leadership of the wives to pass to Mrs. Evans, whose husband was head of the English department, but the headmaster's wife always invited a newcomer to call, and Natica in due course received her bid to the "residence," the huge three-story bulge at the end of the longest and most rambling of the red-brick school buildings.

Mrs. Lockwood's "den" was crammed with red upholstered Victorian chairs and divans, and with papier-mâché tables and étagères bearing bibelots and framed portrait photographs. It was as if she were trying to preserve the tightly linked world of her kith and kin from the catastrophe of modernity in a kind of brocaded time capsule.

"You were a Chauncey, I understand. There was an Ernest Chauncey in the class of 'twenty-five who married my cousin Euphemia Higginson's second daughter, Hetty."

But when Natica, versed in the branches of her family tree, proceeded to explain the exact degree of cousinship, she quickly perceived that Mrs. Lockwood was not attending. Information might proceed from behind the fine shell of that egotism, but not penetrate it. She was a small, plainly dressed woman, with a round, rather featureless face and curiously hard pale blue eyes, who smoked incessantly, a cigarette dangling from her lips as her darting hands worked at needlepoint.

"I'm told you're a great reader, Mrs. Barnes. Perhaps you have read some of Cousin Amy Lowell's poems. They used to be considered rather too passionate to have been written by a respectable spinster, but then Cousin Amy was always a law unto herself. You've probably heard that she even smoked cigars. She started a school in poetry that was called imagism. There was an irreverent fellow — I think his name was Pound — who claimed to be the real founder and that hers was 'Amygism.' Dear me, how my poor mother used to laugh at that! She never quite approved of Cousin Amy. But then our branch never went in for the arts."

And this, Natica reflected, was the woman who had married a butcher's son! Perhaps, like "Cousin Bessie Tudor," as the Virgin Queen had been described by a legendary Back Bay dowager, she considered her state such as to warrant any match or none at all.

They were joined by Mrs. Evans, known to the faculty as the *camarera mayor* of the headmaster's wife, a large fair blond woman of imposing manner and hearty tones, who listened for twenty minutes with studied patience to Mrs. Lockwood's soliloquies. When she rose to leave, she quite firmly took Natica with her.

"It's best not to tire her," she explained when they were outside. "Dear Mrs. Lockwood has a minor heart ailment. Nothing to be really alarmed about, but we must be careful. No doubt you have received full instruction in the genealogies of the 'hub.'"

"She does seem to have them at her fingertips."

Mrs. Evans gave her a quick glance, as if to approve the moderation of her reply.

"She is a woman of great stature. Her patience and courage with ill health has been an example to us all. And it cannot be too easy, having been born what she was, to adapt herself to the life of a boys' school in the country."

Was this a second test? Natica smiled to herself as she gave a sturdy response: "I should think being the wife of the headmaster of Averhill would be good enough for a Bourbon!"

Mrs. Evans's laugh did not conceal her approval. "How amusingly you put it. And speaking of Bourbons, that reminds me. Would you care to join a little group of faculty wives that meets every other Thursday at my house to discuss a selected piece of French literature? We call it our *Cercle Français.*"

Of course, Natica would be only too honored.

When she walked to the river the next day with Alice Ransome, one of the more congenial of the younger wives, she found her only sourly impressed with Mrs. Evans's invitation.

"Oh, if you're in Marjorie's precious *cercle* already, you won't be hanging around with the likes of me."

"You mean she wouldn't ask you to join?"

"The wife of the athletic director? Dream on, my dear."

"Then I don't know if I care to go myself."

"Oh, go, by all means, if only to tell me about it."

Alice was a tall, broad-shouldered woman of thirty whose figure might have been impressive had she not stooped to look smaller.

Her bobbed straw-colored hair made a poor frame for a large nose and fallen chin.

"Is the *cercle* then so coveted?"

"What else is there to covet?"

Natica thought this might be a good point. She preferred Alice to Mrs. Evans, but poor Alice was not in any position to provide amusement. When "Marjorie," as she was now privileged to call the latter, informed her that the newest member always selected the topic for her first meeting, she chose *Phèdre*.

"Well, that's just fine. I was sure you'd give us tone. Watch out, Mr. Racine, here we come!"

✔ ✔ ✔

Mrs. Evans's living room was on the bare side; the walls were painted yellow and the chairs and sofa draped in a dull brown. A small breakfront displayed indifferent plates on teakwood stands. The sentimental watercolor of an Evans daughter hung over the mantel. An open door revealed Mr. Evans's library, more invitingly crammed with books and framed old maps, but Mrs. Evans closed it when the seven ladies were assembled, and the sighing heavy Irish maid toted in the big tray with tea things. Greetings and inquiries as to health were conducted in hesitant and painfully articulated French, but the main discussion, led by the hostess, was not.

"I'm going to start by admitting that I've only seen one play at the Comédie Française, and that was *Le Monde ou l'on S'ennuie*. The title seemed appropriate." Here she paused for laughs and received a couple. "I don't doubt that *Phèdre* is a great play. But I must say — and call me if you will a spoiled American who pines for derring-do — that five acts of Alexandrine verse where the only bit of action is a sword pulled out of its scabbard — never of course used — is what our German friends (if we have any in these Nazi days) call *landweilig*."

"Ah, but, Marjorie, if you had seen the divine Sarah in her greatest role, as I was blessed to in my salad days, you would have had your fill of excitement." Mrs. Knight, wife of the senior Latin teacher, rarely appeared on campus, having somehow exempted herself from the jurisdiction of the headmaster. She was the oldest of the faculty wives, in her middle or even late sixties, and had a long, haggard face, heavily made up, and brooding dark eyes over blue shadow. The added touches of her richly dyed auburn hair and huge amber beads made her seem like a retired actress. She was, on the contrary, a New York heiress who lived away from the school in a big dark Tudor house of her own purchasing and wrote poetry that she was too "free-spirited" to publish.

"You mean Sarah Bernhardt?" gasped Mrs. Greenwald, the wide-eyed, constantly astonished wife of the physics teacher. "You actually saw Sarah Bernhardt, Estelle?"

"Bless you, my dear, I saw her many times. Why, she even came to my aunt's house in Paris and heard me recite a poem. Yes, *me*, poor, scared-to-death little Estelle Tyler! Oh, I almost expired when I heard my mother, who would stop at nothing, ask *cette chère Madame Sarah* if she would be so *gracieuse* as to *écouter la petite*. And then suddenly there I was, standing up before them all, declaiming 'Le Sommeil du Condor.'" Mrs. Knight closed her eyes and clasped her hands. "Oh, why didn't I perish, like Pheidippides, at that summit of joy? For next I heard the famous *voix d'or* actually asking me to her home for a lesson in diction! But *bien entendu*, that was not a milieu for a *jeune fille*, and dear Papa put his foot firmly down. Who knows what histrionic career he may have nipped in the bud?"

"Why couldn't a *jeune fille* go there?" Mrs. Greenwald, in all sincerity, wanted to know.

But Mrs. Evans had had more than enough of her senior guest's reminiscences. "I think we had better get back to Racine. And, Edith, you can find out about your *jeunes filles* later from Mrs. Knight. Suppose you tell us *your* reaction to the tragedy we're here to discuss."

"Well, one thing that puzzled me, Marjorie," the physics teacher's wife confessed, "was all the emphasis on incest. I looked up the word in my dictionary, and it defined it as . . . well, let's say making love, between two persons too closely related to marry legally. Now of course the heroine could not marry Hippolyte at all because she was already married to his father. But if she hadn't been, there would have been no impediment that I could see. I mean she and Hippolyte were not blood relations, were they?"

This provoked an animated discussion of many voices.

"But he was her stepson! Incest doesn't have to be between an actual mother and son, does it?"

"Of course it does. That's the whole point of it."

"Anyway, wasn't she guilty of *moral* incest?"

"Why was she guilty of anything? She didn't *do* anything, did she? After all, Hippolyte wouldn't even look at her."

"But she wanted to do plenty. Oh, didn't she!"

"You mean she *only* wanted to commit an act that would have been *only* moral incest. It seems to me that's getting pretty far away from any real sin."

"What I find unattractive is that Hippolyte was young enough to be her son."

"What makes you think that? She may have been only a couple of years older than him."

Mrs. Knight's voice rose above the babble. "When I saw the divine Sarah in the role, she must have been well in her fifties, if not more, and Hippolyte was played by a strapping youth. I feel all the anguish of an aging woman in the lines. Oh, how can you miss it?" She closed her eyes again tightly, as if evoking a memory too flaming to be hid. The room was silent with surprise and perhaps with awe. "No, that immortal verse speaks with a terrible clarity to those who have been through a certain ordeal. To those who know what it is to feel the passing of beauty in the beholder while it is at its most poignant in the beheld."

Mrs. Evans was plainly disgusted. "I think we are straying from our analysis of the play. I am going to ask Natica to give us her reaction. She, after all, was the one who proposed Racine."

"Well, I think, Marjorie, the reason we find the dramatic situation a bit confusing is that we are not Jansenists, as he was."

"Suppose you explain to us just what a Jansenist is, dear."

Natica supposed she was being warned not to "show off," but she had started and had to go on. "A Jansenist was a kind of French puritan. He believed that all men are saved or damned before they are born, and that there's nothing in the world we can do about it. Phèdre is damned because she loves her stepson, as it was always in the cards, at least in *her* cards, that she would. It isn't in any way her fault; it's Venus's fault. And she knows this and knows that it's hideously unfair. That's her tragedy."

There was another outburst.

"Why, that's horrible!"

"How could anyone believe anything so awful? To be damned for something she couldn't help? What sort of a religion is that?"

"We might all be damned if it was just a question of *feeling*."

"Ladies, ladies!" Mrs. Evans raised a silencing hand. "Natica had made an interesting point, but surely she is overlooking the central crisis of the play. Phèdre falsely accuses Hippolyte of attempted rape, and for this his father has him killed. So she's really guilty of murder. That to me settles the question of damnation. If she's not damned, she's in for a long term in purgatory."

"But she never dreamed Thésée would go so far!" Natica protested, appalled by this oversimplification of her favorite drama. "You remember, her old nurse Oenone told her, 'Un père en punissant est toujours père.' She has been tricked by circumstance into believing her husband is dead. She has been driven almost mad by frustration and humiliation. And she is on her way to tell Thésée the truth, at the risk of her own life, when she receives the body blow of learning that Hippolyte loves Aricie. She hasn't eaten or slept for days; she is half dead, and Oenone works on her fevered imagination . . ."

"I'm afraid someone else's imagination is a bit fevered," Mrs. Evans interrupted icily. "And, if you don't mind, Natica, I think it's time some of the other ladies had a chance to speak."

Natica, deeply mortified, did not open her mouth again during the discussion. Even when a question was directed to her, as one or two were, by women obviously trying to make up for their hostess's rudeness, she simply indicated, with a slight smile and self-deprecating shrug, that she had used up her small store of criticism. But that night she exploded to Tommy.

"Do we really have to stay in this school? Wouldn't you like to have a parish of your own? Or even be a missionary like your brother? I'd rather face the cannibals than Marjorie Evans and her sacred *cercle!*"

He tried to pass it off as momentary pique on her part, but when she insisted that she was serious, he got up and took her in his arms and whispered what it was that she, and he too, basically needed. She pulled at once away from him.

"But we agreed we wouldn't even think about a baby for a year!"

"But there's no law that says we can't change our mind, is there?"

"Oh, Tommy, I *can't* get into that before I know where I am. Don't make me feel trapped!"

He at once relented, and when they went to bed he made love to her, but with the usual precautions. Making love would always be his answer to her problems; she was beginning to understand that. Oh, she liked it well enough, but she was wondering already why he had to do it every time in exactly the same way and why he was so confident that he never failed to confer an ecstasy upon her. After only two months of marriage she was simulating orgasms.

That night she slept fitfully, and her dreams were confused with her waking fantasies. It seemed to her that she was a soul alone, clad in a long white robe, as she envisioned Phèdre at the Française, isolated from the others, some jeering, some passively sympathetic, all peering, set apart by the bleak fact of her damnation. Then she fled across the boards and into the darkness of the wings, flitting as in a ballet, but in the coolness of shadows and by the trickle of streams she found no consolation in the frantic and ineffective devotion of her equally damned old nurse. She might hide herself away from the harshness of daylight and the people who found an inert contentedness in the little niches of the exposed rocky slopes outside, but in the end that daylight would penetrate even to her blackness and shrivel her into a little heap of dry bones.

When she fell at last into a deep sleep it was almost morning, and she awakened late. Tommy had gone to school, but he had left her a note:

I didn't think last night was the time to tell you, but poor Miss Stringham's complaint has been diagnosed as cancer. Mr. Lockwood has asked me if you would consider taking her position. Think it over. It might give you just the interest and distraction you need at the moment.

Natica clasped the note to her breast. God bless Tommy, after all! Miss Stringham was the headmaster's secretary.

6 ....

THE HEADMASTER's office in the "Schoolhouse," as the main classroom building was known, was across the corridor from the principal assembly hall, and when the door was open the roar and rush of boys changing classrooms on the hour was deafening. But when it was closed the large chamber was almost soundproof, and Natica enjoyed the sense of sitting in the eye of the whirlpool of this strange male educational process. From the two French windows she had a sweeping view of the whole circle of the ever active campus, muted like a film with a dead soundtrack. Her own little room adjoining was windowless and bare except for the typewriter desk and file cabinets and a large stained photograph of the Roman Forum, but the door to Lockwood's office was always open except when he had private visitations, and she could see across her machine to the great eighteenth-century French boule table covered with gold and silver mementos which he used for a desk and the Sargent portrait behind it of his clerical predecessor.

Her duties required her to be at the office immediately after morning chapel and to remain there until lunchtime. In the afternoons she could work at home if she preferred, typing dictated letters and reports, and on weekends she was subject to call at the headmaster's study in his residence whenever he needed her.

Having typed since her fourteenth year and having taken courses in shorthand during her Barnard summer, she expected to be adequately equipped for the job, and she could only hope that her new boss would be less exacting with women than he was reputed to be with men. It was encouraging that rumor had him trembling, like the first duke of Marlborough, before a wife who could be something of a shrew.

On her first morning he greeted her as perfunctorily as if she had been working for him a year, and launched immediately into the dictation of three letters to parents. He spoke slowly, with perfect articulation and without a single change or interjection, as if he had been reciting a prepared piece. But she knew he was testing her.

When she came back with the letters typed he read all three carefully before saying a word.

"I think we shall get on together, Mrs. Barnes."

His use of the formal address signified the change in her status.

"I hope so, sir."

"Have you been a secretary before?"

"I've had some experience," she fibbed.

"In my letter to Mrs. Kingsford about her son, Jimmy, it occurs to me that I may have been too harsh. I suppose an adoring mother might object to the application of the term 'egotist' to her son."

"Would 'individualist' be better?"

"But that might be construed as a compliment!"

"How about saying he has an individuality too pronounced for his years?"

"Excellent! Write the letter over that way."

It was not more than a week before she was allowed herself to compose the routine correspondence: the letters of congratulation and condolence to the more distantly connected, the answers to simple inquiries, the replies to graduates who wrote giving news of their careers. And more and more now when he was dictating, he would pause to ask her to suggest an alternate word or phrase. But she was careful never to volunteer one.

"You have a sense of style," he told her after she had worked for him a month. "Have you done any writing yourself?"

"Oh, I've scribbled a bit. Nothing too serious."

"I suppose every woman believes she has a novel in her."

She hesitated. Was this the moment for a bolder note? Was he challenging her? "Maybe that's the only way we women have to live."

"You mean if one lives, one doesn't have to write?" Those small red eyes seemed to bore into her. "What does Tommy think of your writing?"

"I doubt he even knows about it. There isn't, you see, anything much to know."

He grunted. "You're smarter than Tommy."

"I trust, sir, that doesn't mean you think little of my poor husband's intellect."

"No, it doesn't mean that at all. He had the sense to marry you, didn't he?"

She had no desire to write fiction at this point; she would be too busy gathering material out of which it might be made. For what was she but a spy in the holy of holies of a male society? Wasn't it on the playing fields of Averhill that the battles of Wall Street were won? And then, too, she highly enjoyed her new position. She was somebody, even if a small somebody, on the campus now. When she saw other faculty wives wending their dreary way to and from chapel, or to and from the dining hall, she felt in contrast as if she were on a bobbing horse on a merry-go-round. It was all she could do to keep from waving gaily at them and crying out what a good time she was having. The headmaster being everything at Averhill, even his secretary was envied, as the valet who emptied the chamber pot of Louis XIV was envied by the greatest peers of France.

Lockwood sometimes sent her as his messenger to faculty members with instructions about a change in schedule or the need of filling in for a sick or absent master. She was always careful never to allow the smallest note of authority to creep into the mild matter-of-factness of her chosen tone. Indeed, one young master laughed in her face, exclaiming:

"When I think of the difference between how that order must have been given and how it is transmitted! But don't think we don't appreciate it, Natica. We need a velvet glove for that iron hand."

Tommy did not know quite what to make of the change in their lives. He appreciated his own enhanced importance on campus as husband of one who enjoyed the headmaster's confidence, but he was chagrined by the substitution of Lockwood for himself as the primary object of his wife's preoccupation. And even a milder husband would have scarcely relished his spouse's superior knowledge of school affairs.

"I wouldn't count too much on Sandy Rowe as assistant coach for the junior thirds."

"What makes you say that, dear?"

"Between you and me I doubt the old man will renew his contract, come spring. He's made some inquiries about a replacement."

"Natica, should you be telling me that?"

"Don't you want to know?"

"Oh, I suppose so. But it seems kind of sneaky."

"Should husbands and wives have secrets from each other?"

"Perhaps not. Only . . ."

"We have your career to think of. If I keep my eyes and ears open, I may be able to help you quite a bit. Suppose another headmaster wants you on his faculty in a better position than you have here. It's etiquette for him to channel his offer through your headmaster. Well, sometimes those offers get stuck to Lockwood's desk. He writes back that he's sorry, but so-and-so is just too happy at Averhill to think of leaving."

"Oh, Natica, he wouldn't do that!"

"How little you know him. That man would do anything under the sun he deemed in the best interests of his school. And with a clear conscience, too. Even a serene one! So you see, it's to your interest to have a friendly hand opening his mail."

"Oh, darling, it's great of you to want to help me, and I do appreciate it. But do you know what I'd rather have you do than anything connected with Dr. Lockwood or Averhill?"

"Have a baby. I know. But I can't think of that now. Just when I'm really getting started on this job."

"You don't think starting our family is more important than writing Lockwood's letters?"

"Tommy, please! Give me *time.*"

She saw by the sudden whiteness of his face that she had hurt him deeply, but she couldn't help it. Despite her assurance to the contrary, there were plenty of things she had kept from him. One of them was that, with her growing cognizance of what it took to run a school, she was beginning to doubt his capacity for the job. Roy Evans, the senior master and Lockwood's right hand, had qualities of tact, imagination and self-restraint that she now saw were lacking in her husband.

Evans was certainly a very different person from his wife. Natica wondered how he could have married her. He was a quiet, serious, graying man, very thin, with an angular face of sharp lines and eyes of a remarkable gentleness. His deep voice inspired trust. He was always being consulted by Lockwood, often when Natica was within hearing, and he never raised his voice or showed the smallest impatience, even when the headmaster — a regular event — lost his temper.

"But it's right there in the paper, Roy!" She heard Lockwood excitedly slap his copy of the *Boston Transcript.* "Everett Perkins, drunk and disorderly, charged with assaulting a police officer. He'll not only be thrown out of Harvard; he'll be thrown in jail! And rightly so. No, sir, I shall *not* disregard it. I shall send him a stiff note this very morning informing him that he will not be welcome at Averhill for his class reunion this spring."

"I needn't remind you, sir, that his father is a trustee, and a very generous one."

"No, you needn't. You think of nothing but money, Roy. There have to be a few principles recognized, even by Boston banking families. That young man has had every advantage, every blessing, showered on his thick head since he was a baby. I prepared him for confirmation myself. Why, he's even one of Mrs. Lockwood's godchildren! And *this* is how he repays us!"

"I'm not thinking so much of his father's money as of his father's broken heart. I think this may be the time for a gentler word."

"I may indeed write a letter of sympathy to Everett senior. But we are speaking of his son. Only last winter, after that disgraceful incident in that New York nightclub, I wrote Ronnie Slater that he would not be a welcome visitor at Averhill for a year. And his was a far lesser offense."

"Perkins has only been charged with *his* offense, sir. Had we not better wait to learn if it is substantiated?"

"President Conant did not deny it in his interview. Are you assuming that he doesn't know what's going on in his own university?"

"Not at all, sir, but . . ."

"That will be enough, Evans!"

Lockwood dictated his stern letter to Natica when Evans had gone, but the latter returned to the office as soon as the headmaster had departed to his sacred studies class. Evans closed the door carefully behind him.

"Natica, my friend, do us all a good turn. Don't put that letter in the box till tomorrow. I think the old man is going to have a second thought."

She nodded in silent conspiracy, gratified by this further proof of her niche in the citadel. And indeed when Lockwood asked her the next morning, with seeming casualness, if the Perkins letter had gone out, he appeared mildly relieved to learn that it was still in her out basket. A small gleam in his eye might have revealed a suspicion, but a suspicion was not a reproof.

𝟤 𝟤 𝟤

Natica and Tommy were invited to tea at the Lockwoods' after the Groton football game. It was a crowded affair, as Dr. Endicott Peabody attended with some thirty boys and masters from his own school. Natica was eager to see the famous "rector" of Groton, now almost eighty years old and a legend in New England education. The long parlor of the headmaster's house, whose walls were covered with photographs of teams and crews and an occasional landscape, presumably of the Hudson River School, and whose elaborate if rather worn Belter chairs and divans were covered with young males, was dominated by the figure of Peabody, standing with his back to the fireplace, holding a teacup from which he took only a rare sip. He was big and balding and somehow square, and he stood very still and stolid, eyeing Lockwood with a pale gray twinkle behind which, at least on his own territory, might have always lurked the potentiality of a reprimand. He conveyed the impression that it meant very little that Groton had lost the game.

"You've got a fine team, Rufus, and they played a fine game. Nobody minds losing when they have sport like that."

"But really, we take advantage of you, Cousin Cotty. We have twice the number of students to pick our team from."

Natica knew that Peabody was a cousin of Mrs. Lockwood, but the Averhill headmaster's use of the tribal form of address still somehow struck her as hand rubbing: the butcher's son claiming alliance with the Brahmin.

"Numbers make no difference when every boy is worth his metal."

"Have you ever thought of enlarging Groton, Cousin Cotty? You could triple its size, I have no doubt, and still have a dozen applicants for every vacancy."

"No, I've always thought a hundred and eighty was the largest number of boys I could get to know personally. I'm sure with your famed memory, Rufus, you could increase Averhill to a thousand or more."

"You flatter me, sir. But I have thought that with a larger number one could afford to be more cosmopolitan."

"Cosmopolitan, eh? Is that what Averhill is, Rufus?"

Natica likened the two in a sudden fantasy to the Kaiser and his uncle King Edward before the Great War. Lockwood clearly felt socially inferior to the bland, well-mannered and utterly unimpressed older relative; he was too smiling, too glittery-eyed, too glib, but he also had the greater intellect and the larger school. If Peabody had founded Groton, Lockwood had more than doubled Averhill.

"We seek a more representative student body." Lockwood now moved into territory that he considered more his own. "At Groton you draw boys principally from Boston and New York. Whereas here . . . well, take, for example, those present. I select at random. I even close my eyes. Answer with the name of your home town, boys, when I point to you."

With lowered eyelids he suddenly darted a long finger at the nearest row of Averhillians. The boys, amused, rang out their answers loudly. There were four "New York"s and three "Boston"s before he came at last to a feeble "Philadelphia." The room burst into laughter.

Lockwood opened his eyes wide and beamed, turning defeat into a joke. "You see, Cousin Cotty, what I mean! Here is a young man who must have reached his homestead in a covered wagon."

While Tommy that night at supper chatted about the game, going over some of the plays in tedious detail, Natica hardly pretended to listen. It no longer mattered that he bored her; she had developed her own interest in the school. It was really, she supposed, not so much an interest in Averhill as in what she could make of it. There it was, something real, something to hand, something that she could dramatize, even perhaps recreate.

"Tommy," she demanded suddenly, obliterating his analysis of a forward pass, "do you think Dr. Lockwood is a great man?"

"Why, I never doubted it," he said, surprised. "He has that reputation, surely."

"But do people see *why* he's great? Do they see he's a great actor? That he lampoons the world of which he has become the celebrated mentor because he sees . . . because he understands, let me put it, that there's nothing he can do to make the smallest amount of sense out of it?"

Tommy stared. "Are you trying to tell me that Dr. Lockwood doesn't *believe* in Averhill?"

"But is there really an Averhill to believe in?"

"Well, if there isn't, what on earth are we all doing here?"

"A good question."

"Perhaps you've been seeing too much of the headmaster, sweetie. I know that at times he can exert a very confusing influence."

"Oh, never mind me, Tommy. I'm just playing games. Go back to your home runs."

"Home runs are in baseball, Natica."

The next morning when she came to the headmaster's office she found Lockwood there ahead of her, standing by the window that faced the chapel and gazing out.

"What did you think of the great Endicott Peabody?" he asked without turning.

She had been sure he'd say something of the rector of Groton. "He struck me as belonging more to a Calvinist world than to ours. Didn't they believe in signs of grace?"

"You mean that his appearance or demeanor, or perhaps what he said or how he said it, gave you the hint he had been saved?"

"That he was one of the elect. That he had been chosen, even before he was born, for salvation."

Lockwood turned to face her; his face was craggy with gloom. King Lear, she thought. Or was it Dr. Johnson? He seemed to gaze through her as he intoned:

"When you see Peabody in the pulpit in raiment white and glistering, waving a long arm and uttering his sonorous banalities, don't you feel that a Salem Peabody could hang a hundred witches and still be saved? What was it that Saint-Simon said of some dying duke: 'Le Bon Dieu will think twice before damning a man of that pedigree'? Peabody seems to have been put on earth for the express purpose of showing us what it is to be saved."

"You mean as a kind of taunt?"

"Or as a reminder of the damnation to which the rest of us may have been committed."

"We were discussing that at Mrs. Evans's *cercle*. The ladies couldn't understand how Calvinists could have believed anything so dreadful."

Lockwood chuckled. "Poor little souls, how it must have scared them! A lifetime of teas and gossip and household chores and then . . . the flames of hell!"

"But Mrs. Evans can be sure of her own salvation. She has all the signs."

"Perhaps too many of them."

He turned back to the window as if to reconsider the enigmatic message of the chapel tower. He offered no mitigation of the rigor of his comment on Marjorie Evans; she was clearly beneath his further thought. After a few moments of silence she offered:

"But would heaven be any happier?"

"You mean with all those harps and golden streets? Eternity, one assumes, would make joy and pain coevals. I don't profess to know about heaven, but surely hell is not so remote. One of our graduates who came up to school last week was telling me of the prison camps in Germany. He goes to Berlin on business and has one or two friends there who aren't afraid to speak out in private. The sadism, they say, is beyond belief. Wretched Jews are stripped and beaten and starved. I had a nightmare about it last night."

"You dreamed you were a prisoner?"

He whirled around to glare at her. "No, it was a real nightmare. I was a guard!"

She made no reply, and he was at once the headmaster again, very dry and crisp. "Take a letter to school counsel. 'My dear Alfred: I have been told that under a new Massachusetts statute we are now required to file annual reports as to . . .'"

✦ ✦ ✦

On winter afternoons, when the weather was dark and blowy, and the headmaster, who was subject to heavy head colds, chose to stay inside, she would be sometimes called to his study at home where he would dictate long paragraphs for future sermons or addresses in seemingly random order as they occurred to him. Soon her notebook was full of these anecdotes and observations, and at the end of a session she hazarded the suggestion that they might make a book.

"But who would read them?" he growled.

"Well, your graduates, to begin with. You taught them when they were young. Why not go on teaching them?"

"I taught them nothing!"

"Nothing?"

"That's right. We don't teach the boys anything at Averhill. Oh, we try of course. We do our best to drum things into their heads. But their resistance is like that Maginot Line in northern France, an impenetrable wall of turrets. How many of them will read a great poem, or even a great novel, after graduation? How many will go to church, or speak more than hotel French, or ponder the mysteries of the universe? How many will dissect a frog? How many will care for anything but girls and games and the great god Dollar?"

"But isn't it the exceptional boy that the system is designed to produce? What about Elijah Cabot? Isn't he one of our greatest poets?"

"But Averhill didn't even touch Elijah! He loathed the school."

"Well, maybe that in itself was his inspiration."

"On the theory that brutal parents and schools produce great artists? Dickens and that blacking factory? A noble function, isn't it? But we still don't teach. Elijah would have read poetry if he'd been beaten black and blue every time he was found with a sonnet in his hand. It sometimes seems to me, Natica, that we are caught in the devilish vise of a conformity that makes use of our very protests to fool society into believing it is free!"

She was utterly at her ease with him now. "Do you know, you are proving my point? There *is* a book in it. A great book, too. Another *Education of Henry Adams.* Didn't he believe that his education had equipped him for nothing in the world he had to live in?"

"That is true. He never thought he learned anything in school or college. Oh, I've often thought of a book, to put some sort of form into my life and thoughts. But if the book itself had no form, how could it?"

"Why must it have a form? Why not simply dictate it, as it comes?"

"To you, you mean?"

"It would be my privilege. You could do a little each day or week, whenever the mood strikes you. I'd be able to come to you any time you want. Or in the middle of a morning's dictation, you could simply say: 'Natica, this one is for the book,' and I'd jot it down. Maybe, after you have a hundred pages or so, the material itself will suggest the form it will ultimately take."

The long look that he gave her now suggested something between the gratification of a boy and a humility quite uncharacteristic of the formidable headmaster she had known for six months. "Do you know something, Natica? I might just try it. I really might."

7 . . .

ONE MORNING at her desk Natica overheard a livelier than usual argument between the headmaster and Roy Evans. The spring vacation was just over, leaving reports that some Averhill boys had been seen drinking at parties in New York and in the Boston area. Lockwood was much aroused.

"We have to act promptly and decisively, Roy. This idea that when a boy is away from school in the holidays he is beyond our jurisdiction is a repudiation of our whole mission. What sort of a travesty of the Christian moral imperative do we present if a boy can swear and smoke and drink — and perhaps worse, for aught I know — the moment he's off the campus?"

"Your principles are perfectly understood, sir. They've never been publicly challenged by any parents that I know of." Roy's tone, as always, was low-keyed and reasonable. "What we are faced with now is *rumors* of breaches of the school code. We both know that breaches, particularly in the holidays, are inevitable. Many parents serve cocktails every night as a matter of course. It is not unusual, I am told, for them occasionally to allow a seventeen-year-old to have a drink with them. If you have solid evidence of a boy's being inebriated at a party, then you might have a talk with him."

"A talk! It would be a question of suspension, if not outright expulsion!"

"Might that not seem excessive to parents in whose supposed control he was when it happened?"

"To them, perhaps. If they are derelict in their duty should I be in mine?"

"What, at any rate, do we really have to go on? Mrs. Amory Dillon has written to the headmasters of two other schools besides ours to complain of the behavior of certain boys at a party she gave for her daughter in Manchester. One of these was an Averhill sixth former."

"Jackson Bates, exactly."

"But when I telephoned to Mrs. Dillon, she admitted that he had been the least offensive of the group. He had simply tumbled down a stairway."

"He was drunk, sir!"

"He has a boy's light head, and had had one drink. I've talked to him. It won't happen again."

"You've talked to him! Drunk and disorderly, disgracing the name of the school, and you've talked to him! Well, let me tell you something else, Roy Evans. I too have talked to Mrs. Dillon, and I have obtained a list of all her guests at that party. It contains the names of no fewer than twelve Averhill students. She had only complained about those who were intoxicated, but she freely admitted that most if not all the young people present had had something to drink."

"Provided by her."

"Of course, provided by her! I'm not defending the wretched woman. I'm interested only in what our boys did."

"And how do you propose to find out which boy drank what?"

"By asking them, of course! By calling them in, one by one, and asking each precisely what he had imbibed. Do you suggest they will lie to me, if I put them on their word of honor?"

"But, sir, you will be asking them to incriminate themselves!"

"This is not a courthouse, Evans. It's a Christian academy."

"It will be perceived as an inquisition."

The headmaster's sigh was windy. "I sometimes wonder, Roy, if anyone believes in any of the things that I do. We appear to exist in a howling desert of hypocrisy."

"If you will excuse me, sir, I have a class on the hour."

Evans, Natica noted, always knew exactly when to drop an argument. When the headmaster took refuge in exclamatory generalities, his junior took it as a signal that the point was not to be labored. Lockwood was usually too shrewd and too practical to do more than rock his own boat. But Natica was increasingly aware that Evans and other senior faculty members apprehended that they might be living on the edge of a smouldering crater. Lockwood at times seemed almost to be reaching for an issue where he would be able to throw down the gauntlet at a society that accepted him as a god only so long as he behaved as gods should. He was bored — that was really it — so bored that he might be yearning for a catastrophe that would bring down the temple around his gory locks. Was there any role left for him sufficiently dramatic but that of Thomas Cranmer thrusting his recanting hand into the flames before they could reach his martyr's body?

The *Boston Globe* had been running the salacious story of an Averhill graduate divorcing his younger wife for adultery, and Lockwood, unexpectedly entering Natica's office, caught her reading it. He snatched the paper from her.

"That's not fit reading for a young lady!"

"There are few surprises for young ladies these days, sir. And I'll thank you to give me back my paper."

"Take the filthy rag!" He tossed it on her desk and retreated moodily to his own office. When she came in later, in response to his ring, and took her seat before him, notebook in hand, he had the brooding, faraway stare that foretokened an entry for "the book."

"It may interest you to know that the defendant in that sordid case struck me initially as a fine young woman. Another example of how hard it is to find 'the mind's construction in the face.' I had not, however, like King Duncan, built 'an absolute trust' on her. Well, well. Let us see what profit we may derive from an earlier case."

And touching and retouching his fingertips together slowly, as if to keep pace with his reflections, he proceeded, as always in these sessions, to dictate as if he were reading aloud.

"John Winthrop, the first governor of our Bay Colony, records in his journal that one James Britton and one Mary Latham, the latter a young woman of only eighteen years, were hanged for adultery. They had been duly condemned by a court on which he presumably sat. Winthrop sets forth the bare facts: how the woman had been wed to an 'ancient man' who had neither honesty nor 'ability,' and how she had proved very penitent and aware of the foulness of her sin, and how the man, very much cast down, had petitioned for his life. Some of the magistrates questioned whether adultery was death by God's law, but the sentence was carried out, and Winthrop concludes his entry with the expression of a pious hope that Mary Latham will prove a good example to other young women of the colony."

Lockwood's long, silent stare did not seem to focus on his secretary.

"We are appalled today," he concluded, "in reading Winthrop's words. How could a man, who seems in many of the passages of his journal a person quite as compassionate as ourselves, record so complacently so savage a punishment for so common a crime? And yet there is a fascination, almost an awe, in contemplating a community which set its moral tone so high, a community which did not blink at the stain of original sin, a community which kept its eyes fixed on the stern dictates of the Almighty and did not seek its salvation in the modern bathos of exalting love, love, love."

He now abruptly changed his tone, in a way he had, as if an invisible director on a fancied set had called "Cut." "I believe that you and Tommy are dining with us tonight." It had indeed been a rare honor, to meet the visiting headmaster of Saint Andrew's School. "After dinner I shall take Dr. Cotton to my study for a short conference. Please speak to Mr. Roy Evans and ask the gentleman not to linger too long over their cigars. That is something my wife particularly objects to."

Natica was to wonder afterwards if the very satisfaction she had felt that night before dinner in Mrs. Lockwood's cluttered Victorian parlor, looking, she had hoped, at her very best in blue silk with a red scarf, and imagining herself a smoothly functioning cog in the well-oiled machinery of this male institution, might have been the act of female *hubris* that precipitated her expulsion from the works. Yet the only mistake that she could see she had made was to have delivered her message to Marjorie instead of to Roy.

"The headmaster hopes that Roy will speed the gentlemen with their coffee and cigars after dinner. He is going to be closeted with Dr. Cotton, and Mrs. Lockwood doesn't care to be left too long with the ladies."

Marjorie Evans's cold gray eyes seemed to aim her big marble nose dangerously at her interlocutor. "I think my husband and I can handle ourselves socially without *your* help, Mrs. Barnes."

"I never questioned it. I was only doing what Dr. Lockwood asked me to do."

"Did he ask you to speak to *me?*"

"No, I don't suppose he did. But he wanted the message conveyed to your husband."

"Then convey it, Mrs. Barnes. You're taking everything else on your shoulders these days."

Natica, left alone, contemplating one of her hostess's elaborately carved Belter chairs, was possessed of the sudden image of a knife slitting its tightly packed pink upholstery to reveal an ugly cavern of angry broken springs and ominously stained cotton.

She moved over to join the respectful female group around the chair where Mrs. Lockwood, a cigarette dangling from her thin lips, was chatting as she plied her needlepoint. Was it Natica's imagination that made her fancy that the headmaster's wife deliberately failed to notice the two perfunctory comments that she added to the perfunctory talk?

At the dinner table, where ten were seated, there was a dispute between the host and hostess across the board that drew a strained silence from the guests. Natica had heard of these disputes but had never witnessed one. They were rare and were supposed always to result in a total victory for the wife.

Lockwood had perhaps unwisely chosen this evening to discuss the book that he "and Mrs. Barnes," as he facetiously put it, were engaged in composing.

"It will probably never be finished. I cannot seem to become enough of a literary carpenter to put together the box that would contain the impact of the school on the world and vice versa. I should have to be an historian, even a statistician, a biographer, an autobiographer (oh, yes), a novelist (for some things would never be believed) and even a poet!"

"Leave novels to women, Rufus," his wife retorted dryly. "It's their province."

"My dear!" His eyes rolled. "Do you thus dispose of Tolstoy, of Balzac, of Dickens?"

"I'm talking about Americans. Or perhaps I should say New Englanders. We are New Englanders, are we not? Our men are at their best when they are serious, when they write essays or history, like Prescott or Great-Uncle Francis Parkman."

"And Hawthorne?"

"You will remember that Mr. Emerson deplored Hawthorne's novels, though he admired the man. And Henry Adams knew what he was doing when he published those two novels anonymously."

Somebody brought up the name of William Dean Howells, but Mrs. Lockwood rejected him as a Middle Westerner who had settled in Boston and then (worse) abandoned it for New York. The headmaster, uneasy at the curious warp of mind that his wife was revealing, tried to mollify her with a compliment, saying that in eschewing fiction he would at least be within the tradition of the Lowell family, who had written every kind of prose and poetry *but* that.

Natica suggested that Amy Lowell's prose poems were almost short stories.

Mrs. Lockwood, without looking at her, remarked sharply to the table: "If Mrs. Barnes had listened to the discussion, she would have heard me say that fiction should be left to women."

"And Amy was barely that," Lockwood murmured to the lady on

his left. Unfortunately for him, in the embarrassed silence that had followed his wife's pointed rudeness to Natica, the remark carried to her ears.

"I'll thank you not to make unpleasant remarks about my relatives, Rufus Lockwood. They've been kind enough to *you*."

What impressed Natica at this awkward moment was the completeness of the headmaster's rout. He muttered an apology and confined his conversation for the rest of the meal to his immediate neighbors. His wife knew just where and when to implant her deadly dart. No doubt she had had ample practice.

Walking home afterwards with Tommy, she found him upset and bewildered.

"What in God's name have you done to Mrs. Lockwood?" he wanted to know.

"You mean, don't you, what has Mrs. Lockwood done to me?"

"Darling, she *is* the headmistress. Or at least the headmaster's wife."

"And that gives her the right to have the manners of a pig? Whose side are you on, anyway?"

Tommy paused to stare at her in astonishment through the darkness. Never before had she shown herself so tart. "I thought I was on your side. But I thought on our side we could work out together our life at Averhill."

"I didn't reproach *you* for not telling Mrs. Lockwood that her manners were foul. Let us leave it, please, at that."

"But Natica, my darling . . ."

"Let us leave it at that!"

It came as little surprise to Natica that on the following day, which was Sunday, Roy Evans called at the apartment with a very grave countenance. Tommy was at chapel, preparing for the morning service.

"This is a tough one, Natica. But I may as well get on with it. The headmaster does not want you to go to your office tomorrow. He's got a Miss Thurmond coming up from the village to try out as his new secretary."

"He wanted *you* to say that for him?"

"That's it."

"He didn't have the guts to do it himself?"

"Great men can keep their guts for the occasions when other men's won't serve. This is not one of those."

"I see. Is there anything else?"

"He wants you to know that your dismissal has nothing to do with any fault on your part. You have done, he asks me to tell you, an excellent job. But he feels that using a faculty wife for your post has aroused jealousies among the other wives."

"Which ones? Or should I say, which one?"

Roy's studied impassiveness admitted her accusation.

"How have I hurt Marjorie?" she demanded angrily. "Have I taken anything from her she didn't already have?"

"A school is like an Indian tribe, Natica. People resent the new favorite of the chief. It has nothing to do with the fact that they didn't have a chance of becoming the favorite themselves."

"But was it also necessary for your wife to get Mrs. Lockwood to hate me? What did she tell her? That the old man's been making passes at me? Or that I've been inviting them?"

"That was hardly necessary. The idea of the book was quite enough. Something shared by you and the headmaster in which nobody else had a part. Mrs. Lockwood is a very jealous, a very possessive woman."

"And she knows just when to throw her Lowells in the fat red face of the butcher's boy!"

She noted his wince. For all his realism, for all his diplomacy, it was cruelly painful for him to see his idol spattered. But she was remorseless now. "Of course, I see why I'm a threat to you all. You're in a conspiracy to keep the old man from wandering off the reservation."

"What do you mean?"

"I think you know exactly what I mean. You're all dreading the day when he may blow a fuse that will knock the school into a cocked hat. He was damn close to it when he wanted to interrogate and then fire those boys who had taken a drink on vacation. I'll bet you and Marjorie have weekly conferences with Mrs. Lockwood about how to keep him under control. And when you heard he was writing a book! That had to be the end, didn't it? God knows what the old boy would come up with that might scare away half the parents in New York and Boston!"

"And what has all that — even assuming there's any truth in it, which there isn't — have to do with you?"

"I was helping him, wasn't I? I was even the little baggage who had put the idea in his crazy old head, wasn't I? Oh, I had to be disposed of at any cost. Cost? There was no cost. A simple kick in the ass would take care of me."

She thought she could perceive that he was impressed. But he would never show it.

"Do I hear the would-be novelist at work?"

"Perhaps that is the only role you've left me."

"Will you allow me, at any rate, to say how sorry I am?"

"No, Roy, I won't. I'm going to say what I have to say no matter how much it hurts us both. You allow your wife the full rein of her bitchy temper. It's your fault that she gets away with it."

He took it well. He even nodded. "But what can I do?"

"You could leave her."

"Oh, Natica." He closed his eyes as at the hopelessness of explaining such things to her. "At any rate, I can console myself that my problem is not yours. Your Tommy is a fine guy and he loves you."

But she would not let him have even this. "My Tommy's an ass!" she hissed. "And you know it!"

✦ ✦ ✦

Two days later, on a cloudy, cold, misty afternoon, Natica was circling the empty campus for exercise, for something to do, for an excuse to get out of the house. The boys were on the baseball diamonds or in the gymnasium, and the deserted chapel and Schoolhouse, the latter with no windows lit, seemed to question her intrusion. A boy, perhaps fifteen, was walking just ahead of her. When she caught up with him, for he was only strolling, she asked him if he was out for exercise.

"Oh, walking doesn't count as exercise," he replied. He was a tall, gawky youth with black hair that fell over his forehead and a rather winning air of candor.

"Doesn't count?"

"We have to do ninety minutes a day and fill out what are called exercise blanks. Mr. Ransome, he's the athletic director, you know, tours the campus in the afternoon to be sure boys aren't shirking. But I know his beat. When he comes out of the Schoolhouse, I can duck in there and read for the rest of the afternoon."

"What will you read?"

"Well, right now I'm reading *The Idylls of the King*."

"Oh, what fun! I love *Guinevere*. But what about the exercise blank?"

"Oh, I fill it in with fibs. Lots of the guys do that."

She paused to look at him in surprise. "And you tell me that? A master's wife? How do you dare?"

"Oh, I've sat next to you at lunch. You don't remember, of course. But you remind me of my sister. You'd never tell."

"It's true, I never would. But I should think at least your English teacher would like your reading poetry."

"Oh, Mrs. Barnes, you know the system. Everything here falls into pigeonholes. We read poetry from ten-fifteen A.M. to eleven. They think there's gotta be something wrong with a guy who wants more than that."

"And is there something wrong with you?"

"I sure as hell hope so."

"Then you don't like Averhill?"

"Me? I hate it."

"Why don't you ask your parents to take you out?"

"Are you kidding? My old man's a trustee. Anyway, what the heck. In two years I'll be at Harvard, and then I can do anything."

"Lucky you!" she exclaimed wistfully.

When she left him to dart into the Schoolhouse, she reflected bitterly that in two more years he would be out, at least on parole. But she? And then, with a wonderful, surging excitement she felt again the throbbing hope that had been initiated by Roy Evans's remark about her novel writing, and she clenched her fists and wanted to cry out aloud.

For there *was* a novel in the story of the captive headmaster in his prison of red brick and white columns, surrounded by a green graveyard of buried faiths and hopes. Oh, how she might do it! And she would cross every *t* and dot every *i*, too, why not? Was it not her prerogative after the way she had been treated? Dickens and Charlotte Brontë had done the same to their schools. Averhill owed it to her!

And Tommy? What would such a book do to Tommy's career at Averhill? Well, that was a chance she would have to take. Perhaps she would become so famous that other schools would be glad to employ him just to get her on their campus.

But that night, when he gently suggested that now she was no longer working for Dr. Lockwood she might have time to have a baby, she almost screamed at him.

Ruth's Memoir ✦ ✦ ✦

MY NIECE Natica and I have always had a close but slightly prickly relationship. The crises that I have seen her undergo may seem pale in contrast with the explosions of young people in this decade of the sixties, but they were nonetheless searing to her. After all, standards are never the same; people were willing to die at the stake in the Reformation for beliefs that seem the merest piffle to us today. And I suppose that Natica's frustrations must be viewed in relation to the fewer alternatives that were open to women before World War II. My trouble with her was that as an educator I was much more aware than she of the alternatives that *were* available: women were indeed going to law and medical schools in the thirties. It took more grit to make the grade than it would later, but grit I expected of my niece. Natica, on the other hand, considered me an old maid who was basically sympathetic to an establishment that had downgraded me for not becoming a wife and mother. She was never quite fair to me, but I still loved her. She had such a terrible capacity for unhappiness, even though it was balanced by surprising recoveries.

It was in the early fall of 1937 that Tommy Barnes telephoned me to ask if I could possibly come up to Averhill for the weekend. Natica was undergoing what he described as a "mild nervous breakdown" over the rejection of her novel by a New York publishing house. The refusal of the book had been sufficiently definite to cause her to lose all heart and give up the idea of submitting it elsewhere. She was, as he put it, "in a funk." I agreed, of course, to go up. My sister and brother-in-law would have been no good in such a crisis. They would have simply told her to buck up and pull herself together.

I had read the book, which Natica had sent me. It was not really a book, but rather the first hundred pages of one, with an outline of the projected balance. Its rejection had come as little surprise to me, and considerable relief, though I should have thought it might have been accompanied by an invitation to submit a second work. Natica's straight, stabbing style had a certain blunt effectiveness, but it was raw, terribly raw, with no redeeming subtleties or ambiguities. And it was obvious that she was drawing her characters from life; their idiosyncrasies were underlined even where they seemed to have no relation to the theme of the novel. It was, in short, an album of crude snapshots rather than a portrait gallery. Even had the proposed book had the requisite literary quality, a publisher might well have been apprehensive of a libel suit. Certainly it would have been the end of Tommy's career at Averhill. Natica had not shown him the manuscript, writing me that she had no intention of crossing *that* bridge until she had to.

Tommy met me at the train; he was very solicitous about my bag and almost lifted me into his car.

"I'll never forget your kindness in coming up, Aunt Ruth. I haven't been able to do a thing with Natica. She hardly says a word to me. Oh, it's not that she's disagreeable or bad-tempered. But she seems to be in a completely passive mood, almost a daze. It's as if I wasn't there."

And indeed I found his wife in the grip of an uncharacteristic lassitude. But it was soon apparent that this was largely caused by her husband's presence. After a lunch of sandwiches in which very little but family news was discussed she and I took a walk through the woods to the river, and she became much more animated. I asked her exactly what the editor had said about her manuscript.

"Oh, the lady I talked to, a Miss Sims, was very frank. I suppose she meant to be helpful. But she said that it wasn't really fiction at all. That I was too angry. That I had better let some time go by and simmer down. She even pulled the old Wordsworth line about emotion recollected in tranquillity."

"Even if it's an old line, mightn't it still be a good one?"

"But the point is that I write the only way I can, Aunt Ruth! I seethe until I boil over. And what comes out of the pot on the stove is my writing. If that's not fiction, I can't write fiction."

"Then maybe you should try your hand at nonfiction."

"About what?"

"I guess that has to be your idea."

"But I don't know anything! I'm not a scholar, or even an observer of current events. I haven't been anywhere or done anything with my life. I'm like a Brontë sister without the moors and without the genius. If I can't make up my own kind of weird stories, I have no function. Can't you see that?"

"I don't see it at all. I know it's frustrating to be told to count your blessings, but it can be a healthy exercise. You have youth, health, an attractive personality and a first class mind. Don't tell me there's no future for you simply because one publisher chose not to publish one book."

"But I've made a false start, and I don't see how to correct it."

"A false start?"

"My marriage, for one."

I'm afraid my first reaction was one of exasperation. It had been obvious to me from the beginning that she had not really been in love with poor Tommy, and now it seemed unjust that he should be condemned for lacking qualities she had never expected of him.

"Tommy is a good man. He hasn't a mean streak in his body, and he adores you. You can still make something of your marriage, Natica."

"Listen to me, Aunt Ruth." She stopped walking and, taking me by the elbow, made me turn to face her. "I want to tell you something about Tommy. I want to tell you how it occurred to him to to offer me a consolation for my disappointment. He invited me

into the little study in the back of our apartment which he has converted into a kind of male sanctum, complete with pipe rack, sport-
ing prints and a roll-top desk he found in school storage. It is here
that he retires, with his old red robe and Indian moccasins, when
he wants to write a chapter of his 'Talks to Boys.' Oh, you didn't
know that Tommy was also writing a book, did you? Well, he is,
and he has a sublime confidence that literature will somehow grow
out of the right setting. If he can only lounge before his desk, in
the proper Hemingway pose, puff at his pipe and gaze soulfully out
the window . . .''

"Natica, what are you driving at?" I was determined to interrupt
this remorseless shredding of her spouse.

"Simply that I had been invited to his den to be told that I need
not so bitterly regret something that was essentially beyond the ca-
pacities of my sex."

"Do you mean novel writing?" I felt myself immediately sliding
over to her side. "He's never heard of Jane Austen, I suppose. Or
George Eliot or Virginia Woolf?"

"Well, he might admit them to the lower slopes of Parnassus,
but never anywhere near the peak. Oh, he put it very gently. He
twinkled and chewed his pipe and asked me not to take what he
was going to say personally. But did a woman — any woman, he put
it — have the 'blood congested genital drive which energizes a great
style'?"

I stared. "That doesn't sound like him. Where did he get that
from?"

"Oh, he got it from Roy Evans, I'm sure. Roy is an aficionado of
the great Hemingway. He's the ball-less teacher of virility in literature to little boys."

I walked on now, and she followed. For several minutes neither
of us said a word. Nothing she could have told me about Tommy —
no infidelity, or even battery — could have more convinced me of
the hopelessness of that marriage. But what could I tell her?

"Whatever you do, Natica, don't do it in a hurry. You have time.
There are many ways of working out a difficult marriage."

"What experience do you speak from, Aunt Ruth? But at least you haven't urged me to have a baby."

No, I certainly hadn't. I thought she was in no mood to have a baby. We now proceeded to discuss, in an almost normal fashion, the cottage that the school was at last providing for the Barneses, enabling them to move from the restricted quarters of the "Pest House." I was astonished at the abruptness of her change of mood. Had she simply wanted the satisfaction of revealing to someone outside the Averhill faculty the full fatuousness of Tommy's attitude? And now that she had classified him forever, stuck a pin right through the round body between the butterfly wings that no longer deceived anyone, and slammed shut the glass case of her collection of Averhillian entomology, was she temporarily relieved of the duty to analyze and could her mind move on to other distractions?

"Can I see your new home?" I asked.

"We can go there right now."

We turned back to the school. The cottage, vacated by the widow of a retired master who had recently died, was a pretty white farmhouse, square, with green shutters and a tiny garden in back. Before we had inspected the last of the freshly painted, empty chambers I had promised her all of the furniture of my parents that I had kept for years in storage. It seemed the least that I could do. But I couldn't help wondering if Natica hadn't planned it that way. I hoped, anyway, that she had. It might have indicated that she still contemplated a future as Mrs. Thomas Barnes.

Part Two

8 ...

STEPHEN HILL had romantic good looks, with very pale skin and lustrous raven hair, and with moist brown eyes that offered more sympathy than anyone, including himself, could hope to deliver. He was like a youth in an old miniature, in a vitrine with others of beautiful dead young people, discovered on a visit to a boarded-up, mouldering mansion. Yet Stephen considered himself as only potentially romantic; he feared that in some ways he was as precise and literal as his father. The latter was indeed well known for these qualities. In Redwood, the old Kip manor house on the Hudson, inherited by his wife but greatly added to and embellished by himself, Angus Hill would sit silently through the stately service of his dinner, raising his head only at the sound of a distant whistle and commenting, after a glance at his gold pocket watch: "The six-oh-seven to Albany is two minutes late."

Stephen supposed that his father loved him as he more obviously loved his two older sisters; there was nothing anyway to induce him to disbelieve it. Angus Hill was a small, slight, bald gentleman of sober dress, of rare chuckles, mild criticisms and occasional fits of appalling wrath. His mission in life seemed more that of a spouse than a father: to provide the brilliant settings for the radiantly beautiful wife who so gratifyingly favored him. Stephen had read his Veblen and knew that the American tycoon was supposed to hold out to the world a handsome consort, complete with diamonds and a palatial abode, as proof positive of his wealth, his might, his virility. But his father, who had acquired all his means by simple inheritance, seemed rather to hide behind his mother, deferring to her physical and genealogical superiority, to the extent (except for his occasional temper tantrums) of almost blotting himself out.

Yet Stephen, without jealousy, or at least without an awareness of it, regarded these paternal qualities, which he reluctantly recognized in himself, as the appropriate uniform for the adorers of Angelica Hill. For her loveliness was in itself quite enough for any one family; it had to be sufficient function for the rest of them, including his sisters, thin and darkly pretty, though not so much so as to compete with their mama, to perform as acolytes at the maternal altar. And this despite the fact that the quality of Angelica's looks was largely in the aura they shed, in the glowing pink pearl of her skin, the wide serenity of her sky blue eyes, the abundant crown of her high-piled, finely gray hair. In a mere photograph one saw a stylish lady of late middle age, tending the least bit to the stocky, with a lineless heart-shaped face and a beautifully chiseled nose and chin. It took a portraitist in the tradition of Sargent to bring out the glow, the enchanting sense of personal solicitude, the unfailing kindness sometimes in conflict with an inherited puritanism. Angelica was loving but stubborn, full of small superstitions and amiable obsessions, a bit stupid in generalities but shrewd in particulars, and at all times perfectly aware of the absolute power she wielded over her loved ones. She could afford to ignore their constant, exasperated cries of "Oh, Mother!"

Stephen himself was the most vociferous. It agonized him when he saw her sink an indulging spoon into the plate of ice cream she had sworn off the day before, or light the cigarette from which she had pledged abstention, or even reach for the second cocktail in defiance of her resolution to limit herself to one. If he was an acolyte, he was certainly an angry one, constantly officious in his self-imposed duties of preserving the beauty, health and total sobriety of his idol.

Angelica simply laughed at him, blithefully repeating both her reso-
lutions and her defections, and quelling him when he had gone too
far with a mild: "Darling! Remember that I am, after all, your
mother." As if he needed to be reminded!

There had always been friends who had told him that it could
not have been an easy thing to be the only son of Angus and Angelica, that the burden of their rather august and ceremonious existence must have at times weighed heavily on his shoulders. Yet
Stephen was quite aware that they never expected anything of
him but that he should accept the good things of life as complacently as they did themselves. His father had always been the first
to admit that he himself had done nothing with his life but preserve
his inheritance and serve on a few charitable boards. And his mother
simply wanted him to marry a nice girl.

Never in his life had Stephen fretted so much about his parents
as in the fall of 1937 when he returned from a summer tour of European capitals taken with three Yale friends, all like himself newly
graduated, to settle down in the tall, pink Florentine palazzo with
its small L-shaped courtyard and potted plants that an imaginative
urban architect had constructed for Stephen's parents in East Ninetieth Street at the time of their marriage. He had originally planned
to rent an apartment of his own, but as the palazzo offered him a
whole floor to himself, and as his job prospects were still uncertain,
it seemed the indicated temporary residence. For ten years, six at
Averhill and four at Yale, he had lived at home only on vacations,
and he had not been prepared for the problems that the uninter-
rupted proximity of his parents and two older sisters would bring.

What was really wrong, he decided reluctantly, was largely his
own fault. Living at home, he could no longer see himself as at
least romantically superior to his family. At school and college he
had written sonnets and prose poems and reveled in English poetry,
and it had been easy enough to feel himself considered a youth of
great promise by friends who asked only that the compliment be returned. But without his claque, without a job or even a regular
schedule, he hardly seemed as different from his mother and sisters,

with their silly parties arnd routine charity committee meetings, or his father, with his endless talk of accounts and investments, as was imperative to his more aspiring soul. This made him a constantly critical companion. His sisters responded to his describing their committee work as purely formal and banal with tart demands that he identify a single disadvantaged person he had ever assisted, and his father, whom he criticized much more guardedly, suggesting that it was the class of capitalists and not the individual who might have been wanting in public spirit, muttered that it was a pity to have provided a son with so expensive an education only to have him turn out a Bolshevik. And his mother . . . well, she was, as always, lovely, adorable and impossible.

At Yale he had cherished the notion of returning to Averhill after graduation as a teacher of English. He had undergone a religious phase at the age of sixteen, and like many boys at the school, he had fallen under the spell of the headmaster's inspiring sermons. Rufus Lockwood knew how to hold a disciple once obtained. He made no secret of his favorites, and the personality that could be so corrosive to the uninitiated exuded a compelling charm for the inner circle. When on one of his many visits back to the school in his Yale years Stephen confided in Dr. Lockwood his ambition to become a teacher, he was at once taken up.

"Indeed, dear boy, there is no nobler calling, and I deem you in every way fitted for it. Why should you look further than your beloved alma mater for a situation? I think you have a good understanding of what Averhill is and what I want it to be, and you would help me to close that gap."

But Stephen had run into an unexpected opposition. Angus Hill, a trustee of the school, was one of those who were inclined to look a bit askance at the protean headmaster.

"He may be a great man, but there's a shrewd practical side to his spiritual nature. I shouldn't be surprised if your post at Averhill would cost me a hundred G's."

And when Stephen under closer examination was obliged to admit that Lockwood *had* suggested that he might teach a course in art as well as English and that his family might see fit to endow a small gallery with a permanent collection of American paintings, his father simply chuckled.

The project was not abandoned, but Stephen had agreed to postpone it for a year and to consider working in the interim for the bank that had custody of the Hill securities.

His temporary idleness, however, was to bear more exotic fruit than a job in a trust company. He had never experienced a great passion — certainly a requisite to any romantic nature — and he came to believe for a time that he had found it.

Angelica Hill was doing over her living room, and she had engaged the services of a popular French decorator. Madame Annette Godron had come to New York a few years before to establish an American branch of the business she and her husband had founded in Paris, but which their domestic discord had made her feel would be better managed with an ocean between them. She had so many and such interesting ideas for the palazzo, for which her admiration seemed boundless, that Angelica, who found her charming, had greatly expanded her plans for redecoration, inviting her advisor after each morning visit to stay for lunch. Stephen, who rarely left the house before the afternoon, was apt to join them at table and soon came under the Godron spell.

She had something in her air of the smart Parisienne of the 1920s, with bobbed dark hair and a look, in calm hazel eyes, of self-assured inquiry, and she was always dressed, at least for business, in simple black. She made no effort to disguise her age; she seemed to affirm that a woman at forty-plus was where she should be. There appeared to lurk behind her quiet briskness, her unvarying equanimity of temper, an acceptance of more things and people than might have been expected of a Gallic businesswoman. And she was certainly the best listener Stephen had ever talked to.

When his mother went upstairs after lunch for her short daily nap he would talk with Annette over coffee until she had to insist on returning to her office. Missing his old Yale friends, bored with his kin and hungry for sympathy, he chattered with unabashed egotism about himself and his problems. Her total attention freed him of all semblance of shame.

She saw no reason that he should not take a post at Averhill if one were available. "Of course, you're never going to make any money at it, but then you don't need money. We Europeans don't understand why rich Americans so often want to be richer."

"Rich Frenchmen aren't like that?"

"Some, of course. But it's considered a bourgeois attitude."

"But I *am* bourgeois."

"So am I, *bien entendu*. What I mean is that in France the bourgeois attitude is not necessarily the dominant one. We don't *have* to bow to it, the way you seem to here."

"Father keeps saying it's a mistake, after only four years at college, to go right back to the school where I've already spent six. He thinks I should give a year to learning how to handle the family money."

"But you're not doing that, are you? You're sitting at home talking to your mother's decorator."

"That's just because I've persuaded him to let me put things off for a bit."

"Would he mind so terribly if you told him you were going to Averhill now? I've noticed that American children have a way of imagining their parents care more about their decisions than perhaps they do."

"He'd be hurt. And then remember he's a trustee of the school."

"And your mother, I suppose, always agrees with him? At least where a son is concerned?"

"Not necessarily. Oh, Annette, she *listens* to you. Would you talk to her?"

She considered this, but then shook her head. "No. Because your father's not really being unreasonable. What's a year?"

"An eternity. When you're as bored as I am."

"Let me tell you something, Stephen Hill." For a moment she was almost grave. "Young men in Goethe's time liked to affect melancholy, even despair. But with most of them it was a mask. Basically they were happy, or at least happier than they knew. But you are not a man to play that game. You would be really unhappy. And that is never safe. Now I must be off to work."

His mother had a box at the opera, where she went two or three times a week, issuing standing invitations to certain old friends and relations to propose themselves for performances of their choice, and soon Annette was a regular guest, slipping silently into the back of the box shortly after the opening curtain. Stephen, watching her immobile profile in the dimness, felt sure that the music merely provided a tranquil background for her thoughts.

"Oh yes," she confessed when he taxed her with this. "What are those silly plots to me? I love to sit in the darkness and let the music carry me back, way, way back."

"To happier times?"

"Why happier? Do you think the past is always happier?"

"Mine was."

" 'Good Hamlet, cast thy nighted colors off.' "

"I will if you'll agree to go to a nightclub with me after this."

"What a charming idea! I should love to."

But in bidding good night to his mother he said only that he was seeing Annette home. He feared she would find it ridiculous that he should be having a "date" (if she could have brought herself to use the word) with a woman so much older.

There was, however, no such feeling reflected in any eyes that he could see at the nightclub to which he took her. Annette did not so much seem young as ageless. She was amusing and amused; she frankly delighted in the loud music and the smartly dressed people. Two couples, passing their table, stopped to greet her, and she introduced Stephen as if it were the most natural thing in the world that they should be together. And when he took her home afterwards, she took leave of him at her doorway with a firm and friendly handshake.

But it was different, at least for him, after that. He wanted to be with her more now, and away from his family. He took her out to dinner at French restaurants, the most expensive in town, and she "paid for her meal," as she gaily put it, by instructing him in what to order, even giving him little lectures about Gallic cooking which she took very seriously, as indeed she proved when she cooked a meal for him at her apartment.

"What do you really think of our friendship?" he asked her that night.

"I think it's very nice."

"And what do you think Mother would think of it?"

"I don't think. I know. She highly approves. She seems to think I'm good for you."

He was immediately incensed. "The sophisticated Parisienne making a gentleman out of a hayseed?"

"You Americans have such a rage for definitions, for putting things in cubbyholes. Can't you and I simply enjoy ourselves?"

What he had never imagined was that love could grow out of such calm. He had always associated it with the usual images of motion, wind in trees, breakers along the coast. But Annette gave him a new sense of the pleasure of being himself at a particular moment, without any need of a morrow. The fact that she was intently and efficiently busy most of the time when away from him did not impinge on the serenity of her demeanor when present. Indeed, it might have helped to create it.

And when their relationship deepened at last, that too seemed to come easily. One night at her apartment, where they had repaired for a drink after the theatre, she simply said, as he rose to leave:

"You know, you can stay if you like."

"I can?"

"Don't be embarrassed if you don't care to. It won't make the least difference in our friendship."

Looking at her intently, he felt that she really meant this. "But what will your doorman say when he sees me leave in the morning?"

"He'll say I have a handsome young lover and that I'm a lucky old bag!"

⚹ ⚹ ⚹

Their affair was carried on in Annette's little box of an apartment at noontimes. The dusky old Italian prints of ruins, the gilded baroque columns by the fireplace, the strips of crimson brocade, the spindly Venetian chairs, all tightly fitted-in accumulations of years of auction haunting, seemed in their lovely deadness to intensify the emotion enacted before them. Stephen had been in love off and on with many girls, met at parties and in summer communities, but he had not before had an affair; his infrequent physical encounters (and that seemed now just the word for them) had been in brothels. He had had to wait for an idle and jobless existence in Manhattan, where he had nothing to do with his mornings but read novels and with his afternoons but play squash or roam the park, to find the fulfilling experience. In the evenings now he was perfectly content to dine with his family, forgoing all carping criticisms, on nights when Annette's presence was required at the social gatherings of her demanding clients.

She was less passionate than he. Indeed he wondered, in occasional fits of exasperation, if she was passionate at all. She enjoyed their lovemaking, but when it was over, it was over. As he lay on the bed afterwards, smoking and languidly watching her dress, seated before the triple mirror on her bureau, he had the feeling that she was preparing to resume her place in the "real" world. And when, ready to leave, she would move briskly over to give him, still sprawled on her sheets, a quick peck on the forehead, she might have been a benign mother falcon leaving her flightless young in the nest while she departed in search of provender.

When he accosted her with this, she took it seriously enough to turn back from the door and seat herself on the bedside.

"Some of us have to work, you know. We can't all spend our days as you do." She patted his bare stomach. "Go now and play squash with your marker at the Racquet Club. This marker has to hang Mrs. Paine's curtains."

He caught her hand. "You don't have to hang any old curtains. You can be as idle as I am."

"You mean you'll 'keep' me? *Merci du compliment!* I'm not quite there yet."

"No, no, no, don't be ridiculous. I mean as my wife. It's only up to you."

She cocked her head as if to consider a curious proposition. "Aren't you forgetting that I *am* married?"

"But you're separated! You could get a divorce."

"I'm also a Catholic. We don't divorce. And besides, I'm old enough to be your mother."

He seized her other hand. "I don't care! Oh, I know you think I'm feckless and irresponsible, but I'm not, fundamentally. We could get married and live at Averhill." He paused. Even at such a moment it struck him that Annette was unthinkable at Averhill. "Or if you didn't like the school, you could have an office in Boston and carry on your business there. It's only an hour away. And I have plenty of money to set you up there. It's all in trust, but the income's mine!"

Only she could have freed one hand and looked at her watch at such a time without being insulting. "My appointment with Mrs. Paine is at two-thirty. I really must go. If you care for me, dear Stephen — and you *are* a very dear Stephen — you won't talk to me about marriage again. It would not only be absurd. It would be grotesque. Now be a good boy and let me go."

"A good *boy!*"

But she had slipped from his grasp and was gone. He could hardly rush after her naked to the elevator corridor. He could only get dressed and call the Racquet Club to cancel his squash lesson. He would walk in the park and consider what to do next. For a while he was too excited to orient his thoughts, but when he reached the reservoir he became calmer. What had happened to him was clear enough: he had taken the simple, decisive step to true manhood. He had reached out at last to take a firm hold of his hitherto limp and listless destiny and yank it roughly into shape. Annette was everything he had always needed. How he saw it now! She would arm him to face his father and turn the nebulous dream of teaching at Averhill into a shining reality. Now that he properly considered it, she would be far from unthinkable in the school. She would have an office in Boston, of course, but she might have to go to it only three or four times a week. She could redo houses in the wealthy suburban neighborhood. She might even redecorate some of Averhill's buildings! They could do with her touch. And mightn't she even teach a course in French literature? Other schools had women teachers. Why not?

He resolved now to go home and have it out with his mother. She had unexpected tolerances as well as unexpected rigidities; one could never be quite sure where she would come out. And then he was convinced that she loved him better than anyone else in the world, including his father. She would want him to be happy. He did not know how much she knew about him and Annette, but the recent silence of his whole family on that subject was surely an indication that they were watching and waiting for something.

He found her at tea with two ladies, and he had to wait until they left. But she saw at once that he had something on his mind, and as soon as they were alone she suggested:

"Why don't you get us a cocktail, darling, and tell me all about it?"

"I think, if you don't mind, I'd rather talk to you first. It's about Annette. You know I've been seeing a lot of her."

"Oh, yes."

"She says you approve."

"Why not? I'm devoted to Annette, and I have total confidence in her."

He winced. "Confidence that she won't try to marry me, is that it? Your confidence was justified. She turned me down flat. But I am determined to prevail upon her to change her mind."

Angelica rose with a sudden start and took hurried steps over to him. When he jumped up, she threw her arms around him and drew him to her in that strong silky clasp that had always annihilated his filial resistance.

"Oh, my darling boy, I know how hard this is on you now, but believe me, Annette is right. It would never work out."

He found that his shoulders were actually shaking with resentment. For the first time in his life he jerked himself almost brutally free from her embrace.

"I thought you at least would understand. You've always held yourself out as a romantic."

"But, dear child, is this really so romantic?"

"Because of our ages?"

"Well, that's the big thing, isn't it? You and she couldn't have a family."

"What makes you so sure of that? Women older than Annette have had babies."

"But not after a certain thing has happened."

"And what makes you think it's happened to her?"

"Because she's told me. Annette, you will remember, is my friend, too. I'd go along with almost anything that would make you happy, my child, but not something that would mean you could never have children."

He read in the new gleam of resolution in those usually gentle eyes that his case was lost. She and Annette were bound as allies in a bond he could never hope to breach. In a sudden seizure of anger and bitterness he wondered if the bond was between them as women or as old women. Was he only a silly, frustrated boy?

"It's the old French story, I suppose. The mama who wants her baby initiated in the rites of love by an experienced woman. My God, did you even pay her?"

"You are not only being perfectly disgusting. You're being inso- lent. Will you please go to your own room. I have nothing more to say to you."

"Mother, listen . . ."

"*Go,* Stephen! Go at once."

Alone in his study everything seemed to be draining out of him in a horrid mess of love and hate. Of course it was all over between him and Annette. He could no more have made love to her now than to his mother. Annette herself would have recognized this; she must have known that his mother would tell him about her menopause. "To make men pause!" he cried jeeringly aloud. Why had she told Angelica except to provide her with a way of bringing the affair to a close?

His mind was now a feverish arena of imagined and remembered things. The vision of Annette's breasts blurred with that of his mother's, peeked at when he was a boy hiding in her bedroom, as she emerged from her bathroom with her robe parted. He shut his eyes in pain, trying to separate the thought of flesh untouchable from that of flesh touched. And suddenly an ancient but always persistent fantasy of his swept over the disordered landscape of his mind, though in a grotesquely altered form. He had imagined himself as Paris of Troy coming to judge the beauty of the three rival goddesses, boldly smiling, daringly impertinent, insisting that they strip to the skin for his better contemplation of their parts. But as they ambled before him now in wanton naked majesty, their Rubenesque bosoms and thighs and abdomens seemed wrinkled and saggy, and, then, when they appeared ready to close in on their judge, hot and panting in their eagerness to persuade him to give each the award, he feared he would be stifled in their ancient flesh and took to his heels.

He came down to dinner only because he could not bear to be alone with himself any longer. His mother was upstairs; she had pleaded a headache and would have her meal on a tray. His father and both sisters were at the table. It was a family party — a sufficiently rare event. Had the girls been summoned to their mother's chamber and told in no event to go out that night?

The conversation was desultory. Stephen did not utter a word. But at dessert Angus suddenly glanced down the board at his son and raised his nightly glass of champagne in an unusual and friendly salute.

"I have just had Dr. Lockwood on the telephone, my boy. It seems there's a good opening there next fall, and he urged me to persuade you to take it. What could I say but yes? Learning about family securities will just have to wait, I suppose. I assume you'll need the interim to prepare your courses. Including an introduction to American art. For I told him I'd give that gallery my serious consideration."

So he knew too. They all knew. His mother had done quick work. Wasn't it just as well? But in the first flush of his gratitude and in his sudden surge of warmth for this distant and rarely confiding father, he found himself wondering if the latter's impenetrable restraint might not have been a needed armor against the emotional ravages of his spouse.

After dinner Angus retired as usual to his study, and Stephen was left in the parlor with his sisters. Neither Janine nor Susan had their mother's beauty; both were conventionally, even a bit boringly pretty. They had flat, round faces that would probably bear the years ill, but their eyes were appealing and their smiles not without charm, and they dressed well. That they were still unmarried at twenty-five and twenty-three worried no one, including themselves; it was so obvious they were destined for good matches. Janine was the more sophisticated, the more practical of the two; Susan liked to think of herself as romantic, like Stephen, but they were essentially alike.

Janine now revealed that their mother had indeed summoned them to tell them about Annette. She and Susan were sufficiently sympathetic to him, but it was perfectly evident that they considered his affair a bit ridiculous. Susan at least tried to see it as a gainful experience.

"Anyway, you can say you've had a great love in your life," she pointed out. "I thought I might have had one with Brian Emden last winter, but I got over it too soon. I guess you have to work on those things."

"Isn't it rather futile to work on one if you're going to have to give it up in the end?" Janine asked her.

"But doesn't everyone want a great love?"

"Only if it's going to end in marriage."

"But that's so prosaic, Janny!"

"Look at Mother and Father. They had a great love and married."

Susan glanced dubiously in the direction of Angus's study. "I can't really imagine having a great love for Father," she said in a lower voice. "A love, yes, of course, but not a great one."

Janine appealed to their still silent brother. "What do you think, Steve? Do you think Mother and Father had a great love?"

Stephen glanced from one to the other to show them his awareness that they were trying to distract him from a supposed obsession.

"Well, I think Father must have, for her," he replied at last. "At least in the beginning. But Mother, no. I don't suppose Mother was ever subject to great passion. It's not really her thing, is it?"

"What is her thing, then?" Susan demanded.

"To inspire one, I guess."

And looking at his sisters he wondered if indeed any woman was capable of a great passion. Was that why Averhill had seemed to him such a citadel of romantic feeling? Precisely because it was a male monastery?

9 ...

On a cloudless October morning, as cold as it was bright, a month after the commencement of his first term as a master at Averhill, Stephen stood before the blackboard of his classroom and chalked carefully the first stanza of John Donne's "A Valediction: On Weeping."

> Let me pour forth
> My tears before thy face, whilst I stay here;
> For thy face coins them, and thy stamp they bear,
> And by this mintage they are something worth,
> For thus they be
> Pregnant of thee;
> Fruits of much grief they are, emblems of more:
> When a tear falls that *thou* falls which it bore;
> So thou and I are nothing then, when on a divers shore.

As he wrote, a small select English class, the sixth form (or senior) "Upper A," scribbled the daily ten-minute theme on their assigned reading. There were a dozen of them; some had been first formers in Stephen's last year as a student in the school, and they treated him with a friendly if at times sarcastic respect. Two were prefects in his dormitory and helped him to keep order there. He

cherished the hope that he had achieved a precarious balance between intimacy and authority.

Beside the text now he drew two crescents to represent two eyes
confronting each other, labeling one *M* and one *F*. Between and
below the crescents he drew several small circles in each of which
he placed a human figure, using five lines for the body and limbs
and a dot for the head, and differentiating the sexes with oblongs
for pants and a triangle for a dress. Then he turned to address the
class. Their writing time was up.

"What do you think the poet means, Evarts, by the clause 'that
thou falls which it bore'?"

"That got me, sir. I haven't a clue."

"Emerson?"

"Could it mean, sir, that the lady is of easy virtue? 'Fall' could
mean that she had been seduced. And that might explain the
last line. The man and woman have become nothing because she
has lost her virtue and he has been guilty of seduction."

"Well that is certainly ingenious," Stephen commented in surprise. "Though I don't know that in a day of double standards a
successful male lover would be considered a nothing. I suppose
you could argue that the divers shore meant that she was no longer
respectable and he still was."

A grave stout boy with thick-lensed glasses raised his hand.

"Yes, Dixon."

"The lady is certainly going to lose her reputation because we
know she's pregnant."

"I think you're confused there. Isn't it the tear that's pregnant?"

"I suggest, sir, if I may put it so, that the tear is the symbol of
the female egg that has received the male sperm."

Stephen glanced about the class. No one was smiling, but that
didn't mean they weren't riding him. Indeed it probably meant
they were. He decided, anyway, to take the suggestion seriously.

"And I suppose you would then argue," he continued, turning
to the blackboard, "that the impregnated cell is an emblem of
more grief because the lady's fault will soon become apparent to

the world. But why should the tears be fruits of *grief?* There must have been some pleasure in the making of them. And why should the man be weeping? Is that a likely reaction to being told of the lady's plight?"

"Men always weep in poetry. It's a convention."

"But they weep at noble things, not at embarrassing ones. I suggest that he's weeping because they're about to be parted. He may have been called to the wars. At any rate, it seems clear that he's going away."

"I don't see why he should weep at that. Isn't it the best thing that could happen to him under the circumstances?"

The class burst into laughter, and Stephen was sure now that it had all been planned. But he decided it would be better to join in the mirth.

"Let's be serious, gentlemen," he proceeded when the room was quiet. "Craven, will you give us *your* version of what the stanza is about."

"Certainly, sir." Craven now read from the theme he had just completed. "The lovers, gazing into each other's eyes, are weeping over their imminent separation. The image of each, reflected in the eye of the beholder, becomes encapsulated in a tear and necessarily falls and dissolves when the tear falls. Thus the lovers envision their own annihilation in weeping."

"Very good, Craven! That's it, I think. And the tears suggest the sea that will soon be between them, which prepares the way for the great emotive language of the third stanza." Stephen now recited in a full voice:

> "O more than moon,
> Draw not up seas to drown me in thy sphere,
> Weep me not dead in thine arms, but forbear
> To teach the sea what it may do too soon."

After a pause he took his seat at the desk. "To me those four lines are the greatest poetry," he said gravely.

"Sir?" The raised hand was that of Giles Woodward, whose small, dark ferret face seemed to challenge anyone to deny his position as brightest of a bright class. "May I offer a different interpretation?"

"Of course."

"You told us last week that a poem does not have to be chained — I believe that was your term — to the century of its composition. That it could be used as a flexible instrument to serve the uses — or even the images — of a later time."

"To some extent."

"Oh, only to some extent? To what extent?" There was a shade of impertinence in Woodward's inquiring mien.

"Let's have that interpretation, Giles."

First names were not used in classroom, and Giles's grin showed that he was prepared to take full advantage of the slip. He proceeded now with confidence. "Well, the little sticks that you have drawn to show the sex of the persons in each tear remind me of the signs on washroom doors. I seem even to hear the cascade of the flushed toilets within that sweep away the lovers and make them nothing indeed."

Woodward turned with a show of indignation to confront the laughter in the row behind him. "No, I'm serious! The dropping tears, droppings, can represent excretion, the pouring out of love, all cleansed and removed by the water, the sea, the flushing of plumbing. Isn't something like that what Donne's getting at?"

There was no doubt now that he was faced with a serious and challenging impertinence, but Stephen still wondered if he could not make something out of it.

"Are you suggesting, Woodward, that the poet is relating love to a less exalted bodily function?"

"Does he have to? Can't *we*? Isn't that your theory? And what about that Yeats poem we read last week?

> "A woman can be proud and stiff
> when on love intent,

But love has pitched his mansion
In the place of excrement?"

Stephen threw up his hands. "Excellent, Giles. First rate."
And he nodded in approval as the class applauded.

He was still feeling his way with care in his second month at
Averhill. It was his hope that, being the only master who was himself a graduate of the school, and having been out a mere five years,
he might provide a useful bridge between the students and faculty.
In this he was encouraged by the headmaster himself, who used to
insist that the greatest fault of pedagogues lay in their assumption
that the workings of the juvenile mind in any way resembled their
own.

"You must give your imagination daily calisthenics, Stephen.
Academia tends to paralyze it. Our masters adore classifications. If
I had my way we'd have no classes or courses. We'd simply sit in a
circle, like Socrates and his young friends, and merge all subjects in
a single pursuit of knowledge and the love of God."

Stephen of course was aware that Lockwood was prone to such
flights of hyperbole. A master in a physics lab who lectured on
Wordsworth's intimations of immortality might find himself re-
proved for taking his superior's theory too literally. Nobody was
more precise in his expectations of just what ground had to be covered by which teacher than the Socratic headmaster. But Stephen
liked to emphasize to himself the similarity at least of his and
Lockwood's ideals.

He knew that a master at Averhill could not really be a friend
of the younger boys, but he saw no reason that some helpful con-
geniality could not be established between himself and members of
the graduating class, and he cultivated particularly the three prefects in his dormitory, inviting them to sit up late in his study on
Saturday nights drinking cider and discussing their lives and ambi-
tions and what the school was and what it could be. He knew he
had attained some degree of success when the prefects began inviting the prefects in the two neighboring dorms to join them. The
danger was always that when the talk turned to sex, the formality

of the master-student relationship might be fatally eroded, but Stephen tried to avoid this by keeping the discussion on a general plane and outlawing illustrations drawn from personal experience.

His early sense of success, however, received a mortifying blow only a week after his class on the Donne "Valediction." Roy Evans, head of the English department and senior master of the school, a man whom Stephen had much admired as a student and liked and trusted as a cohort, administered the reproof as tactfully as possible.

"I hear you're getting on splendidly with the sixth Upper A," he told Stephen one morning in the faculty coffee room. "You're going to be a real help in proving my theory that these special groups of brighter students should not be held back by the slower ones. But don't you think they're still a bit young for Yeats's Crazy Jane poems?"

"Would Yeats have been, at seventeen?"

"I don't mean that they're too young individually, but as a class. As a group they still tend to giggle at an association of love and excretion."

"So you heard about that."

"I did. And not from any of the sixth Upper A, either. Your little discussion of love and plumbing has been the subject of smirks and tee-hees at my fourth form lunch table."

"I'm hardly responsible for that."

"Oh, but you are, my boy. That's the Averhill system."

"I thought I could decide what I could teach my class."

"And what made you think *that?*" Roy's goggle of astonishment was meant to be comic, but it nonetheless underlined the basic gravity of their dispute. "Do you think *I* can?" He gripped Stephen's shoulder in friendly fashion and led him to a corner, farther away from the other masters. "Look, my friend, you know I wouldn't give a tinker's damn myself. You could have them reading *Lady Chatterley's Lover* as far as I'm concerned. Suppose they do giggle? That's not the end of the world. But you must know from your own experience here that the old man finds out everything that goes on on this campus."

"Dr. Lockwood can be very broad-minded at times."

"Yes, but he decides what times those are. And he particularly dislikes to have them chosen by his subordinates."

Stephen had nothing more to say, but when Roy left him, he took the matter up with Tommy Barnes, who had constituted himself his special friend and advisor. Together they coached third form football. Stephen liked the friendly young minister, whom he remembered with affection from his own school days, though he found his big brother attitude verging at times on the fatuous. And Tommy was indeed horrified at his project of appealing Roy's implied interdict to the headmaster himself.

"You mean you'd actually quote that Yeats poem to Dr. Lockwood!" Tommy demanded, gaping. "Are you out of your mind? When he gets roused on a moral point, he actually *likes* to hurt people. Even his protégés."

"And I'm one of those?"

"Well, you are *now*."

Tommy was so upset that Stephen should even be considering so suicidal an idea that he asked him to come to supper at his little cottage the following night. His wife, he explained, had worked for the headmaster the year before and was something of an expert on the imperial moods. "See what *she* will think of your project," he said, rolling his eyes to express the extremity of her probable view.

Stephen had met Natica Barnes at lunch at the school and at tea at Mrs. Lockwood's and had wondered why that pretty little brunette, who had a reputation for brains, should have chosen so unstellar a mate. In her home the question presented itself more forcibly. There was not much, it was true, that one could do with the tiny rooms, but it struck him nonetheless that Tommy's wife had done the minimum. The prints of flowers and birds on the walls were at worst dull and at best conventional, and the too bright new chintz in the living room seemed to proclaim its owners' need to have it take on all the job of decorating. The meal was adequate but, in Dr. Johnson's phrase, "not one to ask a man to." Stephen got the impression that her husband bored Natica, not by any sullenness of her demeanor or even by any failure of attention, but by the quickness with which she apprehended what he was trying to say and the slight sharpness with which she interrupted him.

"I know the poem you mean, dear," she put in, after Tommy had spent minutes trying to put delicately what Yeats had expressed more forcefully. "It's where love has pitched his mansion, isn't it? I quite agree that Dr. Lockwood would find that objectionable in any master's class at Averhill. It's conceivable, I admit, that he would be capable of introducing it in one of his own. There's no telling where his self-dramatization might lead him. But if Stephen is thinking of asking his approval to include the Crazy Jane poems in his own course, yes, I agree, he had much better forget it."

Stephen expressed his surrender with a smile. "I guess that's that, then."

The telephone rang towards the end of their meal, and Tommy answered it. It was a summons from the headmaster, and he left after a hurried final bite and a mumbled apology.

"The school does reach a rather long arm into your life, doesn't it?" Stephen commented. "It must be hard at times to be a master's wife."

"It's not always easy, certainly."

She was distinctly more relaxed with her husband away. She went into the pantry to get the bottle of white wine he had frugally recorked, and refilled both their glasses.

"You must sometimes wish that Tommy had a more impersonal boss, like a bank or a business."

She glanced about the room in mock fear of eavesdroppers. "Are you seeking to entrap me? How do I know you're not a spy sent by the most high?"

"Me? The tiniest cog in the academic machine?"

"But that's not the way we see you here at all. We see you as the son and heir of a powerful trustee, a favorite of the headmaster, in short, a comer."

"I can never seem to get away from the money," he said disgustedly. "And the worst part of it is that there's always some truth in it. Dr. Lockwood *is* interested in what my old man can do for the school. Any headmaster would be."

"Oh, you're taking me much too seriously. It's only envy, after all. Everyone says you're doing very well indeed. Tommy thinks the world of you, I know."

"And as a matter of fact we're not all that rich," he continued in the same vein. "Plenty of Father's friends are much better heeled than he is."

She nodded. "I can appreciate that. I grew up on the north shore of Long Island with my pauper's nose pressed to the grilled gates of the great estates there. I could see that wherever there's a huddle of millionaires, some are going to be poorer than others. Indeed, some may be so much poorer that they can almost kid themselves they're ordinary folk."

"Now you *are* laughing at me. I must have sounded like an awful ass. But still I *am* ordinary. And at least I know it."

She shook her head firmly. "Ah, but you're not. And you never will be. People *look* at you."

"What makes you think that?"

"Because I did. When I came up to the Halloween dance with Grant DeVoe. You were a sixth former, and if you don't mind my saying so, a very handsome one." Her smile was that of the matron who could afford, in her domestic security, the luxury of extravagant language. Or was the smile a mask?

"Did we meet? I'm embarrassed that I don't remember."

"We didn't actually meet. But you were pointed out to me."

"By Grant DeVoe?"

"Presumably."

He decided to give her a dose of her own candor. "Do you mind my saying I never liked him? You were far too good for him."

"He thought it was the other way round."

"That proves I was right and that he's a fatuous ass. Was that the only time you were at Averhill before you came here with Tommy?"

"Yes. But the memory is a vivid one." She gave him the sense of holding back important things, as if in a game they were playing.

"May I ask you a personal question? Why did you quit working for Dr. Lockwood?"

"It was he who decided that. Or rather Mrs. Lockwood decided for him. She paid me the compliment of being jealous. It was not, I believe, that she suspected me of amorous designs on her venerable spouse. But she found me officious."

"I'm sure she was wrong."

"She was quite wrong. But at Averhill it doesn't necessarily help one to be in the right. Certainly not if one is only the wife of a poor curate."

He smiled. "You must have decided I'm not a spy if you tell me that."

"Or that I don't care if you are."

He frowned. "You're not really happy at the school, are you? I hate to think that."

"Why should it matter to you?"

"I guess because I love Averhill so."

"And it can't be heaven unless everyone in it is happy?"

"That must be it. Why do you find it so bad a place?"

She considered this. "I don't suppose it really is, for the boys anyway. And I imagine the brand of education is at least equal to the best of the other preparatory schools. But Lockwood is certainly a despot. I concede that may not always be a bad thing for a headmaster to be. It enables him to get a lot of things done, and the boys expect it of him, and anyway they'll be out of here soon enough. But it can have a bad effect on the faculty, who are exposed to it permanently. If they kowtow they tend to become meek and oily, and if they protest they're fired or ignored, and in the latter case they become bitter."

"And which do you think I'll become?"

"Neither. I tell you, you're different. Your relationship with the headmaster is different."

"I'm afraid I have a very different view of Dr. Lockwood. Of course, he's a bit of a tyrant at times, but that's just part of the headmaster act. It has nothing to do with the great heart behind it."

"Are you so very sure of the greatness of that organ?"

"Absolutely sure! It's too easy to exaggerate the dictatorial quality of any headmaster. And isn't it a smallness in any teacher to become bitter or intimidated by a little brusqueness of manner?"

"You agreed, didn't you, just now that it would be unwise to go to him about the Crazy Jane poems?"

"But that was only a minor matter!"

"Isn't that the way intimidation starts?"

He found her persistence irritating. "Of course, you think it's only my money that makes me talk so bold."

"I think it's part of it. But not all. You have some fire in you. Don't lose it."

When they rose from the table, he thought they would retire to the living room, that she might even offer him a drink. But instead she led him to the front door to bid him good night.

"I see you're surprised I'm making it such an early evening. But Marjorie Evans can see this door from her front windows. She may have already noted that Tommy has gone and that you're still here. Young bachelor masters and masters' wives are not encouraged to have tête-à-têtes at Averhill."

He stared. "My God, can the place be that petty?"

"You have a lot to learn, my friend. And now, good night!"

10 ⋰

STEPHEN HAD known Mrs. Estelle Knight as a schoolboy knows the semi-reclusive wife of one of the older masters — little more than by sight. But as Mrs. Knight's family mansion on the Hudson had been a neighbor to Redwood, and as Angelica had been a childhood friend of Estelle's younger sister, she had insisted that her son, now a master himself, call on her.

"She's an odd duck, I admit, full of airs and fancies, but she's basically rather an old dear, and I think she's had a hard life. Wilbur is a good man, but too much the pedagogue . . . Oh, I'm sorry, darling, I keep forgetting you're one yourself now. Still, you knew Wilbur at school; you know what I mean — the solemn Latin teacher who makes his class greet him with a *Salve, magister*. Didn't you tell me that yourself? That wasn't the life Estelle dreamed of in the old days in Rhinebeck. She likes to think of herself as a poetess, but she bought up the whole edition of the one book she managed to get printed. Apparently she got cold feet just before publication. But be kind and go to see her."

Stephen performed his duty on an October Sunday afternoon. The Knights lived in a large Elizabethan red-brick house, somewhat apart from the other faculty residences, which they had built. The long dusky living room, with red damask curtains partially drawn, into which he was ushered to await his hostess seemed to proclaim the independence from the school that a private fortune conferred. The walls were paneled in dark linen fold, and the carved cream-colored ceiling bore the roses and portcullises of the Tudors. A good deal of silver, platters and chalices, glinted on side tables; the thin cushions of the high Jacobean chairs were a faded pink. Estelle's entrance, after he had waited ten minutes, struck him as emulating a great actress in retirement.

"So! Angelica's boy has come to see me at last. Do you realize, Stephen Hill, that you never once set foot in this house the whole time you were a boy at school?"

He knew that she was several years older than his mother, which put her certainly in her sixties, but the very violence with which she combated the years made her seem older. Was all that high-piled reddish auburn hair a wig? The thick powder and painted blue under her large black eyes made a kind of mask of features that untouched might have been fine enough: the distinguished aquiline nose, the high brow, the firm chin. And her slow pace across the room, the short train of her black velvet tea gown trailing behind her, was not without a certain regal dignity. She might have been an aging Elizabeth giving audience to a potential Essex. Indeed, it occurred to him that such was exactly what she was mentally enacting.

"I doubt that Dr. Lockwood would have approved of his boys making social calls."

She drew herself up at this and then took a rather stately seat in a high-backed chair, indicating with a gesture that he should do the same. "There are many things of which Dr. Lockwood doesn't approve. He's a great one for slamming doors and windows. I wonder if he isn't a bit afraid of the out-of-doors of life."

It seemed an odd remark from one who had encased herself in such a gilded shell, but Stephen said nothing, and she proceeded to ask him for news of his "beautiful mother," who, she told him, had been dubbed the "Rhine maiden" by the Hudson River neighborhood of their younger days.

"Your mother was the loveliest of the Kip sisters, yet they were all lovely. My mother used to deplore the fact that I didn't have Angelica Kip's golden hair or Dotty Kip's dainty feet. I was so mortified! But tell me about yourself, young man. How are you getting on with your English classes? Do you find that you strike any sparks? Are there any young Keatses or Shelleys in that assemblage of bankers' sons? Alas, I fear not. You'd have as much chance of finding a poet in my accountant. 'Ode to a Capital Loss Carryover'!" She threw back her head to give vent to a throaty laugh.

"Some of the boys are intelligent enough," Stephen countered. "And some even have rather wild imaginations. Though I can't help suspecting that to them Donne, for example, is a kind of double acrostic to be solved. That they have no concept of the lyric poetry that explodes out of his elaborate technique."

"No sense of the mortal moon passage, you mean?" And once more the auburn pile of tresses was tilted back, and the deep voice suddenly soared. " 'Weep me not dead in thine arms! Teach not the sea to do what it may do too soon.' "

He was startled to hear her deliver, and with such vigor, his favorite lines. "How feelingly you recite that! Is it true what Mother told me about your suppressing your book? Wasn't that a loss to poetry lovers?"

"It's not quite a loss. I believe the copies are in a warehouse somewhere. And a number of the poems appeared in magazines. There was even one in *The Atlantic Monthly*."

"Would you lend me a copy? I'd love to read them."

"My dear boy, I'll be happy to give you one! It's entitled *Weep Me Not Dead*. So you see how dear the 'Valediction' is to me."

"Is it too personal for you to tell me why you wouldn't let the book appear?"

"I don't think so. Unless you feel it might be disloyal for you to hear something not wholly laudatory about your sacred headmaster."

"Dr. Lockwood disapproved of your publishing?"

She shook her head slowly, sadly. "Rufus Lockwood never took me seriously enough to approve or disapprove of anything I did.

What is a master's consort in his great academy? The only thing he deigned to object to in me was that my private means made me less subject to the absolute control he loves to exercise over his little court. Oh no, it was not my poor poems that he cared about. My dear husband, who is the noblest as well as the most loving of men — I know the boys find him stuffy; you undoubtedly did, too . . ."

"Oh, no."

"Anyway, you *will* appreciate him, I know, in time. You're too intelligent not to. But to the point. Wilbur had long urged me to gather my little efforts into a book and exhibit them to the world. But I'd always had a horror of the idea of being held up to the sneering gaze of Philistines. Indeed it was all he could do to get me to consent to appear in the little magazines. He sometimes even sent in poems without my knowledge. But at last he prevailed upon me to do as he wished. A publisher was found, and this pretty booklet was duly printed." Here she picked up a blue leather volume with a flower border, evidently specially bound for herself, from the table at her side. "But a few weeks before the publication date an event occurred that took the heart out of me."

She paused so long now, staring fixedly across the room at nothing in particular, that he felt constrained to ask her if the experience had not been too painful to relate.

"No, no," she answered hastily. "I feel I can tell you anything. You are *très sympathique*. My husband had once been offered the post of headmaster of a small boys' preparatory school near Rhinebeck, close to my old family home and also, of course, to your dear mother's. It was not a great institution, but he had always dreamed of a school of his own, and for me it would have been sheer heaven, back to the river, close to my brother and many old friends. I have sometimes felt, foolish as it sounds, that my muse, if I dare call it that, can flourish only on the banks of the glorious Hudson. But Rufus Lockwood decreed otherwise. He promised Wilbur the post of senior master, as soon as it should become vacant, if he would stay. He persuaded him that he was committed to Averhill, that his and the school's destinies were somehow intertwined, that it was even his *duty* to remain. And poor Wilbur, as he well knew, is very vulnerable to the word 'duty.' Of course, all that Lockwood wanted was an expert Latin teacher. They were getting very hard to find. So we stayed on, and when the then senior master retired . . . well, *you* tell me what happened."

"It was given to someone else?"

"It was given to the man who still holds it! To Roy Evans, though he was a decade younger than Wilbur, and so young at the time that we had never even considered him a candidate."

"How did Dr. Lockwood explain it?"

"God doesn't have to explain. I believe there was something said about the trustees finding Wilbur too classical, but we all know that Rufus Lockwood dominates his board. No, my friend, he never had any intention of making Wilbur senior master. He simply didn't want to lose a good Latin teacher. What was it to him that by the time he made his appointment of Evans, Wilbur was too old to be considered for another headmastership? The accent had swung to youth."

"How shocking!"

"The only really shocking thing was that Wilbur and I had been naïve enough to believe him. But the whole wretched business filled me with such a sickness of heart that I lost all desire to show my poems to a world in which such a man as Lockwood was esteemed and admired."

Stephen decided that he had better not comment on this. She had talked freely to him; she might talk with equal freedom to others. He had not enjoyed hearing her story, but after all, had it come as a complete surprise? Even as a sixth former he had taught himself to excuse certain of the headmaster's highhanded acts as the fruit of a noble passion to place his school above all other interests.

"Would it be asking too much to have you read one of your poems?"

It was a happy notion. Rufus Lockwood and his opportunism

vanished away as Estelle at once opened the little blue volume.

"I shan't try your patience. I'll read you the shortest one in the book! What I call a *chinoiserie*. But promise you won't laugh."

He held up a hand in affirmation, and she turned the leaves.

"Ah, here it is." She cleared her throat. "It's called 'On Watching a Child at Breakfast.' "

> "It must be very nice to feel
> Ecstasy
> About oatmeal."

The oddest thing about her performance was that it gave a certain validity to the silly jingle. Reciting the first line, she leaned down as if addressing a child and spoke with the saccharine condescension of a fatuous adult. Then she threw back her head, closed her eyes and almost cried out the word "ecstasy."

"That has always been one of my favorites, Estelle."

Stephen turned to face Wilbur Knight in the doorway. Grave, gray, with chiseled features, a rigid posture and a beautiful tweed sports jacket which he wore like a morning coat, the head of the classics department seemed the symbol of all that was needed in a rational world to keep his wife's exuberance in check.

"Mrs. Knight has been entertaining me so well, sir, that I've overstayed my leave. I really must get back to my dorm before supper."

"Well now you know the way, as the saying is!" his hostess exclaimed. "If you like reading poetry, how would you care to come in some afternoon and read with me and Natica Barnes? I find her uncommonly intelligent, a real oasis in this academic dryness."

"I'd love to, but you know what my schedule is. I'll certainly try."

Wilbur Knight attended him to the hall, and Stephen felt that he must cut a sorry figure in the older man's eyes, listening to an old woman read her silly verse on a beautiful afternoon when all youth should be out-of-doors. But Knight's words expressed no such reaction.

"It was kind of you to call on my wife, Stephen. She has few amusements, I fear. I'm sure that reading poetry aloud with a bunch of women is not your idea of an afternoon sport, but if you ever have a free hour to spare her, I should much appreciate it."

Walking hurriedly back to school in the darkening air, Stephen decided that the old Latin teacher was very likely the saint his wife deemed him.

11 ....

STEPHEN WAS able to discount much of Mrs. Knight's grievance against the headmaster as the exaggeration of a perfervid imagination, but he had more trouble reconciling Natica Barnes's cool assessment of Lockwood with his own high admiration of the man. She had been willing to exempt the boys from the ill effects of what she had called Lockwood's despotic regime, but only because their subjection to it was of limited term. But wasn't that term the most impressionable part of their lives? Hadn't it been of his own?

He had chosen to see Lockwood as a kind of craggy creative genius, forgivably indifferent, even callous in his treatment of lesser beings who stumbled between him and his goals. He had conceived of him as a man whose passionate sense of divine light and fierce need to convey some rays of it to his boys made any idea of ordinary human rights on his campus seem secondary or even irrelevant. And his impression of the headmaster's idealism had bathed the school in a romantic light that had persisted even after his college years had considerably dulled his religious faith. Indeed it was this that had really motivated his return to the school.

Could he now afford to have much to do with a woman whose radically different opinion, if accepted by him, would strip Averhill and his own life of a juice so apparently essential to his imagination?

But he seemed to have lost his choice in the matter. The image of Natica Barnes was constantly in his mind. At lunch in the dining hall when she was sitting by Tommy at a neighboring table, he would try not to be too obviously glancing her way. He noted that the sixth formers at his own table were equally aware of her, and he could recall from his school days the kind of lewd comments that were being whispered. Of course she had little competition from the other wives, on the whole a dowdy lot, or from the waitresses, all of middle age or elderly (Lockwood notoriously vetoed the employment of any female who might arouse the lust of his boys), but even among her peers Natica would, Stephen felt sure, have made a neat, trim, lively and shapely impression. Poor Annette seemed old and faded in his suddenly disloyal memory. Why on earth had she married a clod like Barnes?

"How would you like to bang her?"

Stephen almost started to hear the question, from one boy to another, several seats down the table. But he restrained the impulse to reprove them when he saw they had been watching him watch her and that the question, ostensibly private, had really been mockingly aimed at himself. He pretended not to have heard.

It was the custom for the masters and their wives to enter the dining hall ahead of the student body and take their positions at their tables while the boys filed in. One day, to Stephen's surprise and quickly guarded excitement, Natica walked over to stand behind the chair on his right.

"I don't see why the poor bachelor masters shouldn't have a hostess every now and then. I've told Tommy I'm going to sit here today. If you don't mind, that is."

"The boys will be delighted."

"Only the boys?"

"They will be only delighted. *I* will be enchanted."

The headmaster's table was on a dais in a large bay. When Lockwood had completed his thundered grace and taken his seat with the rest of the assembly, Stephen fancied that the eye that had briefly swept that crowded chamber had taken in Mrs. Barnes's altered seat.

The sixth formers around him were effusive in their welcome of her. Their talk fell on the subject of the mother of a first former who had had the brass to ask the headmaster himself to take her on a tour of the school pantry and kitchen to check on their cleanliness. Natica asked what his response had been.

"Oh, he agreed to be her guide," one boy replied. "He said he'd always wanted to see the kitchen!"

"That sounds like him," she noted. "Only of course it wasn't true. I'm sure he knows every pot and pan. But I'm glad one mother at least stood up to him. The poor parents come up here to find their sons completely free from their control. They have to shed their authority like tourists taking off their shoes in a mosque."

"Sometimes their sons even assume it over *them*," another boy offered. "I heard Dicky Daniels asking that obese mother of his if she couldn't manage to look a little thinner when she went to talk to Dr. Lockwood."

"Oh, poor woman!" Natica exclaimed with a fine show of dismay. "And did she comply? Did she manage to suck it in?"

There was general laughter. Then Giles Woodward, of the Donne plumbing theory, took a determined conversational lead.

"But it's not only the headmaster's stern stare that the poor parents are subjected to. The whole school feels free to inspect them as if they were slaves at auction in the old South. Hadley Clark, coming out of chapel with his mother last Sunday, had the humiliation of hearing the shortness of her legs discussed by a bunch of fifth formers."

"But you boys are terrible! Stephen, tell them how terrible they are. Didn't young Clark resent the remarks?"

"He's only a third former, Mrs. Barnes."

"He wouldn't have left the place in one piece."

"Shall we tell Mrs. Barnes what we did to that snotty Eustis kid who got so hot at our calling his old man a crook?"

"You didn't!"

"But he *was* a crook, Mrs. Barnes. We read about it in the *Times*. He only got off by pleading the statute of limitations."

"Even so, poor boy, you shouldn't have thrown it in his face."

But her tone showed that she was with them, and Stephen had a happy sense of the unity of their little group. He even recognized, with a pang of envy, what a pleasant thing it might be to have such a wife at school.

As he and Natica walked out of the hall together she observed: "Children are often ashamed of their parents. I know I was of mine. And I was even more ashamed of being ashamed! But *you* couldn't have felt anything like that."

"Why do you say that?"

"Oh, because the Hills are such a famous family. And Mrs. Knight tells me your mother's a great beauty."

"But I used to be terribly embarrassed by the ostentatious way they arrived at school when I was a boy here."

"How do you mean?"

He noted her attention and played up to it. "Well, there was one particularly awful Sunday that I remember when Dad and Mother arrived in *two* cars, just after chapel, while the whole school was coming out and could see them, right there by the Cabot Gate. Dad was driving one of my sisters in a big yellow Hispano touring car, and Mother, who didn't like to be blown, was in a green Rolls limousine with my other sister. You never saw such a circus."

"I'll bet the boys loved it!"

"Maybe. But I wanted to curl up and die."

"It would have been the happiest moment in my life!" she exclaimed in a tone of real conviction. But then she added more soberly: "Which is nothing to be proud of, believe me." And she left him to join her husband.

✔ ✔ ✔

The invitation from Mrs. Knight was written in a large purple hand on a stiff card with a gold border and an eagle crest.

If you could spare an hour on Sunday at four we might read Maxwell Anderson's delectable drama *Elizabeth the Queen*. Dear Natica Barnes can join us at that time, and I dare to foretell that we shall prove a congenial threesome. Perhaps we shall not rise to the empyrean heights of the incomparable Lunts, but we can but do our best.

It seemed a most un-Averhillian way of passing even a Sunday afternoon, but Stephen knew at once that nothing would keep him from accepting the invitation.

At the appointed day and hour he found Natica ahead of him. She and Mrs. Knight were in the midst of an earnest discussion of who was to read which part.

"No, no, Elizabeth is just the part for you," Natica was insisting. "So full of twists and turns and shades of mood. You must read it all. And Stephen, of course, will be Essex. I'll read the other parts. I've penciled the cuts in the three copies you've so generously provided."

"But, my dear, I want *you* to read the main role — or at least part of it."

"No, I have it all worked out." Natica was very definite. "And our reading should take no more than an hour. Stephen, I'm sure, will have to get back to school. So let's start right away with the scene where the council members trick Essex into accepting command of the fatal Irish expedition."

As the reading progressed Stephen found himself strangely drawn into the playwright's version of a romantic past. The close atmosphere of the dark Tudor parlor, the scent of incense and his hostess's throaty utterance of her lines seemed to turn the house itself into a stage without an auditorium, while the hovering school and campus beyond, even the great gray chapel itself, receded into shadows. He tried to bring himself back to a semblance of reality by putting more force into his reading. He wanted to emphasize that if Essex's life would be short, it would still be brilliant. He might be doomed in the end by the false old monarch, but he would make a splendid finish, young and brave, bowing his head to the block and flashing out his scarlet-sleeved arms to signal his readiness for the axe. He glanced at Natica. Was she having fun?

He couldn't tell. Only when she read the part of Penelope, the queen's lady in waiting who was also in love with the hero, was there any emotion in her voice, but then her tones rang out loud and clear. He wanted to fancy himself as the man whose love she disputed with her mistress. But the fancy was suddenly stifled in the heavy atmosphere of the chamber; he heard his own voice weaken and pause. He had to clear his throat; Mrs. Knight offered him a glass of water. When, on his quick refusal, she resumed her role, now almost crooning in her ecstasy, he wondered if he could even breathe the air that seemed to intoxicate the older woman and at least invigorate the younger. It was as if everything that was female in the predominantly male world of Averhill had fled or even been chased from a hostile campus to be boxed up between Estelle Knight's dark panels where it would defiantly throb and expand until it exploded, shivering the red brick and white columns of the beautiful circle and shaking the square Gothic tower of the chapel to its very foundations.

But when Natica happened to glance up from her book at him and smile, it was as if the whole gaudy chamber, the wig and the incense, had fallen away, and youth and truth were there alone.

" 'Give me the ring, give me the ring!' " shrilled Mrs. Knight in the old queen's final vain plea to her stubborn favorite to invoke her mercy.

Natica's gaze was now expressionless, except for what he thought he could make out as the smallest yellow glint in her eyes, and then he realized with a start that the reading was over and that he shouldn't be staring at her.

Outside, accompanying her back to her house, he felt compelled to reconstruct some kind of bridge to the renewed reality of Averhill.

"Mrs. Knight really got a kick out of reading that part, didn't she?"

"Shouldn't she have?"

"Oh, sure. But do you know something funny? When I called on her, I fancied she was playing the part of an old queen receiving a young courtier who might become a favorite. I guess it's pathetic, really."

"What is?"

"Oh, the idea of shutting herself up in a make-believe palace and dreaming of love while intoning inferior verse. But at least she hasn't lost all touch with reality. She doesn't pick Juliet to play. She picks a part her own age, and that of a woman who ruled her world, so she can adjust her fantasies closer to her facts."

"And what are her facts?"

"Well, you know. The painted wife of a superannuated Latin teacher sitting on a pile of unpublished and probably now unpublishable poetry."

"You could see *me* in much the same light!" came the unexpected and shockingly tart rejoinder. "I may not be painted or married to an old Latin teacher, but I'm certainly married to a teacher, and what do I have but *my* fantasies? Indeed, I'm worse off than Mrs. Knight, for she has money, and somebody actually wanted to publish her verse! It's easy enough for you to sneer at our little compensations. You're rich and can travel all over the world in the long vacations. You can teach the boys what you wish, and if anyone stops you, you're free to quit. And you can buy all the beautiful things you want, even if your family do go in for flashy cars!"

They had stopped walking and were facing each other. Indignation had given her a becoming glow.

"I can't bear to think I've hurt your feelings!" he cried.

She blinked with surprise at the violence of his outburst. Then she shrugged. "Oh, you haven't hurt them, really. It's more that you've aroused them."

"As if I could be superior about *you*."

At this she simply turned to walk on.

"I can't stand it if you're not my friend!" he called recklessly after her.

She turned back and smiled. "Oh, I'm your friend." They had reached the little gate to the brick walk to her cottage. "I wouldn't have flared so if I hadn't been."

Walking back to the school, elated but spurning analysis of his elation, he passed the rear of the chapel and rounded the darkening campus on the way to his dormitory. Ahead of him he spied the short, thick, slowly progressing figure of the headmaster. Had Lockwood seen him part with Natica at her gate? Had he even spotted them coming down the lane from the Knights' house? And if he had?

He quickened his pace to catch up with his principal.

"Good evening, sir."

"Good evening, Stephen. And a very good evening it is."

"I've come from a cultural session. Mrs. Barnes and I were reading poetry at Mrs. Knight's."

Lockwood's brief glance seemed to evaluate the oddness of this abrupt confession. "And did you read some of Mrs. Knight's own verse?"

"Oh no, sir."

"Oh no, you exclaim? Well, I imagine that might not have provided unmitigated delight."

"I can't say, sir," Stephen replied in some confusion, anxious not to seem for a second time disloyal to his hostess. "I haven't seen more than one of them. No, we read a play of Maxwell Anderson's."

"Indeed." The tone made it clear that no further details were called for.

They walked on in silence until they reached the headmaster's house. Here Lockwood paused before entering.

"*Verbum sapienti*, my friend. I am aware that Mrs. Knight is an old acquaintance of your mother's and that some degree of social intercourse with her may be required. But before you embark on any regular course of meetings under her roof, please bear in mind that she is not disposed to be friendly either to myself or to the school. Her husband, on the other hand, I need hardly add, is one of the finest and most loyal of our masters. Good night, Stephen."

Stephen, alone again, wandered to the middle of the campus to stare up at the square Gothic tower of the chapel. On clear days it radiated a message of peace and serenity, with perhaps just a shade of smugness. But in the shrouded twilight it seemed to cast a sterner spell, to warn if not actually to reprove. It occurred to him that Averhill might be beautiful to him, that Averhill might be romantic to him, precisely because it evoked the sweet sins the chapel could never condone. Were the tower and the Palladian Schoolhouse and the rounded campus and the stocky, vigorous figure of the headmaster himself not just as essential to his vision of love as the winding river with its overhanging foliage and canoes on a holiday in early spring? But that vision had not initially been the love of women.

12 ⸴ ⸴ ⸴

IN HIS FIRST two years at Averhill Stephen had not been much attached to the school. As a quiet, good-looking boy, adequately competent at sports, never in any kind of serious trouble and sufficiently quick with his fists if mocked, he was at least tolerated by the rowdier leaders of his form, and the masters considered him a good if rather passive student. But the springs of his enthusiasm had not been touched; he regarded school terms as periods to be got through, and he marked off each day on the little calendar on the bureau of his cubicle with a neat penciled cross before going to bed. It meant twenty-four hours less before vacation when he could return to Mother and Redwood, the beautiful old white mansion with the high columned porch that looked down a sloping lawn to the broad Hudson. For knowing his passion for her ancestral home, Angelica tried to arrange to be there and not in the city on his Christmas and spring holidays as well as all summer.

His homesickness was of the deep, brooding sort that did not go away, even after a vacation had demonstrated that home was not all it had appeared in his visions at school. Indeed it began to seem to him that his discontent at Averhill was creating a kind of idealized Redwood, where the deer leaping through the woods and the blue jays in the dappled sunlight and his mother in white reading in the marble pagoda near the edge of the mighty river had become figures in a painting of the Hudson River School, remote in time and pregnant of tears. And then the school, with its jangling of bells and continual announcements from daises, with its bustle of boys through varnished corridors, their vapid joking and coarse laughter and bawling of evangelical hymns in chapel, was only cacophony.

But in the spring of his second year at Averhill something happened that marked the beginning of a change in his attitude. His old Irish nursemaid, Ellen, beloved by the family, who had been kept on at Redwood in the factitious post of seamstress after the children had outgrown their need of her, died of a sudden stroke, which, as Angelica explained in her letter, was perhaps in the nature of a blessing. But to Stephen it came as a catastrophe. On his last vacation, preoccupied with his bird list and boating on the river, he had paid scant attention to the poor old woman, who, though she adored him and he her, had grown tediously garrulous and forgetful. Now she was translated into the symbol of all he had lost, of his unrecoverable childhood, nor could he ever make up to her for his unkindness by hugging her until she had to push him away to catch her breath. He knew, right there in the mail room where he had read the letter, that he was going to break down and weep unbearably, and to avoid the disgrace of being witnessed he rushed upstairs to his empty dormitory and threw himself on his bed to sob.

The sleeping quarters, however, were out of bounds in daytime, and the dormitory master, Mr. Coster, working in his adjoining study, heard him and walked down the aisle to his cubicle.

"What is wrong, Stephen?" he asked in a tone of simple kindness, devoid of any hint of reproach.

Stephen jumped up to explain his loss in a burst of jumbled words. But Mr. Coster, a grave, silent man of some thirty years with beautiful silky premature gray hair and soft eyes that bespoke a constant guarded sympathy that their owner never seemed to expect to be asked for, who taught English as precisely as if it were mathematics and who was known as a strict but utterly just disciplinarian, did not appear to find that Stephen's grief for an old servant was out of proportion. He put an arm around the boy's shoulders and led him into his study where they both sat down.

"I'm glad you feel the way you do for poor old Ellen," he said gently, after Stephen had told him more about her. "And I'm glad she didn't suffer. Your tears are a tribute to her. Don't be ashamed of them. That would be to be ashamed of love. We're much too stiff upper lip at Averhill. Love is what living is all about. And you shouldn't worry too much about having neglected Ellen lately. The dead don't judge us by our last acts. They have the whole picture. She knows that you love her."

Never before had an adult talked to Stephen with anything like this sympathy. Oh, there was Angelica, of course, but she wasn't an adult. She was . . . well, she was Mother. His father had always been embarrassed by the least show of emotion, and the family friends had treated him as a child. But now a world opened before him in which the categories of age, of teacher-student, even of disciplinarian and law breaker (for what was Stephen doing in the dormitory in the daytime?), fell away, and he and Mr. Coster were simply two human beings who could talk about life and even love. When Stephen left, the dormitory master actually gave him a small hug of reassurance.

The categories soon enough reestablished themselves, nor was Stephen so unwise as to take the least advantage of his brief moment of intimacy with Mr. Coster. The latter was once more his friendly, mildly sarcastic, essentially formal self; he treated Stephen as before, as he treated the other boys, with the unvarying courtesy that he must have felt was the due of every student not actually misbehaving. Stephen showed his gratitude by asking him to be his counsellor for the following fall: each third former was entitled to ask for one. He also took the stories and poems that he was now beginning to write to his new mentor, who gave him good advice, mostly in the matter of restraining the growing exuberance of his language.

For Stephen's heart was becoming exuberant. Homesickness faded, and the red-brick school buildings and the gray chapel began to take on for him some of the charm of Redwood. He found friends now among his formmates and took pleasure in sports, particularly rowing on the river. His grades shot up, and he won the third form debating prize for his affirmative argument on the topic: "Resolved: that we should join the League of Nations." And now even God came to permeate the campus through the homilies of the headmaster.

In fourth form year, aged fifteen, he elected to join the church and attended Dr. Lockwood's pre-confirmation classes, often staying afterwards to ask the great man questions. The headmaster's obvious sincerity as a proselytizer diminished the awe of his presence, and Stephen found himself bold enough to offer even probing inquiries. Did the sanctity of the Communion service prevent the passing of dangerous germs via the sacred chalice? "Well, I always give it a good rub with my cloth after each person's sip." Wasn't the prospect of eternal life more frightening than consoling? "Only because we cannot imagine what it will be like to have the concept of time extinguished." Had true Christians not been guilty of burning heretics? "Misguided priests are always with us." Why did Christ descend into hell? "He may have wished to give hope even to the hopeless."

The early spring of Stephen's fourth form year was a damp and misty one. On a Sunday morning when he rose at six to attend Communion and walked to chapel with his best friend, Charlie LeBrun, he felt the soft moist air like silk on his cheeks.

"Mr. Coster says that Browning is bumptious," he exclaimed to his companion. "But don't you feel today that God *is* in his heaven and all's right with the world?"

Charlie was a small but muscular and very blond boy who admired Stephen but did not share his flights of fancy. "It might be righter if I could think of a topic for my essay in current events."

"Oh, to hell with current events. *These* are the current events all around us; the sky, the elms, the birds!" Stephen gesticulated enthusiastically. "Let's go canoeing this afternoon. It should be glorious."

"No, I've got to work on my essay," Charlie retorted glumly. "I'll have to think of something."

"I'll help you with that after chapel."

"Will you really, Steve?"

"If you'll go canoeing with me."

And during the service in the green and yellow light filtered through the stained glass Stephen listened with pleasure to the "comfortable words" of our Lord in the mellifluous tones of the headmaster and delighted in the warm presence of Charlie beside him.

The river that afternoon was sluggish and deserted; it was too early in the season for regular canoeing. They drifted along, close to the bank, not speaking except when Stephen, peering into the clustered bushes, identified a warbler. But he was more interested in the vision of Charlie's back before him. His friend had stripped to the waist, and his fine rounded shoulders and curly yellow hair offered a contrast so charming as to make Stephen see his feeling for his companion in a startling but highly exciting new light. Only weeks before he had indignantly spurned the nocturnal advances of a boy in the adjoining cubicle, but now the mysterious and tabu matter of schoolboy love, darkly denounced from the headmaster's pulpit as "sentimentality," struck him suddenly as a natural and delightful thing. And wasn't Charlie feeling the same way? Why else had he taken off both sweater and shirt on a chilly day?

"Let's pull over and go swimming."

"It's too cold."

"I'm going anyway."

They pulled the canoe ashore and climbed up the bank to a small clearing where Stephen rapidly stripped, his back to his friend. Then he turned around and boldly exposed his state. Charlie stared and whistled lewdly.

"Well, look at you! And we all thought you were such a goody-goody. I'd never have dared suggest anything like this."

✓ ✓ ✓

There was no oportunity for it to happen a second time, for the spring vacation started on Tuesday, and Stephen went home to Redwood and Charlie to Baltimore. But Stephen looked eagerly forward to a resumption of their intimacy when they returned to school, and now it was the holidays that he marked off on his calendar. He had no feeling of shame about what they had done. It simply seemed to him they had discovered a beautiful thing totally outside the laws and morals that were expressed so definitely at Averhill and at home. The all too obvious fact that his father and the headmaster would have denounced it in horror and disgust did not dismay him, nor did it even lower their standards in his estimation. Their world was a good and proper one; it belonged to them and to Stephen so long as he outwardly conformed to its rules, and it should not be disturbed or even affected by love that would be always concealed. Who knew, after all, what things they, with equal propriety, might be concealing from him? And wasn't it an essential part of his new joy that *only* he and Charlie knew about it?

But Charlie, back at Averhill, seemed changed. He made no response to Stephen's covert references to the river expedition and talked rather tediously about a girl he had met at some silly Baltimore party. Stephen allowed a few days to pass to give the effect of the holidays time to wear off and then suggested that they canoe again on the river.

"Sure. Let's get two canoes and ask Phil Trigby and Bill Skates."

"You don't think we might have more fun, just the two of us?" And then, even as he hated its vulgarizing effect on a noble feeling, he allowed himself to wink.

"No, I'm through with that kid stuff." Charlie deepened his voice to take on the semblance of the new adult his holiday romance had made him. "I had a frank talk with my older brother Ben the other day. He asked me about some of the things we did at school and admitted he'd done them too. But he said it was only because there were no girls around. It's the same way in prisons and naval ships too long at sea. But he said it shouldn't become a habit and we should quit well before the end of fourth form year. And that's only two months away."

Stephen, deeply hurt, never mentioned the subject again. He simply tried not to hate Charlie, and they remained ostensible friends. What caused his particular mortification was the loftiness of Charlie's new masculinity; Charlie, the veteran of many such adventures, had the nerve to look down on Stephen, who had had only one! And why? Because Charlie was the first to renounce schoolboy love. The first by two weeks!

But Stephen recognized as he brooded over the incident, burying it deeper and deeper into his secret self, that the real basis of Charlie's superior attitude was that he had somehow inferred, consciously or even subconsciously, that what they had done together was more important to Stephen than to himself. The real shame, Stephen now began to see with burning cheeks, was not in doing it but in consecrating it. So long as it was a form of masturbation, it was adequately manly, but if it involved love, it became degrading, even degenerate. Well, Stephen would know how to behave in future.

That summer he fell in love with an eleven-year-old girl, the daughter of the caretaker at Redwood. The situation struck him as grotesque; he was a man, celebrating his sixteenth birthday in August, and she was still a child, although renowned in the neighborhood for her remarkable beauty. He never told a soul of his love, but he took every opportunity available to be in spots where, without arousing suspicion, he could spy upon her. Back at school in the fall the emotion faded to a pleasant recollection. The Christmas holidays he was now willing to spend in the city, where subscription dances were the order of the day, and he even invited Charlie to come up from Baltimore to go to one with him, and they necked with two girls in the taxi going home. But the romantic haze in which Redwood had been enveloped for him in his earlier years still clung to the square Gothic tower of the Averhill chapel and the sluggish flow of the river in early spring.

A horrid incident marred the glory of his final year at school, where he was editor of *The Averhillian,* president of the debating society and handball champion. Mr. Coster, in the middle of the winter term, abruptly resigned from the faculty and disappeared from the campus. It was officially announced that he had a heart murmur and that his doctor had prescribed a period of absolute rest, but rumor had it otherwise. Rumor had it that the summer before he had written letters of a "sentimental nature" to a boy whose father had found them months later and forwarded them to the headmaster.

The incident was much discussed. Mr. Coster had not been suspected of such inclinations, but his past was now reexamined meticulously in the new light of his guilty correspondence, and many of his remarks and gestures were coarsely reinterpreted. Stephen did not join in any of these speculations. It filled him with sorrow and an odd kind of targetless anger that the love and sympathy he had found so welcome in that dear man might have come from *that.* Yet wasn't that love too? Stephen, anyway, had learned the cruelty of which his world was capable. It was terrible indeed, but he could only hope that it was the poet in his nature that derived an indignant comfort from the notion that there could hardly be light without dark or beauty without ugliness.

13 , , ,

AFTER THE reading at Mrs. Knight's Natica became a near obsession to Stephen. Between classes, at his desk, his mind would wander from the text he was preparing for assignment to recapture the sharp quick step with which she entered the dining hall and the open friendly smile she would toss in his direction as she passed his table. In chapel he would look for her and wonder irritably what she was doing if she wasn't there. And soon his fantasies were taking a bolder turn. He imagined her joining him in the throng after a Sunday service, suddenly clutching his arm to draw him aside and whisper miserably that she couldn't stay with Tommy another day. She had fallen in love with him, hopelessly in love with him, and she had to tell him that very minute! At night in bed he would toss and turn with lustful thoughts.

She seemed now the sole female element in a world of unrelieved maleness. It was as if she had sprung from the middle of the green campus, like Botticelli's Venus from the sea, thrusting into the shadows of the surrounding buildings stray members of the cruder sex and withered examples of her own. She had come to incarnate all the romance he had once so strongly sensed in the school; without her the masters and their wives, like the gods and goddesses of Valhalla after the abduction of Freia, became old and gray.

There were brief, angry periods when he would try to shake himself out of his preoccupation. Venus from the sea? That busy trim little creature in tweeds who cast so bleak a golden stare at the foibles of Averhill? Who had married a bumbling curate to get away from parents she despised, very likely for no better reason than snobbishness? And who probably, in any case, was a cold fish? Perhaps it was indeed time, as his mother was always suggesting in her letters, that he should be cultivating the families in the Averhill neighborhood with marriageable daughters. There was even a country club that had already indicated that young bachelor masters would be pushed ahead on the waiting list of potential members. Might not the persistent image of Natica be the simple product of his own repression?

He had become almost intimate with one of his dormitory prefects. Giles Woodward, that small sharp weasel of a boy, brightest and most impudent of the sixth form, he had won to his side by the simple expedient of asking him to act as his "executive officer" in maintaining discipline. From a sarcastic but never openly insubordinate critic Giles had overnight become his warmest supporter, and he often now sat up late at night in Stephen's study, reading while the master read or wrote, but always ready for a chat when the latter wished.

It was thus that he happened to be present one night when Stephen was talking on the telephone with his mother.

"I trust my beautiful boy is behaving himself." Angelica's bantering tone rarely implied sarcasm. Her admiration of her son's looks was quite as sincere as his of hers. But she reduced Averhill and even its headmaster to the rank of minor things. However, there were few things that she regarded as major.

"How would I not be, Ma? The campus is not exactly fraught with temptation."

"What about all those faculty wives?"

"You should see them! And anyway they're most of them a generation older than me."

"That hasn't always stopped you."

"That's a low blow. And there aren't any Annettes among them."

"But I hear there's one quite pretty and apparently brilliant one. Madeleine DeVoe was telling me about her when I mentioned that you were teaching there. A Mrs. Barney or Barnard, would that be right? She used to live down on Long Island and married a minister."

He could only marvel at the way his mother always seemed to know everything, at her way of taking over his life before he had even started to live it. But still he wanted to talk about Natica.

"Barnes, you mean. She married Tom Barnes."

"You know her?"

"Of course, I know her. Everyone knows everyone up here. She's very nice. We had a poetry reading the other day at your friend Mrs. Knight's."

"Just the three of you?"

Was she a mind reader? "No, Mr. Knight was there. Don't worry about me, Ma. I lead a monk's life."

"That's what I'm afraid of. I wish you'd join that country club. I'll make you a present of the dues."

When he rang off, he noticed that Giles was watching him over the top of his book.

"Is your mother warning you off?"

"What on earth do you mean?"

"Mrs. Barnes. Mothers are wonderful, aren't they? Yours could sniff that out all the way from New York."

"Sniff what out?"

"That Mrs. Barnes is giving you the eye."

"Does it occur to you that you may be treading on rather thin ice, young fellow?"

"Just trying to be a pal, sir. Just trying to be a pal. I'd hate to see a nice guy like you get muddied up with a minister's wife."

Stephen knew that he should send him straight off to bed. But his immediate need to know on what Giles based his impudent and fascinating assumption prevailed over every caution.

"What makes you suppose that a lady as perfectly proper as Mrs. Barnes is giving me what you vulgarly call 'the eye'?"

"The fact that she came over to join you at your table, leaving

Mr. Barnes's. No one's ever seen a master's wife do that before. And then she looks at you, too, when you're not watching. I've seen her. And finally, she's bored by her boob of a husband. I've seen him sneak up behind her in the kitchen and kiss the back of her neck. I could see she hated it, too."

"How could you see any such thing?"

"From a window in the infirmary. When they lived in the Pest House. It was right next door."

"You mean you were a peeping Tom!"

"Me and a dozen others."

"And what else did you see?"

"Ah, you *do* want to know, don't you?" Giles's laugh was a triumphant rasp. "But never mind. I didn't see anything else. Barnes is the kind that always does it with the lights off."

Stephen, his pedagogic authority in tatters, now sent his informant to bed.

The next day he received a letter from Mrs. Knight, hand delivered by her husband in the faculty coffee room.

"My wife tells me that this is important," the Latin teacher said solemnly, turning at once away, as if not wishing in the smallest degree to exceed the limitations of his embassy. Stephen opened the scented purple envelope.

> Elizabeth Bergner will be coming to Boston in January to do *The Duchess of Malfi*. Natica says she wouldn't miss it if she had to walk to it on bare feet over a road strewn with tacks. What strong imagery the dear girl uses! But of course we must refamiliarize ourselves with the divine Webster. Come on Sunday. Don't fail us!

It never occurred to him to do so. He would have defied the specific prohibition of the headmaster himself, and he telephoned Mrs. Knight to assure her of his presence.

"There's a good boy. But this time I want darling Natica to read the main part. She's a kind of duchess of Malfi herself, poor dear."

Stephen was actually struck by this when Natica read the part at their Sunday meeting. It was evident that she knew the play very well. There was a firmness in her tone to manifest the ineluctable will of the beautiful and virtuous heroine to enjoy her love despite all that a raging world could do to prevent her. The very motiveless-ness of her brothers' opposition to her morganatic marriage now appeared to Stephen as Webster's finest touch. For the playwright had taken the simple and innocent love of the duchess and her steward and arrayed against it all the gleaming and monstrous paraphernalia of a Renaissance court. It was a pastoral idyll interrupted by a violent tempest, a natural passion smothered by a civilization that could not endure the contrast that it offered to its own obscene artificiality.

His voice trembled when he read the famous lines of the villain: "Cover her face. Mine eyes dazzle. She died young."

When he walked with her afterwards to her cottage, he was talking a bit wildly.

"You read that so beautifully! I couldn't help but think of you as somehow imprisoned in all of this." With an indignant sweep of his arm he sought to encompass the chapel they were passing and the green circle beyond it. "And of Lockwood himself as the grim cardinal brother."

"Dear me, I must really have carried you away. Elizabeth Bergner had better look to her laurels. But what could his eminence, Cardinal Lockwood, hold against me? My marriage to poor Tommy?"

"Not that at all. Not that at all."

She paused. "What are you trying to tell me, Stephen?"

"I'm afraid if I answer that, you might give up the readings."

"Is that your way of making me do so?"

"Promise me you won't, Natica! Promise me you won't do that to me!"

He had risked everything now. If she didn't give them up, she would have permitted him to hope.

She hedged. "Maybe it would be better if we added a few others to the meetings. That would make them less intimate, don't you think? Anyway, here we are. Good night, Stephen."

The Christmas holidays were upon them; he would not see her again until January. Back in New York he was inclined to be restless and bored with his family, but the engagement of his sister Janine to Abel Lockhart, the affable (too affable, Stephen thought) and rather stickily conventional heir to a Chicago stockyard fortune, absorbed all the attention of the Hills, and Stephen's moods went unnoticed.

His mother was concerned about a hint of doubt that Janine had let fall as to the wisdom of her choice.

"Abel is a dear, of course, but nobody would accuse him of being a great catch if it weren't for his money," she confided in her son. "He snores in the back of the box at the opera, and I doubt if he's read a novel since *Treasure Island*. If indeed he even read that. He does everything Janine wants and agrees with everything she says . . ."

"Which makes him not only a dunce but the perfect husband for her."

"I don't suppose it really matters, if he's going to hunt and fish all his life," Angelica continued pensively. "But the poor girl is worried that she may be getting married just to be married."

"What better reason?"

"Oh, hush. You're always so superior where your sisters are concerned."

"It hardly makes me very lofty."

"She was actually thinking of breaking it off the other day when Mrs. Lockhart, who's just as sweet as she can be but dreadfully common, arrived with a trunk — a whole trunk, mind you — of the most expensive linen in the world, all hopelessly monogrammed JHL."

"Ah well, now she's stuck."

"She can't throw her life away just because of some table covers and napkins!"

"Don't you see, Ma, it's providential? All Janine needs is to have her mind made up. She and Abel will rub along very well together."

"You're being horrid."

But in all seriousness he felt that he was right about his elder sister. When he returned to Averhill in January the wedding had been set for June.

Natica was not at lunch in the school dining hall on the first day of term; Tommy answered Stephen's inquiry with the news that she had gone to her parents in Long Island. Her mother, it appeared, had had a mild heart attack. Stephen attempted to stifle the unreasonable feeling that she should have told him. But a week later she was at her usual place at Tommy's table, and he went up to her before grace. Yes, her mother was much better, thank you. He looked around. Tommy had not yet made his appearance.

"Shall we be reading again?" he asked.

"Oh, yes. Mrs. Knight will be after you. We're going to continue to concentrate on Webster. *The White Devil*. And a week from Saturday I'm going into Boston for a matinée of *The Duchess*. I have my ticket!" She held up her purse as if the repository of so sacred a means of admission was not to be allowed out of her sight.

"Tommy's not going?"

"Of course not. He's coaching hockey or doing something much more important like that."

"If I get two tickets, will you sit with me?"

"Heavens, no." Her eyes rolled in mock fear to the stolid figure of Marjorie Evans, two tables away. "The sacred *cercle* may all be there."

"Will you dine with me afterwards?"

Her acceptance was agreeably prompt. "On condition that you take me somewhere where we shan't run into them."

He nodded. He had already thought of a seafood place near the Navy Yard where it would be almost inconceivable to meet Marjorie Evans. Yet it only looked rough; it was actually very good and very expensive.

Mrs. Knight called him that evening to invite him to a reading the following Sunday, but when he arrived at the appointed time he found her alone, standing rather dramatically erect in the center of her living room.

"Once again the great Lockwood has thrust his blackjack into my prison! At the least sign of life from my cell he tries to thrash me senseless. Ah, but I'm not dead yet!"

"What on earth do you mean?"

"Read this!" And she handed him a note from Natica.

My poor, dear Estelle, our harmless little sessions have been pronounced treason by the most High! Lockwood spoke to Tommy last night and told him that his professional advancement would not be accelerated by his wife's visitations to a house where the headmaster and school were known to be held in open contempt! Tommy and I had a terrible scene when he asked me not to come to you on Sunday, and I only agreed when he consented to my going to my matinée (I had not told him I had a ticket), and to my spending the night in your apartment in Boston, so long as I didn't tell anyone!

Stephen did not at first realize how odd his response must have sounded. "I didn't know you had an apartment in Boston."

"It's really hardly that. A simple pied-à-terre. My refuge from Philistia."

"And will you be spending Saturday night there with Natica?"

"I was, but I can't now. My daughter Trudy and her husband are coming for the weekend, and they would take it very ill if I hightailed it into Boston. So Natica will be quite alone in the flat. Unless you'll be good enough to keep her company. There's a small maid's room where you could be perfectly comfortable. There's really no reason you shouldn't, you know. It would all be perfectly proper, and anyway, nobody need know."

Stephen stared at her, almost in awe. "And will you tell her that?"

"That I've asked you? Well, I could hardly have you breaking in on her, could I? But don't worry. We've already talked on the telephone. She hasn't the least objection to your staying there. So even if I must miss my reading, I'll have the satisfaction of thinking of you two enjoying a wonderful matinée and talking it over afterwards in my little flat."

Mrs. Knight, despite the absence of Natica, still insisted on reading aloud several scenes from *The White Devil*. Of course she read, exuberantly, Vittoria's lines. It took a great effort for him to concentrate on his cues.

His only colloquy with Natica before the day of the matinée had been a brief one after a school lunch in which they had agreed to go in separate taxis from the theatre to his waterside restaurant.

He arrived first and picked the most secluded booth. He then ordered two martinis, as she had told him to. When she came in she walked directly to the booth as if knowing which he would have chosen. Sitting down, she pulled off her beret and fluffed up her hair. When the drinks came she took up her glass eagerly and swallowed a gulp.

"There!" she exclaimed with a sigh of satisfaction. "I love this. I'm free, if only for a night."

"What do you love? The cocktail? Or being away from school? Do I dare hope you might love — just a little bit, anyway — being with me?"

She laughed, without even a trace of constraint. "Don't be coy, Stephen. Love would only complicate our friendship."

"Is that all it's going to be — a friendship?"

"What is that French phrase? An *amitié amoureuse*? Why don't we call it that?"

"Except . . ." He paused to take a good gulp of his cocktail. "Except I thought that phrase meant a platonic relationship."

"Possibly. But don't forget, it's a *French* phrase."

"You mean there's still hope?"

"Look, my dear, do we have to dot every *i*?" She took in the eagerness of his expression and gave it up. "Yes, I guess we do. Very well. Are we going to spend the night in Estelle's flat in the way the dear old pander intended? We are. There. Now are you satisfied? Can we enjoy our dinner?"

"Why don't we go there now?"

"You mean to get it over with?"

"No, no, no. To have it sooner. We could dine later. And then go back to the flat for more."

"Dear me, how carnal the man is. But no. I mean to have another cocktail and then a very good dinner. I want to savor this whole free day. I want to enjoy every minute of it. Who is to say which is the best? I won't be hurried. I'm younger than you, but I've had a harder life. I've learned that the greatest joy may be anticipation."

"I'll try not to be a disappointment," he retorted wryly.

"Then start now" was her inexorable reply. And she proceeded to discuss Elizabeth Bergner's rendition of the role of the duchess.

"It's of such a searing simplicity. Her love may be innocent and lawful, yet if she gives in to it she will surely die. So she gives in and dies. Without a word of fear, a syllable of protest. So Elizabethan — or Jacobean, I suppose I should say. They knew that life was abominable, but that it contained a few things that made it worth the candle — *if* you had the will to die for them."

"Is that how you see life?"

"Oh, no. Ours is a different era. We live rationally. By rules. We take only carefully measured risks. You may say the duchess concealed her pregnancies as well as her marriage, but she knew all along she would never get away with it. At least that is how Miss Bergner interprets her. Take us tonight. If Tommy should learn of it, he would be horribly hurt. I don't want that to happen. Yet it might. That's the chance I take. But if I *knew* he was going to find out, I wouldn't be here. Which is the difference."

"I'm like the duchess. I'd take any risk."

"But you have nothing to lose."

"How about my job?"

"Oh, your father could buy you a new school."

He adapted himself to her mood. He listened to the story of her marriage, and he told her about his affair with Annette. She showed a certain interest in it, but not so much as a trace of jealousy.

They found Mrs. Knight's four-room flat a crowded replica of her Tudor mansion.

"Give me ten minutes and then come in," she told him at the door to the master bedroom.

✔ ✔ ✔

Yet it was the first time that he had encountered passion in a woman. Natica in bed lost all her detachment; she clung to him fiercely, greedily, with a kind of desperation. He had preferred to think of the act of love as the union of two equal partners. But that night it was as if she were trying to lose herself in him. In the very intensity of his satisfaction he could still find a little corner of his consciousness in which he wondered if he really existed for her except as a means of self-annihilation. She was as unlike Annette as it was possible to imagine.

Then he heard her voice in the dark, once more detached. "The trouble with this is that we're going to want to repeat it."

"Like right now," he replied, and they did.

But this time he had a different fantasy. Was it really her own annihilation that she sought? And he tried to ward off the intruding image of certain female insects . . .

"I'll bet I know what you're thinking," she said with a sudden dry laugh. "That I should be more demure. Well, maybe I'll learn. Believe it or not, this is my first adultery."

How could a woman's moods change so fast? He found her utterly bewildering.

In the morning she refused to let him drive her back to school in his car. She had come by train; she would return the same way. She departed without even discussing a second rendezvous.

When he arrived at his dormitory just before morning chapel service, he found Giles Woodward sitting at his desk.

"Where have you been, sir? Dr. Lockwood called to ask if you could take Mr. Evans's English Three tomorrow. He has the grippe. I told him what you told me, that you'd gone to New York at your father's request. He said to call you there, and I did. But the butler said you weren't there. That you weren't even expected!"

"I hope you didn't tell the headmaster that."

"No, sir! I told him you'd gone out with your parents and that I'd left the message."

"Good boy! I'll call him now and tell him I took the early train from New York."

"He'll be at chapel by now. You can tell him after the service. But sir . . ." Giles actually put the arm of comradeship around the young master's shoulders. "*Do* be careful, will you?"

14 ˌ ˌ ˌ

HE AND Natica met in secret twice more. The first time was in her house. Tommy was away for the weekend as visiting preacher at a school in Pennsylvania, and she slipped a note into Stephen's mailbox in the Schoolhouse to inform him that she would be home all Saturday afternoon and that he might come (if, of course, he wished) at any time he was "reasonably assured" he wouldn't be noticed. He did not like the idea of betraying poor Tommy in his own bedroom, but he came. Natica was as passionate as on their first occasion, but showed the same quick return to her more characteristic phlegm.

"You'd better go now. Use the back door. The hedge will protect you to the road, and then you'll look as if you'd been hiking to the village."

He dressed, as fast as he could, before trying a parting appeal. "Can't you say something nice, Natica?"

"What do you want me to say? That I needed that badly? Well, I can promise you I did."

"Just that? Not me?" He was suddenly irate. "Would someone else have done as well?"

"Oh, don't be a fool. You were great, and you know it. Don't fish for compliments."

The second time was again in Boston and in Mrs. Knight's flat, to which Natica had been given a key. His excuse for driving to town on a weekday afternoon was an ostensible dentist appointment; hers, a luncheon with an old school friend. This time they had an hour to lie in bed afterwards and talk. She spoke musingly of the possibility that she would leave Tommy one day, but she didn't indicate any connection between this and their affair.

"I think I owe it to Tommy to wait until he's sufficiently established so it won't ruin his career. Suppose, for example, he became the popular head of some smaller school. He's not up to Averhill, of course, but I can see him doing quite nicely at one of those minor academies in Connecticut where they take rich boys who aren't bright enough for Groton or Saint Paul's. I could pretend I had sinus or something that made the cold winters impossible and disappear, presumably to a warmer clime, for long periods at a time. And eventually I wouldn't come back at all. I doubt people would even notice, do you?"

But he wasn't going to put his mind on that. "Would I figure at all in your plans?"

"The last thing you need is a divorcée in your life. Believe me, I'm taking as good care of your career as I am of Tommy's."

"But what *am* I to you, Natica?"

She had been gazing at the ceiling as she smoked. Now she turned, propping herself on an elbow, to contemplate him with a kind of affectionate curiosity. "I think that you, my beautiful man, are not quite real. You're like Cupid visiting Psyche in the dark, except I'm allowed to turn on the light and look at you. So long as I don't tell anyone, that is. And I think that's just the way you and I had better leave it. I've wronged one man, and I don't want to wrong another. No, I mean it, Stephen!" She pressed a hand to his lips to still his protest. "And now I really must get dressed and catch my train. Tommy is going to meet me at the station."

Stephen in the next days was uncomfortably aware of the beginnings of a reaction on his part that he hated to recognize as relief. But relief at what? He had no desire to give up the affair or even to contemplate an Averhill without Natica. No, it was more likely simply relief that nothing more would be expected of him than what he was only too willing to provide. Natica, in other words, was permitting him to have his cake and eat it, to be an idealistic teacher at a church school and have a passionate mistress on the side. What was it about him that made first Annette and now Natica so determined to let him off the hook? Why were they so keen on protecting him? He did not quite relish Natica's calling him, as did his mother, her "beautiful boy."

Yet it certainly simplified life at school to regard the affair in Natica's fashion as something not quite real. His classroom teaching was going very well at last; his dormitory ran almost without problems. And he was beginning to feel that he was having some success in establishing himself as a liaison between the faculty and the sixth form; the headmaster himself had commented on it. Making love to Natica was far less distracting to his academic duties than always dreaming about it; his life fell into two separate compartments which perhaps did not have to conflict so long as one contained elements of fantasy. Indeed, when he saw Natica, so trim and cool and neat, taking her place at Tommy's table at lunchtime, it seemed hardly possible that she could have been naked in his arms the week before. Did her peremptory nod of recognition not almost deny it? Their lovemaking in his memory seemed to take on more the aspect of guilty thoughts than of guilty deeds, and what man could blame himself for the former?

Giles Woodward alone seemed to know what was going on, but his loyalty to Stephen was now such that he too had become part of the fantasy.

"I wouldn't have too many more of those dentist appointments if I were you, sir. Your teeth look just fine to me."

"You sound like Brangäne in the second act of *Tristan*."

"Shall I wave my scarf? Remember, when she did that, it was already too late."

What, however, contained no note of fantasy was Wilbur Knight's visit to his classroom one morning when Stephen, alone there, was correcting tests. The Latin master, even more solemn than usual, closed the door behind him and approached Stephen's desk, but did not take a seat.

"I have a matter of the utmost gravity to take up with you, Hill. I have been apprised of your assignations with Mrs. Barnes in my wife's apartment."

Stephen, flushing, jumped to his feet. "Mrs. Knight has told you?"

"Mrs. Knight has told me nothing," was the gravelly retort. "What would my wife know of such matters? It was the janitor who informed me when I visited the apartment yesterday. He wanted me to know the kind of use that Mrs. Barnes was making of the flat so generously loaned. When I told my wife, and suggested that you might be the man, she was appalled, almost incredulous. She said she had merely suggested that you pick Mrs. Barnes up there and drive her back to school. There had never been any idea of your spending a night."

"May I ask what you plan to do about this, sir?"

"Needless to say, I have passed a sleepless twenty-four hours. My first duty, of course, is to the school. I wish to avoid a scandal if it can be done without dishonor. And I find it hard to believe that you are a man who could fall into the sin of adultery without the strongest temptation. I have known and liked you since you were a boy here, and you have been kind to my wife. I have even obliged myself to consider that Mrs. Knight may, all inadvertently, all innocently, have created a kind of hothouse for the passions by inviting young persons of opposite sex to read erotic poetry in her parlor on afternoons when they should have been outside breathing the fresh air. Anyway, I have resolved to give you the opportunity to redeem yourself. If you will give me your word of honor that you will at once break off your intrigue with Mrs. Barnes and not renew it, my lips will be sealed."

Stephen hesitated. The offer was too generous to be spurned. But Natica, with the collapse of her fantasy, seemed to burst upon his brain with a new reality. He found himself actually trying to bargain with the old man.

"I give you my word of honor that I will not meet Mrs. Barnes again in that manner while I am a member of the faculty of this school."

Knight frowned. "I don't like the qualification. Are you considering resigning?"

"I am not, sir. But as you mentioned the school as your primary consideration, I thought I should tie my promise to my connection with it."

"Dear me, I had not thought you so lawyerlike. But very well. I suppose I must be satisfied with that. I had hoped you might demonstrate some shame at your conduct. But I reckon that is not within the scope of your generation's allowances."

"May I thank you for your moderation, sir?"

"No sir, you may not. I cannot so soon forgive your abuse of my wife's hospitality. Time, however, may mitigate my rigor. It will depend on your conduct in the future."

When he had left Stephen felt, absurdly, like a boy at school again whose twenty demerits, the maximum he could receive at a time without expulsion, had been forgiven by a kindly master whose good will he had now sedulously to recultivate. He knew, at any rate, that he could not risk seeing Natica alone again; he wrote her an account of what had happened and slipped it into her hand as the school assembled to enter the dining hall for lunch. Her quick glance seemed to indicate that she knew just what his letter contained (Mrs. Knight, of course!); she put it in her purse without a word.

Nor did he hear anything from her. He waited until after chapel the following Sunday and then sought her out in the garth where she was waiting for Tommy to change from his robes. Some visiting parents were also in the garth, waiting for sons who were choir members, but the flagstone paths between the flower beds led to secluded corners, and taking her by the elbow he guided her to one. He asked her softly if she had had time to think things over.

"What is there to think about?" Her tone was impatient, almost angry. "We knew it had to come to this sooner or later. We're lucky to have been caught by Knight and not someone else. He can hardly let it be known that his wife was running a bawdyhouse."

"Is *that* all you have to say?"

"Well, what more can I say? We knew the chance we were taking."

"But I need you, Natica! Don't you need me?"

"You know I do. What's the point of going on about it?" Then, seeing a couple approaching, she paused to be sure that her voice was under control. "My need, after all, is greater than yours. A handsome rich bachelor is never going to be at a loss for a mistress. Believe me, my dear, if I sound cool it's because I've been preparing myself for this so long."

"Couldn't we meet in vacations? I know I gave my word, but I'm not really on the faculty when I'm away from school, am I? Suppose you and Tommy were to borrow one of the family's cottages at Redwood next summer?"

"And carry on under your mother's eye as well as his? Dream on, my friend. No, no, this has to end. There's no other way."

"Natica!"

"Well, can you face the consequences? Public disgrace for us both. *And* for Tommy." She seemed to be almost panting now with controlled exasperation. "The loss of your career here. The anguish of your parents?"

He was silent.

"Well, can you?" Her tone had a rasp.

"What can I say?"

"Well then, there you are. Be a man. It shouldn't be too hard, when you hold most of the trumps."

She waved her hand at someone, and he turned to see Tommy approaching them.

He did not see her privately again in the next two weeks, and the time passed in the strange blankness of suspended animation. He tried to lose himself in his classes and in his new assignment of third form gymnasium, and he fought down his shame at the possibility that he was succeeding.

Succeeding? Was he trying to lose himself or find himself? Had Natica ever been quite real to him? Certainly he could not fool himself that he was real to her. He knew that she was simply frustrated, crazed with her restricted life. She had not even tried to make him think otherwise. There would be other men for her. Ultimately she would leave Tommy. And wasn't the deeper reality for himself in the school and the teaching life that he had counted on to sustain the ideals and aspirations of boyhood?

And then he found a letter from her in his mailbox.

When I told you that our affair was my first, I said nothing but the truth. And I have been as careless as inexperienced. When I missed my period by two weeks I went to a doctor in Boston who confirmed my suspicion. When I told him my predicament he had the humanity to write the name of another doctor on a card. The latter has agreed to do the necessary — it will be very simple and riskless, being so early — but I shall need a thousand dollars, and I have no hesitation in applying to your fuller purse. There can be no question of my having the child (in case you have scruples about abortion, though I can't imagine why any man should), as Tommy has not had what I believe the lawyers crudely call 'access' since our first so pleasant but costly night at Estelle's flat. Please make the check out to cash. I know I can count on you.

What was most to elate him in the days that followed was that he had not even for a moment considered giving her the check. Destroy his own child? It was unthinkable. In one blinding moment, standing in the hall of the Schoolhouse, her letter in hand, oblivious of the passing crowds of boys at recess, his doubts and fears vanished. There was only one thing to do, and the absolute imperative made all consequences trivial.

He went directly to her cottage, careless now of who might be watching. He found her in the kitchen, uncharacteristically watching a pot on the range. She gave a little cry when she saw him.

"Why have you come here? It's most indiscreet, in the middle of the morning."

"Listen to me, Natica. Listen to me first, and then nothing else will matter." She took in the new firmness of his tone and sat down at the kitchen table, rubbing her hands in her apron. "I want you to have that baby. I want you to divorce Tommy and marry me. I want you and I want my child. Nothing else in the world matters to me."

Her tensely staring eyes gave no indication of what she might be thinking.

"It doesn't matter whether you love me enough to be my wife. Anyway, you certainly care for me more than you do for Tommy. Now our first duty is to the baby. Oh, Natica, don't tell me you don't want to have that child!"

She appeared to be thinking hard. "I want it if I can give it a decent life. Suppose Tommy refuses to give me a divorce?"

"Then we can go off together. To Europe maybe. And have the child there. Those things always work themselves out in the long run. And the advantage of my money is that we can wait for the long run."

"But oh, Stephen, the school and your job! I can't do that to you, even for the baby."

"What was it you said yourself? That my father could buy me a new school?"

"Maybe he won't after this."

"What's a job compared to the life of my son?"

"Your son?"

"Or daughter. Or triplets, if you like."

"Good heavens." She covered her face with both hands and remained so for several silent, motionless moments. When she spoke, her voice was hoarse. "Oh, Stephen, don't tempt me!"

"Only promise me this. Don't do anything until I've talked to a lawyer friend of mine in Boston. He's the most brilliant man I know. I'll see him tomorrow if I have to cut every class!"

When he left, he not only had her promise. He was convinced

that she would have the baby if he could provide a feasible way. And he was convinced that he wanted that baby more than anything else in the world.

15 ....

STEPHEN SAT in Joel Sapperthwaite's narrow white-walled office in State Street, confronting the concerned, handsome features of his former tutor. Joel was not yet a partner in the famous old firm of Saltonstall & Meyers, but everyone knew that he soon would be. He had fairly reeked with the aura of future success ever since, a stocky Yale senior from Montana on a "football" scholarship, he had spent a summer at Redwood as mentor to the twelve-year-old Stephen. Stephen had made a hero out of Joel, who, like everyone else, had made a heroine out of Stephen's mother, and the tutor and all the Hills had maintained a warm relationship ever since. Stephen even suspected that his father had put Joel through Harvard Law.

"Let's clear up one thing, Steve. Have you told your parents? And wouldn't they rather you went to their lawyers in New York?"

"I haven't told them, and I'm not going to until I have to. I want to present them with a *fait accompli*. What's the point of upsetting them when I'm absolutely determined in my own mind what I'm going to do?"

"And Mrs. Barnes agrees?"

"She has promised me to do nothing until she hears what you advise. But I'm convinced she wants the baby if it can be arranged."

"And Mr. Barnes?"

"I don't know what his attitude will be. But does it really matter? He can't stop her from leaving him. He can't stop us from going off somewhere until the baby is born. Surely, no matter what he does, we can eventually get married somewhere, can't we? And I don't care where."

"You're really prepared to face the music? It will be very loud, you know. Losing your job and making a thumping scandal. Not to speak of what you'll be doing to that poor minister."

"It's terrible, I know. Don't think I haven't sweated it out. Averhill has meant the world to me. Perhaps too much so. I even wonder if it hasn't been an evasion of life. And here comes life in the form of an innocent baby. I've got to guarantee *his* life. I'm sorry about Tommy, but she's bound to leave him eventually in any case. She's told me so. She can't stand him, really."

"Yet she married him. I don't suppose anyone forced her to."

"Oh, Joel, don't moralize. I'm way past that. What would *you* do in my case?"

Joel got up quickly and reached a hand over his desk for his client to shake. "I hope I'd do just what you're doing. It's a sorry business, but I agree the infant comes first."

"And do you know something else? It's the first great decision I've made in my life. All along I've let things happen to me. I've been what my friend Annette used to call *va-comme-je-te-pousse*. But now I'm taking not only my own life but that of two others into my hands, and I'm damned if I won't make a good thing of it!"

"And you really love this girl?"

"Yes!"

"And she loves you?"

"Yes."

It was no longer the time for doubts. Joel gave a strong nod and reseated himself at his desk. "And now to business. Here is what you and Mrs. Barnes must do."

"Call her Natica, please. She too will be your client, although the bills come to me."

"Natica. She will leave immediately for Reno where she will establish the required residence. If I can induce her husband's lawyer to persuade him to consent to a divorce, so much the better. Obviously, we will not ask for alimony. But hate and jealousy can make people take strange positions, and we have to be prepared for his refusal. A divorce obtained without his consent would not be good outside of Nevada. Very well, you and Natica will marry and live in Nevada. Eventually, of course, with two genuine Nevada residences, the divorce and second marriage will be valid everywhere, but believe me, you will not have to wait that long. Barnes will come around. They always do in the end."

"How soon could we be married?"

"In Nevada? Six weeks. Speed is of the essence. We don't want Barnes claiming that baby."

"How could he do that? There's no way it could be his. Natica told me he hasn't had 'access,' if that's the right word."

"Access is just what he *has* had. Natica obviously doesn't understand the term in law. It doesn't mean that he's had sexual relations with her. It means that he *could* have, while they were living under the same roof. But you tell me he doesn't know she's pregnant. Be sure to keep it that way, as long as you can, anyway. If the child is born seven months after your marriage nobody will have much reason to suspect it was conceived before."

"Oh, Joel, how can I ever thank you?"

"You won't have to. You can pay me. Through the nose, too. Messrs. Saltonstall & Meyers are not cheap. But what's that to your exchequer? And speaking of dough, you had better leave me enough to get your beloved to Reno and put her up in a proper hotel."

When these details had been worked out, Stephen called Natica, and learning she was alone, told her the plan.

"How about it? Are you game?"

Her answer was as strong as he could have wished.

"I *am* game. I've thought of what I'd do if you came up with something immediate, as, thank God, you have. I shall leave Tommy today. Within an hour. He's gone somewhere with Lockwood and won't be back till late. I've already packed two bags which is all I'm going to take. Ask the good Mr. Sapperthwaite to get me a room in a hotel in Boston for tonight. I'll call him from the station. And tell him I'll be ready to leave for Reno on the very first plane."

Stephen was taken aback by such a show of resolution. "You don't think you owe it to him to tell him to his face?"

"No, dear, I'm way beyond that kind of guilt-ridden honesty. When you know exactly what you're going to do, there's no point in anything but doing it. Tommy would just rant and rave. It would be a painful scene, to nobody's advantage. I should never have got into his life and now I'm going to get out of it as quickly and cleanly as possible."

"But what will I tell him when I get back to school?"

"Why should you tell him anything? He doesn't know about us. All he will know and all *you* will know and all the school will know is that I've bolted. It won't come as much of a shock to many of the faculty, at least to the wives. They've pegged me as an oddball from the beginning."

"But when I come out to marry you in Reno, they'll know."

"But that will be later. Then we won't care. That will be your part of the plan. Let's take one step at a time. The first will be mine. I'm leaving Tommy a letter telling him I've gone for good and that he'll hear from me later."

"You won't tell him that . . ."

"That I'm pregnant? Of course not. What business is that of his?"

When Stephen told Joel, who had been listening, the part of the dialogue he had been unable to hear, though considerably softening the brisk efficiency of Natica's tone, he did not quite like the look in his lawyer's eye.

"Well, it seems we're all set, doesn't it? I like clients who don't dally about making up their minds."

Stephen did not know what to expect when he returned to school, but he was still surprised to find everything the same. Roy Evans had taken over his morning English classes on his plea of a family legal emergency — the awe in which the Hill family was held at school made this perfectly credible — and his absence seemed to have been hardly noticed except by Giles Woodward, who made a grinning allusion to a dentist appointment to which he did not respond. But the next morning, when he was sitting in his empty classroom preparing for the next hour's session on the "Ode on Melancholy," Tommy Barnes, his face crinkled and gray, burst in and slammed the door behind him.

"Do you know where Natica is?" he demanded hoarsely.

"Why? Has she gone?"

"Don't you know where she is? She left me this note." He waved a paper frantically. "She says she's left me. Left me for good!"

"Oh, Tommy!" Stephen rose, hating himself, to adopt a sympathetic stance. "I'm so sorry. But why should I know anything about that?"

"Because you're her friend! Because you've been reading poetry together and God knows what."

"Reading poetry together doesn't mean I know where she's gone."

"Do you mean to tell me, Hill, there's nothing between you and her?"

Stephen, to prepare himself for the ordeal that was bound to come, had resolved to fix his mind on the image of his unborn child. Once the idea had been firmly established that he owed everything, down to his very existence, to the guaranty of a decent start in life for the foetus he had called into being, lies and deviations and disgrace itself would simply fix themselves into the ineluctable pattern of his destiny.

"I don't mean to say I have never felt an attraction to your wife. But she is perfectly innocent of that. There has been nothing between us."

Tommy stared at him blankly for a moment and then collapsed on one of the desk chairs and began to sob. His shoulders shook. He appeared no longer aware of Stephen's presence.

Stephen forced himself to stand there silently and watch. In his mind there arose the image of a blond-haired boy, well made, a quizzical and faintly sultry look on his handsome features.

A sharp knock on the door was immediately followed by the appearance of a very different boy. He stared at Tommy in astonishment.

"Giles, get out of here!"

"I'm sorry, Mr. Hill, but the headmaster says you are to see him immediately."

"But I have a class in five minutes!"

"He said that didn't matter. That he would send Mr. Sykes to take it."

Tommy, hearing this, seemed to recover himself. "I told Dr. Lockwood about Natica," he explained to Stephen. "I'm afraid I may have got you into trouble. But you can tell him what you told me. I suppose she just hated my guts. Deep down I've known it all along."

The young minister now hurried from the room, leaving Stephen and Giles to stare at each other.

"Is this *it*, sir?"

"This may be it."

"I'm very sorry."

Stephen reached out a hand which the boy took. "You've been a real pal, Giles. I'll never forget it."

"Thank you, sir."

"Oh, you may as well call me Steve now."

"It's that bad?"

"I'm afraid it's that bad."

Downstairs in the headmaster's study Stephen faced a Lockwood whose very benignity was ominous.

"Close the door, Mr. Hill. We shall need to be private. Are you aware that Mrs. Barnes has left her husband?"

"Tommy just told me, sir."

"You did not hear it from herself?"

"I did not, sir."

"Stephen, are you telling me the truth?"

"Why should I not, sir?"

"You have been intimate with Mrs. Barnes, have you not?"

"Intimate, sir?"

"You have met her at Mrs. Knight's without her husband. You have read poetry with her."

"That is true, sir."

"Look into your heart, Stephen. I speak to you as your minister. As the man who confirmed you. Have you never entertained unlawful feelings about that woman?"

"I cannot deny that, sir. But Mrs. Barnes's behavior in my regard has been at all times beyond reproach."

"Really?" The bushy eyebrows soared. "How strange. I should never have believed Wilbur Knight to be a liar. Perhaps it was jealousy about your relations with his own fair spouse that drove him to malign you."

Stephen closed his eyes to intensify the image of the blond-haired boy. Lockwood's mocking laugh at his own ludicrous supposition was almost demonic.

"What did Mr. Knight accuse me of, sir?"

"What you know all too well!" came the answering roar. "He said he had promised not to expose you so long as you kept away from Mrs. Barnes. But when I informed him an hour ago that she had fled the campus, he concluded that you had not kept your part of the unholy bargain and he told me all. Now will you deny your criminal relations with Mrs. Barnes?" Stephen was silent. "That's better. For let me tell you that you're a very bad liar. Guilt sticks out of you. Perhaps that's just as well. Perhaps it means that you're still redeemable. Let me tell you what I've decided to do. For the sake of your family and in view of my affection for you and them, and considering that this wretched woman has gone for good, I offer you a renewal of Knight's unholy bargain. If you will give me your word that all is now over between you and Mrs. Barnes, I shall not ask for your resignation. You understand that I am sticking my neck out for you, that I am risking considerable scandal. But Wilbur Knight, I feel assured, will go along with any course I recommend, and I believe I can handle the unfortunate Tommy. It will appear to the world that his wife has simply absconded. Some tattling tongues may mention you as a possible cause, but that will die down in time. And remember this, Stephen." Lockwood's face had now the sternness of granite. "If I do this for you, you must do as much for me. Not only will you pledge never to meet that woman again, but you will give me your solemn oath to have no carnal knowledge of any other woman." Here the headmaster's features were relaxed to something like humor. "At least until your marriage, which I hope, in view of your lusty nature, will not be too long delayed."

"I must tell you at once, sir, that it may not be. Your offer is unspeakably generous. But if Mrs. Barnes should obtain her freedom, it is my firm resolution to offer her myself as a second husband."

The eyes of a grand inquisitor in Toledo in the time of Philip II could not have shone with a more vivid animosity than those he now confronted. Even at such a moment Stephen could still reflect that there must have been an actual pleasure in sending infidels to the fire.

"Very well, Stephen Hill. Have it your way. You will pack your things and be off the campus by nightfall. I shall call your father and tell him of my decision. I have no doubt he will thoroughly approve. My only regret is that I deviated from my principles in even *offering* you an alternative."

"No one need ever learn of that, sir. And I shall always be grateful."

"I don't want your gratitude! Nor do I care a fig whether or not my ill-advised offer becomes known."

"I trust, anyway, sir, that my dismissal will not affect Tommy Barnes's position in the school."

"His position? What position?"

"I mean his future at Averhill."

"Mr. Thomas Barnes has no future at Averhill. What sort of place is there in a church school for a divorced priest? I don't say that he will have to go immediately, but to speak of his future here is a misnomer."

Stephen could not for a moment seem to grasp this new horror. "But it wasn't his fault, sir!"

"Fault?" exclaimed Lockwood haughtily. "You mean because no

woman could resist you? Don't add fatuity to your other sins. Barnes has disgraced his church by giving our Roman adversaries a new argument in favor of celibacy of the clergy."

"Oh, sir. Have you no pity for him?"

"Had *you?* To my mind Barnes is lower than an adulterer, which is pretty low. For he has proved himself either a *mari complaisant* or an ass. Take your pick."

Stephen could only gape. "An ass, sir?"

"Why yes. For either he knew of his wife's infidelity and chose to look the other way, or he was the only member of the faculty who did *not* know, which turns him into a long-eared, braying animal, does it not? And now, sir, I suggest you have some packing to do."

Stephen, walking dazedly across the circle to his dormitory, reflected that the knowledge of the harm he had occasioned to Tommy was perhaps not the worst blow he had received in the past hour. For he had suddenly identified the face of the boy he had imagined as his son. It was that of Charlie LeBrun.

Ruth's Memoir . . .

It was in the late spring of 1939 that I took a week off from my school (the headmistress had allowed me to give my two classes a "reading period") to be Natica's guest in the luxurious but garish hotel just outside Reno where she was completing the sixth and last week of her required legal "residence." If her husband should decide to file an appearance by a Nevada attorney and not contest her suit she would be able to obtain a valid divorce in twenty-four hours and marry Stephen the same day, but they had decided to marry in any event, and she wanted, as she frankly put it, at least one "respectable" family member to be present at the ceremony. As her mother had flatly refused to go out, both on her own behalf and her father's, and as her brothers could not leave their jobs, there was no one available but the old maid aunt.

At any rate, I was glad to go. I had been much upset by Natica's seemingly brutal abandonment of the affectionate and good-natured Tommy and suspicious of her motives in pursuing a man about whom I knew nothing but that he was wealthy, but my niece has always appealed almost as much to my curiosity as to my heart. She was indubitably an interesting person, and I didn't want to miss any part of her development. And then, too, it was a theory of mine that Natica's hardness was to some extent the needed armor of a brilliant woman in a man's world. I did not then foresee how dramatically the doors of the professions were going to open to women, but I was under no illusion that the only ones so available in the 1930s which had room at the top were teaching and nursing, and the woman without interest in either of these had to put together her own career as best she could.

There was still another factor in my desire to be with Natica in her time of need. My sister's shrill denunciation of her daughter's conduct had been bound to create an almost indignant reaction in me.

"Really, Kitty, to hear you go on, one would think Natica had invented divorce. Do you know that almost a fifth of the girls in my classes — theoretically from the best families in town — come from split homes?"

"But their fathers aren't ministers. How can any decent woman divorce a minister? Doesn't Natica know she's ruining his career?"

"I will admit that makes it worse. But I don't see why the cloth should guarantee a man an unbroken marriage. Anyway, everyone will know it wasn't Tommy's fault. And if they don't, I'm sure Natica will be a good enough sport to enlighten them."

"How can you take it so lightly? I was telling Harry, Natica must have got her callousness from his side of the family. But now you make me wonder."

I had to remind myself as usual there was no point in arguing with my older sister.

Natica was at her best when she met me at the airport. She looked very trim and smart in a brown tweed suit (always her favorite color) and a yellow silk blouse; it was apparent that everything on her was brand new. She drove me out to the vast white gleaming hotel in a rented Lincoln Zephyr, and when I protested at the size of my suite she explained with a shrug:

"Stephen has directed his bank to keep the balance in my checking account at ten thousand bucks. It's like having a little magic well."

"I hope you're not thinking of the money too much," I said sternly.

"But I think of it all the time!" she exclaimed cheerfully. "Who wouldn't, I'd like to know, who's been as poor as I have? Oh, Aunt Ruth, don't look so shocked. I'll be a careful spender, I promise. Only I expect to get my money's worth. Very few of the rich do. They haven't had my long hard training!"

She was in the best possible mood that night at dinner in the hideous Spanish-Moorish dining hall where I, enchanted to be safely on the ground (I was still a nervous flyer in those days), allowed myself to join her in two rounds of cocktails and a bottle of wine. I was soon inclined to be a good deal franker than usual, but she seemed to welcome even my criticisms for the chance to rebut them.

"What will Stephen do now he can't teach at Averhill?"

"He might start a school of his own. If his father would back him to it. But Mr. and Mrs. Hill have been ominously silent on the whole subject of me. Stephen says his mother is bound to come around in the end, but I wonder. I *am* rather a dose to swallow."

"The baby should do the trick."

I caught at once her warning glance. She had told me of the baby but it was to be a secret as long as possible.

"Nobody can hear us," I apprised her. "You *are* sure about the baby, aren't you?"

"You mean about my condition? Of course I am. Did you think I might have made it up? To trap poor Stephen? Really, Aunt Ruth, what a fiend you must think me! I wonder if it isn't a sort of compliment, really."

"No, no, no, I only meant you could have been mistaken. Plenty of women have been."

"Well, there's no mistake about this. You're welcome to ask Dr. Whittaker, my Reno gynecologist."

I returned to my original inquiry. "Couldn't Stephen fund his own school?"

"Hardly. He can't touch his principal without the consent of his bank trustee, and the bank does what Daddy tells it. But in any event we shouldn't even think of that for a couple of years, until the scandal has died down. Parents aren't going to want to send their little darlings to an institution where the wicked Mrs. Barnes could corrupt them."

I questioned her tone. "You seem to find those parents unreasonable. But I suppose they may expect schools to teach morals."

"I don't judge them. They have their opinions and standards; I mine."

"Would you object if I probed that a bit?"

"Not in the least."

"How do you really feel about what you've done to Tommy?"

"I'm sorry about it. Very sorry, really. But in no way ashamed of it. And in no way regretful. It was a mistake that had to be rectified. Why throw one's life down the drain for a sacrament one doesn't even believe in?"

"You haven't thrown yours down any drain. I was thinking of Tommy's."

"I suppose you might put it that Tommy was a kind of war casualty."

"In what war? That of the sexes?"

"Yes! I like that. He had to have a wife if he was ever to get his own school. Bachelor headmasters went out with Freud. Parents and school boards are afraid that every unmarried teacher over thirty is either an active or repressed homosexual. And they so often are! As for myself, I had to have a husband to escape from my family's clutches. To get my head above the surface of my own little slough of despond. We both did what was expected of us. Everyone applauded. When I found I had plunged into a deeper slough, I had to struggle out, that was all. But don't think Tommy's case is hopeless. Stephen may one day be able to do something for him."

"You mean when his father dies? There's the money again."

"As you see, I never forget it."

"But would Tommy ever take money from Stephen? Hasn't he his pride?"

"There might be ways of helping him without his knowing it. Oh, Aunt Ruth, there's so much you can do with money and just a little imagination! And so few rich people have any."

"You seem pretty sure Stephen will give you a free hand with what he's got."

"It's an assumption, that's true. Perhaps a presumption. I could be quite wrong. He may turn out the most terrible miser."

"What would you do then? Leave him?"

"You really do think I'm horrid, don't you? But it's still wonderful to have you here. I've been *so* lonely."

"Why hasn't Stephen come?"

"Because he has this terror that if people think we were intimate before we were married, Tommy might get the idea that I became pregnant while I was still his wife and claim the child."

"That doesn't seem very likely to me," I commented in surprise.

"Hell hath no fury, you know. It goes for men as well as women."

I had the disagreeable impression that Natica was not in any particular hurry to have her beloved arrive in Reno. "Don't you *want* him to come?" I asked bluntly.

"Not really. He'd be so bored. Look, Aunt Ruth. You can't start building up my obligations to Stephen because I've failed in what you consider I owed Tommy. Oh, I know how your mind works. You're a great one for expiation. But please get one thing straight. Stephen is the one who does most of the owing in our situation. I was willing to have an abortion. I had actually arranged for it. All he had to do was pay a sum that meant nothing to him, and there he would have been, free as air, to go on with his life at Averhill as if nothing had happened. It was *his* decision that I should have the baby, even at the cost of my marriage to Tommy. He could hardly not offer me his hand after that, could he?"

I admit I was startled. I had no idea she had played so fair. I had thought of Stephen as even rather reluctantly trapped by the situation. But now it appeared that it had been he who had taken the ultimate responsibility. And mustn't a man have been very much in love to do that? Could any man have been pushed quite so strongly by a sense of *moral* responsibility?

"You do love Stephen?" I permitted myself to ask.

"Of course, I love him."

Her tone was hardly convincing. What was more, I didn't feel she was even trying to convince me. Love was something that Natica seemed to feel could be taken for granted in a marriage, that went along, at least initially, with a "Mr. and Mrs.," like a tin can attached to the rear bumper of the departing vehicle. I could only hope that if she had everything she wanted and if her young man was really as much in love as I supposed, the combination might suffice for a happy union. Natica, I suspected, might be that *rara avis* among egoists, the one who is capable of becoming permanently agreeable when she has attained her ambition.

Stephen arrived two days before the end of Natica's six-week residence and took a room ostentatiously distant from her suite, but he had all his meals at our table. I was much impressed with his romantic good looks. An unworthy side of me played with the idea that no one could too harshly blame the woman who had left Tommy Barnes for so rich an Adonis. But I sternly repressed the notion. He was full of small, conscientious attentions for Natica and even for myself, but he seemed tense and nervous, and the chatter over the dishes was largely between his future bride and her aunt.

"Has he any more news about his parents?" I asked the next morning at breakfast before he had appeared.

"Not a word."

"Hasn't he been with them?"

"No, he's been staying at the Yale Club. It's been a matter of pride. Which side will make the first gesture."

"So we'll just have to wait for the baby."

"And that is another reason for keeping Tommy entirely out of it."

"I still don't see why. If he *knows* it couldn't be his child."

"Oh, of course, he knows," she retorted with a slight show of exasperation. "I've told you there had been nothing between us for months. But I'm talking about what a man might do if he's crazed . . . Hush, here's Stephen."

But it was a new Stephen who sat down at our table. He was waving a telegram and he was radiant. "It's from Joel!" he exclaimed. "Tommy will appear by attorney and he won't contest. In two days' time, Natica, you and I will be validly married in every state in the union!"

I watched Natica as she stared at him. At first she seemed hardly to take in the good news. Then a glow slowly covered her features, and her eyes actually shone. It was joy! I had never seen or even imagined Natica joyful before. But it was to me that she first spoke.

"Ah, dear Aunt Ruth, I promise you I shall make this up to Tommy. But the first thing we owe him is to be happy. If we are building on his sacrifice, we must build well." Now she turned to her husband-to-be. "We *must* be happy, Stephen! Promise me that you'll be happy!"

Part Three

16 · · ·

Natica on her honeymoon in France felt at times as if she had married a stranger. He was not, to be sure, in the least a disagreeable or sinister stranger. He was the same pale, beautiful and occasionally passionate young man who had so deeply intrigued her at Averhill, and he was a charming companion and guide to the historic sites which they visited, so well known to him, from his many trips to Europe with his family, and so deliriously new to her, who had never been. But there was a moodiness in his nature of which she had not been aware, except for a hint on his first arrival at Reno. He would have periods of silence, lasting as much as an hour at a time, when he would respond to her questions only in polite but reluctant monosyllables, and he would sometimes moan in his sleep as if he were having a nightmare, though he denied it when she inquired in the morning. She tried on two occasions to get him to "talk out" his guilt feelings about Tommy and Dr. Lockwood, but each time he firmly changed the subject, insisting that he had fully accepted his acts and their consequences and that now they must let the dead bury the dead. But she was left with the uncomfortable feeling that he was trying to protect her from the pain of sensing his own pain, or even perhaps to protect himself from the pain of sensing that she had none.

His best times were at dinner when he would wax lively again over gin cocktails and vintage wines and recount long and, at least to her, fascinating stories of his childhood, his schools and camps and trips abroad, his parents and sisters, even his many uncles and aunts. It was not that he was unduly self-centered or lacking in interest in her antecedents. It was she who abruptly turned the talk from any inquiry about her own childhood, which thoroughly bored her, and brought it firmly back to the saga of the Hills and Kips, as if she were learning the new language of the fascinating country that was to be her future abode.

"I keep thinking you're going to accuse me of being the most awful bore," he protested once. "The Kips were the dowdiest sort of poor white Hudson River *déclassés*. And Grandfather Hill simply had the luck of being a small-time creditor of the young John D. Rockefeller, whose debt was paid in oil stock. He wasn't even a robber baron!"

"But it's all new to me. Can't you see that?"

"So are your family to me."

"My family, except for Aunt Ruth, could never be new to anyone. That's not snobbishness or superiority on my part. It's simply gospel truth. Just wait. You'll see for yourself, all in good time. But let's not anticipate it."

She resolved that one of the first things she would do on their return to New York would be to go down to the Standard Oil Building on lower Broadway and see for herself the gray entrance lobby where the names of the original partners were carved on medallions in the archways: Rockefeller, Pratt, Harkness, Jennings, Archbold, Flagler, Brewster, Bostwick, Hill. She had learned them all, like the kings of England.

And Stephen's seeming at times a stranger had its romantic side. It was intensified by her being alone with him in a strange land. They had left Reno immediately after their marriage and had taken the *Yankee Clipper* from New York to Europe without pausing to meet either family. They had agreed to postpone all resumptions of old connections until their return from a two-month honeymoon, with the sole exception of Mr. and Mrs. Hill, who would be making their bi-annual visit to the French capital and on whom they could hardly not call. Natica was seeking to associate the great new sights — the cathedrals of Amiens and Chartres and the lofty monastery of Mont-Saint-Michel — with her new husband and the new life on which she was embarking. She was determined that everything about it should be beautiful and elevating. It seemed at moments as if she had died and come to life in a new and enchanting existence where it should be as much a pleasure as a duty to learn the new standards of what was brave and virtuous and what was not. The French newspaper headlines of threatened war were like the distant ringing of an alarm clock to one still asleep. She had no time for the irrelevance of Hitler.

Best of all was Chartres, where they stayed a full two weeks, reading Henry Adams and roaming the peerless church. Stephen tired of it before she; he rented a bicycle and got his exercise pedaling across the countryside. But her appetite for stained glass and saints in niches and soaring buttresses seemed inexhaustible. She could not have enough of the cathedral. Sometimes she joined tours and sometimes hired a guide of her own, but at length she preferred to sit and walk by herself, letting the vast blue coolness penetrate her until she felt almost a part of it.

"I'm like Henry Adams!" she exclaimed one night at dinner. "I'm in love with the past. With the twelfth century, anyway. With a world that worshiped the Virgin. Like Adams I have no use for our terrible modern world."

Stephen was studying the wine list. It was something he was beginning to take seriously. "But Adams didn't believe in the Virgin. She was just a myth. And she was just as much a myth in the twelfth century as in our own."

"But she was a force. A great force. She built all the finest cathedrals in France!"

"That was the force generated by her myth. It doesn't make her any more real. How about a Pouilly-Fumé?"

"But maybe what Adams believed was that the force of the illusion actually created the Virgin. Or recreated her! Why not? You remember that little poem he left when he died, 'The Virgin and the Dynamo'? I think he actually believed that he had become a part of his ancestors' Norman past. 'When Ave Maris Stella first was sung, I helped to sing it there with Saint Bernard.'"

"What wine do you want?"

"Anything you say. The Pouilly will be fine."

"One and a half bottles? One is too little; two too much."

"Oh, one is plenty. I only want a drop. And Stephen?"

"Yes, dear?"

"If it's a boy, can we call it Bernard?"

"What a ridiculous idea! What's come over you tonight?"

"Please, Stephen I really mean it."

They argued about it through the first course of dinner, but he dropped the subject when she became excited. He was always afraid of doing anything that might adversely affect her condition.

She was surprised in the next two days at the tenacity of her new superstition. She had suddenly taken to heart the concept of bracketing her unborn child with Saint Bernard of Clairvaux. If it should be a girl, it would be Bernadine. She had become so intrigued with her own theory about Henry Adams that, having like him no faith, she had begun to take seriously the idea that she might create one by a sufficiently imaginative reconstruction of the past. Might not the invocation of Saint Bernard in some fashion atone for the sorry state of not knowing which of two men was the father of the new life within her?

She did not think she was becoming irrational. She was confident that even the unreality of her honeymoon abroad and her isolation from old sights and familiar faces had not shaken her basic common sense. She knew that her fantasy about Saint Bernard might be the result of too many hours of brooding in a dim religious light filtered through the most beautiful stained glass in the world. But still, if she *chose* not to scorn it or debase it? If she chose to build on it? What but her own will power had brought her the few things she had valued in her life? And she certainly needed something like faith now.

She had not at first doubted that Stephen was the cause of her pregnancy. Their lovemaking had been a source of mutual satisfaction far more intense than anything she had experienced with Tommy, and she had taken no precautions, though why, she was still not sure. Her mood at the time had been reckless, defiant — perhaps even, so far as her reputation was concerned, a touch suicidal. With Tommy she had always used a contraceptive, and besides, she had discontinued sexual relations with him after the start of her affair with Stephen, pleading a bad case of cystitis.

But there had been one exception. The morning following her second meeting with Stephen in Estelle Knight's flat, the headmaster had grumbled to Tommy, while they were robing for Sunday chapel, about masters leaving the campus overnight for matters that could be as well accomplished in the neighborhood and had cited Stephen's trip to a Boston dentist of the day before. Tommy, who had apparently been secretly resentful of his wife's friendship with the new master and suspicious of their poetry readings, had instantly connected Stephen's disappearance with her decision to stay that night in Boston and had confronted her on her return with angry inquiries. She had taken a very high tone and denied seeing Stephen at all, but for once she had been unable to appease him, and she had at last found it politic to convince him of her innocence, or at least to stun him into a kind of acceptance, by making violent love to him on the spot. For further assurance of her supposed passion she had dispensed with a contraceptive. It had worked, for Tommy had been naïve enough to suppose that no "lady," in less than twenty-four hours, could have gone from the arms of one bare man to those of another.

When she had discovered her pregnancy, she had refused at first even to consider that this single act of appeasement could have been its origin. It had not only not been repeated, but she had reduced Tommy to a state of contrition by complaining that his strong activity on that occasion had worsened her cystitis. And when she counted the number of times that she had achieved orgasm with Stephen on their three prolonged encounters, it seemed absurd to seek elsewhere for an impregnator. But the doubt so roughly smothered soon enough made its struggle felt, and she began to be haunted by the image of a growing boy, growing each year into a more ominous likeness of the wretched Tommy, until she would read suspicion in every eye that fell upon the fancied child. In vain she told herself that such striking resemblances were very rare and that one could always simply refuse to recognize them, and even if the matter should turn out as bad as her fantasy painted, could she not always explain to Stephen how it had happened?

Yes. But not why she had lied to him.

Well then, she asked herself irritably, what could he *do* about it? But she was not sure what this new Stephen, so different from the malleable youth at Averhill, would do. And men could be such idiots about these things.

She was distracted from this concern, however, by a cable from Stephen's father's office in New York announcing that his parents would arrive from London at the Crillon the following Monday and would expect them to call the next afternoon at six.

✓ ✓ ✓

Mr. Hill met them in the lobby, a small dry balding presence garbed in a black suit that seemed to defy the Paris spring. His matter-of-fact air was devoid of either welcome or reproof. Nobody watching him greet Natica would have dreamed that he was meeting a daughter-in-law for the first time. He might have been a bank manager greeting a new but not very important client.

"Mrs. Hill wishes to see you alone, so you're to go right up to her suite. I'm to take Stephen for a stroll in the public gardens."

Stephen kissed her before following his father, who had already turned to the front door.

"Don't be afraid. She won't eat you."

She found his mother even more beautiful than she had expected, against the happy setting of her Louis XV salon with its green panels and Boucher prints and pink marble mantel with gilded candelabra. Mrs. Hill, serenely reclining on a chaise longue in a pink dressing gown with wonderful lace (there was the excuse of some minor indisposition), seemed as much at ease in the century of the Pompadour as the famed royal mistress herself smiling down at her from an oval portrait, but there was still a distinct Yankee note of holding off from such frippery in the figure that was ample without being stout, in the face that was lineless without (one felt somehow sure) ever having been lifted and in those clear, penetrating blue eyes. She had even brought some of her own things to claim the room from its too exclusive adhesion to its own era. Natica took in the large silver-framed portrait photographs of her daughters, one in bridal dress, and a snapshot of Stephen's father, looking oddly jaunty in a white flannel suit and a Panama.

Mrs. Hill did not rise but sat up and reached out her arms to embrace her visitor. Not a word was spoken but Natica felt herself hugged.

"There now," her mother-in-law murmured as she released her and patted the seat of the chair beside her. "Sit down and let us have a good talk. You're even prettier than I've been told, my dear. I wanted to see you first alone because it's the women of the family who really get things done, don't you agree? Our minds are not always cluttered up with what we *should* be doing or thinking. Men are always striking attitudes."

"I confess I was afraid you might have struck one about me."

"Well you and I must understand each other. Of course, I didn't like the circumstances that led up to your and Stephen's marriage. How could I? I was brought up with very strict ideas of the sacredness of the marriage vow. But we live in a different world now, and I am willing to start fresh with you as Stephen's wife. What went before is not going to be any concern of mine. I'm simply going to love you."

After a brief silence Natica found herself sobbing. She did not even try to conceal or explain it. She simply knew at once that she loved this woman as she had never loved a human being before. What was wonderful was that Mrs. Hill seemed to find her reaction entirely natural.

"That's all right, dear. You can always weep with me. I can

imagine that you must have been through a good deal of hell. But I trust that you and I will do some laughing, too."

"Oh, Mrs. Hill, if you *knew* what your kindness meant!"

"You see that I'm on your side. Not everyone has been, I'm sure. But that's over now. You will find that Stephen's sisters will be very welcoming. My husband may take a bit longer, but he'll come around in the end. Don't try too hard with him, that's all. Just be natural. The person we're going to have the hardest time with is Stephen himself. Now don't misunderstand me. I don't mean because of you. As a matter of fact, I can very well imagine that you may be just the wife he needed. But it's going to take him some time to accept the fact that a teaching career is out of the question, at least for a while."

"Oh, I know! It haunts me."

"The great thing will be to see that he's occupied. All the Hill financial interests — that is, of my husband and of his sister and brothers — are handled by Bennett & Son. George Bennett is Mr. Hill's brother-in-law and the 'Son,' who is considered the real genius of the firm, is his nephew Tyler. I know Stephen doesn't like Tyler, but I think it might be good for him to work with him for a while and learn how to handle money."

Even in her excited state Natica was struck by the name. "Would that be the Tyler Bennett who married Edith DeVoe?"

"Yes. Is she a friend of yours?"

"I tutored her once."

"Well, I'm sure she was the better for that. Maybe she and you can make Tyler a bit more palatable to Stephen. I suspect it's just jealousy on Stephen's part. The family are always going on about how brilliant Tyler is. But now to more important matters. I want to buy you and Stephen a nice apartment in New York."

"Oh, we won't need anything elaborate."

"Nonsense, my dear. You'll need something charming. Oh, don't think I don't know how you feel. When I first married Mr. Hill I was very worried about the money. As Stephen has probably told you, my family, the Kips, were poor as church mice. Proud as you like, I grant, but still poor. I shall never forget what my sister-in-law Grace, who had married my husband's older brother, told me: 'Don't worry about the money. Just concentrate on making yourself entirely comfortable.' Well, I did just that."

Natica was silent for a moment before she spoke. "Mrs. Hill, I think I am going to do in every particular exactly what you tell me."

"Well, that may be a bit excessive. But for a few months, anyway, I think I may be of some assistance."

"Indispensable."

Natica rose now and walked to the window and stood looking down on the crowded white splendor of the Place de la Concorde. She did not feel that she had to explain her sudden detachment from their conversation. Mrs. Hill, she was sure, would sympathize with her need to take in the full wonder of her welcome. But what she suddenly could not bear was that this woman, whose friendship, whose possible love, seemed everything in the world that she had imagined to make her life worth living, would be barred from her forever if she were to learn that the adored Stephen's wife was not bearing Stephen's child.

How could it be that she was standing in the very heart of Paris with everything that she had ever wanted being stuffed into her outstretched arms and still be wretched? How could she let her persistent, nagging, neurotic vision of a staring boy, staring with Tommy's bewildered and foolish eyes, and with that gaping countenance that her former husband assumed whenever life even for a moment failed to resemble his own idiotic concept of it, stand in the way of a virtually guaranteed bliss? How could she, a priestess of the life of reason, allow a silly fantasy to soil the goal it had taken a near miracle to enable her to achieve? Only the presence behind her kept her from stamping her foot.

What it seemed to reduce itself to was that Angelica Hill's love could not be accepted but on a basis of truth. Natica had never before, that she could remember, found it uncomfortable to wear a mask, even with close friends. Were they not wearing them too? The one exception had been Aunt Ruth, but she had been like a confidante in a French classic tragedy whose function had been to know all. There was something about the proffered friendship of Stephen's mother that seemed to require an absolute candor to assure its validity. Yet surely Mrs. Hill herself wore a mask for her husband, perhaps even for her son. Was it that a greater loyalty was prescribed among women?

"What is it, my dear? Are you all right?"

Natica turned back to gaze for a moment at her interlocutor. She felt suddenly dizzy and sat down. "It's just that I'm going to have a baby. And I don't know for sure . . ." She broke off, appalled. Had she really been going to say anything so crazy?

"You're not sure, but you think you may be?" At this Mrs. Hill rose and stretched out her arms again. "Oh, my dear, I do hope so. It's just what you and Stephen most need. But we must take care of you." Natica was once more folded in the silken embrace. "I wonder if we hadn't all better sail straight home. There's always the chance they may be going to start another horrid war over here."

Natica did not trust herself for the rest of her visit to do more than nod and mumble monosyllables to her mother-in-law's many solicitations. But that was all that would be expected of her now. She was to relax and be made "entirely comfortable."

When Stephen came up and took her out to an early dinner at nearby Larue, she was still in a semi-daze. But as she drank her cocktail, her lips silently articulated a prayer that she might miscarry. Was she a monster? Was she the most unnatural of women? She visibly shrugged, even as he stared at her. What did it matter what she was? She was what she was. Or she would be what she showed herself.

He wanted to know how his mother had been.

"Oh, wonderful. Perfectly wonderful."

His smile was a touch sour. "She wins everyone over. I suppose you told her about the baby."

She stared. "What about the baby?"

"Why, that you're having one, of course. What else?"

"Oh." She pondered. "Yes, I told her that. She seemed very pleased."

"She didn't think it rather soon?" He grinned.

"Well, I said I wasn't entirely sure."

"Good. What else did you talk about?"

"About what you should do when we came home. She thought you ought to work with your cousin Tyler Bennett. That it would help you to learn about the family finances."

His countenance at once darkened. "And what did you say?"

"Why, I thought it was a fine idea. Why isn't it?"

"Because I detest my cousin Tyler and everything he stands for! And Mother knows that. But does she care? Of course not. Just another silly man's idea, that's what she thinks. The poor creatures have to be kept quiet and put to work in some harmless occupation where at least they can take care of the money that buys all the things the girls want!"

"The girls?" Natica mused. "Does that mean your mother and me?"

"Well, if Mother has anything to say about it, it will. She twists people around her little finger. I'm afraid she's got you tied up already."

Natica was intrigued by his obviously very real anger. "And is that really such a bad thing? Don't you want me to get on with your mother?"

"No! She's a castrator, that's what she is."

"But she can hardly castrate me, can she?"

"Don't make a joke out of it! She can turn you into what she is. And maybe it won't be so hard at that!"

She gazed curiously into his dark eyes. Never had she seen him so violent. "Dear me, I guess I know now what people mean about recognizing the moment when the honeymoon is over. We're really married now, aren't we?"

He blanched. "My God, what have I been saying, darling? Can you ever forgive me? And in your condition, too!"

She allowed him to apologize for the rest of the meal, and then she insisted on going immediately back to their hotel and going to bed. For she had suddenly begun to feel very ill indeed.

She woke up in the middle of the night with a high fever, and

Stephen, desperate, called the hotel's doctor. He diagnosed her condition as flu, but when in the morning she was worse Stephen insisted that she be admitted to the American Hospital. In the ambulance she lost consciousness.

✦ ✦ ✦

It was Mrs. Hill, sitting by her bedside, who informed her gravely and sadly, in a low sweet tone, that she had miscarried.

"But everything is all right, my poor dear child. You will be able to have another baby after a proper rest. Stephen wanted me to tell you. He simply couldn't himself. He's in the most terrible state, blaming himself for upsetting you."

Natica reached out a hand to take her mother-in-law's. Her first thought was that she was going to let Stephen feel guilty, at least for a while. There was no telling how many ways it might come in handy on their return to New York.

"It's all right," she murmured to Mrs. Hill. "Maybe it's really for the best. I couldn't seem to get over the notion there was something wrong with the poor baby."

And still holding Mrs. Hill's hand she lay back and closed her eyes. She wondered if she was not perfectly happy.

17 ...

Mrs. Hill was good to her word, and Stephen and Natica were able to buy a small stylish duplex apartment in upper Park Avenue with a marble-floored foyer and a winding stairwell and furnish it with colonial and federal pieces from rooms in Redwood which Angelica had chosen to do over in French styles. Stephen went docilely if a bit sullenly to work for his cousin Tyler Bennett, and Natica found herself pleasurably occupied in decorating her new home, buying new clothes, reading books and cultivating the many members of her new and, to her anyway, interesting family.

The coming of Armageddon to Europe and the period of its curious suspension known as the "phony war" blended with the initial unreality of her new life, making the transition easier for her, perhaps with its implication that nothing need be taken too seriously as nothing was likely to last. Her greatest gratification was in the unexpected welcome that she received from the Hill aunts and cousins. Her father-in-law and his two brothers, Erastus and Fred, both very much like him, were distinctly reserved, even a touch chilly, but she was quick to note that they were thus with others of the family. Their wives and children were distinctly friendly. Angelica had struck the opening note of cordiality, and it was obediently followed. Stephen's sisters were frequent callers, urging her to join them in bridge afternoons or discussion groups. Janine and Susan were certainly not stimulating companions, but Natica cared nothing for that at present. She reveled in her new sense of being included, and she was determined to let nothing interfere with whatever brief period it might continue to amuse her.

Stephen was her one disappointment. He was certainly discontented with his work, if what he did downtown could be called that, for he never discussed it and left the office early to play squash or drink with friends at the Racquet Club, but so long as he did not complain to her — and a lingering guilt about his possible role in her miscarriage kept him silent — she decided to put off facing the problem of his ultimate occupation. Here again, might not the war take care of it? Her doctor had told her that she was well enough to start another baby, but she had persuaded him to take the position with Stephen that it would be wiser to wait a year. She needed the time to reorient herself comfortably in her new world.

As in French society an erring wife was tolerated so long as her husband condoned her conduct, so in its American counterpart a past overlooked by a mother-in-law was overlooked by all. For the first couple of months after her establishment in New York Natica found herself constantly in Mrs. Hill's company. She lunched with her mother-in-law at the Colony Club; she sat beside her in her opera box; she accompanied her on calls to such great ladies as Mrs. Cornelius Vanderbilt and the Misses Wetmore. Everyone appeared to find Natica charming; her intelligence, her good manners, her modesty, were much praised. It was generally concluded that she must have had some good reason to leave her first husband.

Reconciling her own family to her new situation proved an even easier task. When her father was invited to use Uncle Fred Hill's fishing camp in the Adirondacks, he forgot the very existence of Tommy Barnes, as did her mother when Angelica Hill engaged the contracting firm in which both Natica's brothers worked to rebuild the decaying barn and stables of Redwood.

Even Edith DeVoe, now Mrs. Tyler Bennett, did not appear to begrudge her former tutor her elevation into her own circle. She took the arbitrary and often quixotic rules of the social structure entirely for granted: if Natica was accepted, she was quite content to accept her, just as she would presumably have turned her head the other way at the spectacle of her even undeserved downfall. Besides, she welcomed an ally in the Hill family, where she was not finding herself quite as happy as she had expected to be.

"They're more of a clan than anything I've ever known," she confided in her new cousin-in-law. "There must be something about a shared fortune that holds people together. In my family we only saw the uncles and aunts at Christmas or get-together weekends. Of course, some of them lost their shirts in the crash, and Mummie used to say they only came around for a handout. But Tyler's mother telephones her sisters-in-law every blessed morning in the week. What can they have to talk about that much? Maybe all that intimacy comes from the lowly origin of the Hills. Do you suppose so? After all, the grandfather started as a clerk in a general store in some hick upstate village. They must have had to lend each other a hand in the early days of the social climb. Maybe the habit stuck."

"I didn't think they cared that much about society," Natica objected. "The men, anyway. Aren't they too serious for that sort of thing?"

"They may be *now*. But they weren't always. Have you noticed they all married into old families? Mr. Bennett, Tyler's father, is a descendant of Peter Stuyvesant on the distaff side. At least he's always telling me so. And Stephen's mother was a Kip, and Uncle Erastus Hill married a Schermerhorn. It can't all be a coincidence."

"At least they didn't go in for European titles."

"But that was earlier. That had gone out of fashion. Besides, it never worked for the men. No, the Hills are smart. They always get their money's worth."

"I guess I'm the exception to that rule."

"Well, of course they didn't choose *you*. As a matter of fact, my dear, you had to be cleaned up a bit. It's quite wonderful to watch their organization once they get started."

Natica was intrigued. "How did they clean me up?"

"Don't you really know? Aunt Angelica laid down the party line.

Your first marriage had to be socially annulled. They spread the story that your impoverished parents had bludgeoned you into marrying the first halfway respectable male that came along, while you were hardly old enough to know your own mind. When he turned out to be a callow lout . . ."

"Oh, Edith, poor Tommy!"

"I think they even implied he was impotent. That it was really a *mariage blanc*. And so, when the beautiful Stephen came along . . . well, what could anyone expect?"

Natica reflected, with only mild shame, that there was an element of excitement in receiving the protection of so strong and united a tribe. But was it truly united? "I'd be surprised if my father-in-law had much to do with my rehabilitation."

"Oh, they leave the character assassination to the women. Who don't, I might add, need much help."

"But aren't you and I, as in-laws, the gainers from that kind of family loyalty?"

"I'm not quite in your boat, dearie," Edith retorted, but with more amusement than resentment. "I was a virgin bride, thanks to darling Mama's eagle eye and strong chaperonage. And I may not have been quite a Stuyvesant or Schermerhorn, but the DeVoes weren't nobodies by any means, and Tyler had done a couple of deals with Daddy at the bank . . . Oh, yes, I fitted into the general scheme. Don't think my ever-loving spouse would overlook the smallest item in my list of assets!"

"Now don't tell me Tyler's mercenary. And anyway, why should he be? I'm sure he adores you, Edith."

"Are you kidding? Tyler doesn't adore anything but making money. That's why they all admire him so. They think him a throwback to Grandpa Hill. And of course his lordship must have heirs to leave the bucks he makes to. That's where I come in. Do you know, he wants six kids? Can you beat it? Well, he's got one, the sacred son, and I can tell you he's going to do some waiting before Yours Truly goes through *that* again. I envy you Stephen. He seems to do everything you say."

"He coddles me because of the miscarriage. I don't suppose that will last forever."

"Well, gather ye rosebuds, as they say."

"I'm sure you handle Tyler more than you let on."

"If only I could! Nobody handles Tyler. To tell you the honest truth, I think I'm a wee bit scared of him."

Natica decided to reassess Edith's husband after this. Tyler Bennett was slight of build and oddly boyish looking for a man in his middle thirties of such reputed ability. His hair was crew cut; his face freckled, his small nose snubbed and his eyes were a staring pale blue. And if boyish looking, he had a boy's stubborn tenacity of purpose. At family gatherings, when he sat next to Natica, he gave the impression of faintly sneering at everything and everybody, including the sacred Hill uncles, whom he seemed to consider fortunate to have a Tyler Bennett to look after their major interests.

"Edith tells me you're a smart one," he informed her. "I'm certainly glad to hear it. This family, at least my generation of it, could do with some of that quality."

"I don't know that my record shows so much smartness. What have I got to my credit? I can hardly point to my first matrimonial venture with great pride."

"You got out of it, didn't you? And without landing on the buttered side. I'd call that pretty smart."

The bluntness of this apparent reference to her improved financial state took her aback. But she thought it better to offer him an out. "You mean that I substituted a happy marriage for an unhappy one?"

"That's it, exactly. You certainly didn't think I meant the money?" His chuckle was almost insulting. He allowed his pale stare to flicker over the great porcelain centerpiece on the Angus Hills' dining table in which Orion was being rescued from shipwreck by dolphins. "Though speaking of money, if you're as smart as they say, how would you like to join your husband in my office? We could find a place for you."

"As a secretary, you mean?"

"Don't be silly. Why would you want to be a secretary? We could train you as a portfolio manager."

She wondered if he were mocking her. "But I don't know the first thing about stocks and bonds!"

"Who does? Brains and no preconceptions is all I ask. You could learn."

"You use women in jobs like that?"

"I use some. I don't look below the waist if the bean's okay. Hetty Green made as big a fortune on the market as Jay Gould."

"You tempt me. I'd love to get my teeth into something serious after I'm a bit more settled. But why should you need more than one member of our branch of the Hills in your office?"

"I'll be frank with you, Natica. The one I have right now is not much good to me. What I need is a kind of principal assistant to help me with the Hills. Someone who is also a member of the family. You see, they may think I'm a whiz, and I am, too, but they're always leery about my taking risks. Every time I go into a new venture, I need a bunch of family consents. Even from the trust beneficiaries. You could be a great help here, once you knew the business. Janine and Susan, for example, might listen to you, whereas I tend to scare them off."

"I don't think Stephen would much take to the idea of my marching downtown with him in the morning."

"Hell, you could work at home. I'd send up up everything you need, including a steno. Don't let Stephen talk you out of something that's fun just because *he* can't do it."

She marveled at how much contempt he could put into one flat sentence. "Give Stephen time. He may learn to like the business."

He didn't deign to comment on this. "I tell you what. Think it over. There's no hurry. I'll send you a batch of reports on different things I'm thinking of going into, and you can read them at your leisure. What can I lose? And what can *you?* You've got nothing else to do."

She bridled. "That's not quite true. Edith has suggested I go on the Carnegie Hill Settlement Board with her, and Mrs. Hill has —"

"Don't give me those stupid ladies' boards," he interrupted rudely. "If you're worth anything at all, you're too good for them. One board meeting every quarter where the paid director flatters the old girls and gets his padded budget okayed." Here he raised his voice to a mocking falsetto in crude parody of a lady chairman. " 'Will someone move to adopt the budget? Second? All in favor? Contrary-minded? Any new business to come before the meeting? Then do I hear a motion to adjourn? Good. And now, girls, I hear there's the most divine new place to lunch near Park at Fiftieth.' "

Natica had to laugh. "Well, you can certainly send me those reports. I promise to read them, anyway."

"Do that. And let me give you a tip. Don't let Edith waste too much of your time. She's the laziest white woman east of Central Park."

"Woman! I thought you didn't look below the waist."

"Where brains are concerned, that is. With Edith there's no other place to look."

✦ ✦ ✦

Tyler did send her the reports, some dozen of them, by hand delivery directly to the apartment, and she spent several mornings reading them with care. She found that with the aid of a dictionary of commercial terms she could understand them readily enough, and she began to think that Stephen's cousin might not be wholly wrong in envisaging a role in his business for her. For the first time since she had worked for Rufus Lockwood she was using her brain, and she found an exhilaration in it that made an afternoon discussing "Should America remain neutral?" with her sisters'-in-law Current Events Club seem singularly fruitless. Perhaps she could develop a flair for the stock market. Had she not been almost a school administrator under Lockwood? But she thought it politic not to tell her husband of her new interest. It would be time enough if she decided to take the job.

One morning she determined to fulfill her honeymoon resolution of visiting the entrance hall of the Standard Oil Building, and she took the subway down to Bowling Green. She roamed pensively through the gray foyer, avoiding the people hustling to and from the elevators, and gazing up at the large carved names in the medallions, pausing as long as she comfortably could under the "Ezra Hill."

"And here I stand," she whispered to herself, "his granddaughter-in-law. I wonder what he would have thought of me."

She went from there to the Wall Street offices of Bennett & Son, which she had never seen, on the chance that she might find Stephen free to take her to lunch.

The Bennett space had consisted initially of a series of large paneled rooms in which the three sons and son-in-law of Ezra Hill could get away from their wives and daughters, cut their coupons and contemplate prudent charitable enterprises, but when son-in-law Bennett in more recent years, aided by his energetic son Tyler, had formed a corporation for investment purposes, he had kept leasing additional space until the original suite had been isolated like an ancient Romanesque chapel in a Gothic cathedral. Natica, conducted by a secretary to her husband's small office in the new part, noted as she passed, through open doors, two of his uncles secluded in dusky interiors reading newspapers at their desks. The Bennett area had more bustle; there was a large room with bare white walls cluttered with metal desks for telephoning men and a ticker tape machine in the middle. Her glancing eye recognized that Tyler wasted little of the family money in decoration. Other than a statue of a bull and bear fighting and a pompous portrait of Ezra Hill in the foyer there was hardly a picture in the place.

"I'm sorry, Mrs. Hill, Stephen must have gone out," the young woman informed her. "Perhaps he went for a cup of coffee."

"Then he can't be far. I'll wait for him in his office if I may."

"Farther than you think, Natica," came a strangely familiar voice, and she turned to find Grant DeVoe standing in the doorway of the adjoining office. "He'll have to go down to Sloppy Joe's on Water Street. My brother-in-law permits no such levities as a coffee wagon in these august precincts. It might for as much as five minutes distract the mind from the chase of the dollar."

The secretary, seeing her charge taken care of, departed.

"I'm so glad to see you, Grant!" And indeed she was. The pleasure of finding herself on equal terms with the children of her family's old landlord had not yet worn off. Grant had hardly changed at all. His somehow tentative stance, his restrained smile, his cautious friendliness, seemed of a piece with an attitude of not committing himself until assured of a favorable reception. "I had no idea you were working here. I thought you were representing your father's bank somewhere on Long Island."

"I was. But Daddy decided I'd better learn the market with Tyler. He thinks the world of his brilliant son-in-law."

"Everyone seems to."

"Exactly. So here I am."

"It's the same with Stephen. I was hoping he'd take me to lunch."

Grant looked at his watch. "I doubt he comes back in time. Sometimes he doesn't come back at all."

"You mean he has an appointment outside the office?"

"Or an appointment with the Marx Brothers. He's become quite a movie fan."

She looked at him suspiciously. Had he decided that she was an old friend with whom candor was safe? Or was his sarcasm the evidence of his resentment of her too sudden rise to fame and fortune? Or did he simply want to tell her that her husband, like himself, was only the reluctant tool of Tyler Bennett?

"You imply that Stephen's heart is not in his work?"

"Well, I don't believe he was cut out to be a money man. Why should he be? If I had a fraction of what he has, you wouldn't find me in this joint."

"I thought the DeVoes were very well off!"

"My old man may be. But he doesn't believe in sharing the wealth."

"What would you do then if he died and left you your share?"

He studied her as if to determine how serious she was. "Would you really like to know? I think I'd like to keep kennels. I've always been very fond of dogs."

And she suddenly remembered that he had been. The day he

had taken her sailing in Smithport there had been a chow with him, too big and restless to be taken on the small boat, which had been tied up at the dock while they were out and pathetically joyous in greeting Grant on their return. It now struck her that all of his snobbishness might have been a fear of people, a fear of committing himself beyond any of his immediate circle.

"Why don't you tell your father? He might just blow you to it."

"He? Never." He paused. "You don't think it's a silly thing to want to do?"

"Not at all. Why isn't a dog as good as a bull or a bear?"

He laughed. "So long as Stephen has pooped out, how about my taking you to lunch?"

"How nice. I'd love it."

But on the way out of the office Grant's plan was frustrated. They met Tyler in the corridor and stopped to greet him. Good manners required Grant to ask him to join them, as good manners should have required Tyler to decline. But that was not what happened.

"As a matter of fact, Grant, I'm expecting a call from your old man a little before one. It's about the Marston deal, which is really more your matter than mine. He wants someone to read him the tax covenant, which you'll find on top of the pile on my desk. Only a paragraph — Marcie will show it to you. And I'll take Natica to lunch. She won't mind, will she? It's all in the family."

Grant turned to Natica with a sour little smile. "As you see, I've been outranked. Another time, maybe."

When he had gone, Natica was left staring at her substituted host. "Well, I must say, that was pretty cool."

"Oh, come on, he won't die over it. I wanted to talk to you, anyway. We can go to my club. It's just across the street."

Amid green walls covered with Audubon prints Natica gazed from the window by their table over the panorama of the harbor. She had found it was idle to protest his treatment of Grant; Tyler simply wouldn't listen. He wanted to know if she had read his reports, and when he learned that she had, he delivered a short lecture on four textile mills in Massachusetts acquired by the Hills three decades before and now considered a poor investment which should be liquidated. He discoursed in his dry but lucid fashion on costs of production, declining sales and bitter labor agitation. She followed him with close attention.

"So what do you do?" she asked at last. "Dump the whole thing and swallow the loss? Grin and bear it? I suppose it's some comfort it's so small a part of the empire."

"But I hate to lose any part of it! My job is to make it grow."

"You're like a Roman Caesar. No matter how wide your domain you keep your ears tuned for the tiniest barbarian rumble on the remotest frontier."

"Well, look what happened when they stopped."

"It's true." She thought for a moment. "I suppose there is *an* alternative."

He leaned forward. "And what is that?"

"It was in those papers. You know it, of course."

"Tell me."

"It was in the report of the man who pointed out the advantages of moving that business south. Everything is cheaper there, particularly Negro labor, and there wouldn't be any union trouble, at least for a while. Most of the machinery could be transported and all the expert personnel. The expense could be made up in four years of a profitable operation."

Tyler nodded in approval. "And with a spreading war and the need for uniforms we could do it in two. But how would our gracious aunts and some of our bleeding-heart cousins take to the idea of an antilabor policy vigorously enforced? Which would be the only way to make it work."

She smiled. "You're testing me, aren't you? You want to find out how well I read all that stuff?"

"I don't deny it."

"Well, it's all there in the proposal. If you keep out labor organizers by paying your workers more than organized labor gets in a southern state, why should even liberal-minded shareholders object? And anyway, our 'gracious aunts' would never interfere in a labor question. They leave those things entirely to the men. And as for the bleeding-heart cousins, I can't think of any but Bill, Uncle Fred's son, who voted for Roosevelt because he's a fellow philatelist."

"What about Stephen?"

"Stephen isn't interested in politics."

"Look, Natica. Of course, I gave you those reports as a test. There were five proposals as to what to do with those mills, and you picked the only feasible one right off. Come on down and work with us here. I'll give you an office and a girl. You can have a salary if you like, but I don't take one myself. Who needs income, to give it to Uncle Sam? Capital gains are the thing, and those you will have, my friend. We're bound to get into this war, and the industrial boom that will follow is going to blow away the last traces of the depression the son-of-a-bitch New Dealers have been making such hay out of. How about it?"

"Stephen would hate it," she said pensively.

"Stephen is going to hate your doing anything better than he does, I'm afraid, Natica. I'm going to have to be brutally frank with you for your own good. Do you mind?"

"Go ahead. I can take it."

"Then here it is. You've married a born loser. I've known my cousin considerably longer than you have, and I've observed him. If you see things his way, you're going to lose along with him. Now you may say, what the hell, I'm rich, aren't I? I'll always have the good things of life. But that's where you're wrong. Everything Stephen has is in an iron-bound trust that will go to his children when he dies, and if he has none, back to the Hills, in equal shares, as the lawyers say, *per stirpes*. Not a bloody cent to the widow! That's how the Hills do things."

"But that's not true of my mother-in-law," Natica protested, appalled. "She has money of her own. I know, because she bought us our apartment. And she's always telling me how poor the Kips were."

"In Aunt Angelica's day they still made marriage settlements.

But if one was made for you, my dear, Tyler Bennett is ignorant of it, and Tyler Bennett is ignorant of precious few things that go on in this office."

"No, I'm sure none was made. They couldn't have done it without my knowing, could they?"

"And wouldn't, believe me. Of course, Uncle Angus, who owns what he has outright, could make any disposition of it he wants. But what will he want where you're concerned? I'm not telling any secrets out of court when I tell you how bitter he was about the whole Barnes divorce business. And he has pretty much the same opinion of his son, Stephen, that I have. He's never going to leave him anything out of trust. No, Natica, you'd be wrong to count on a fortune or even a decent maintenance, if you survive Stephen. The only way you'd ever see a penny of Uncle Angus's dough is through your children. So if you don't come to work with me and make your own fortune, you'd better start filling that nursery!"

"Well, that's certainly putting it straight on the line."

"Which is where I like to put things."

Natica put Tyler's offer — without, of course, his warning — to Stephen that very night. It went even worse than she had anticipated. She had waited until he had finished his first cocktail before outlining the proposal. She had considerably softened the edges of it, implying that most of her work could be done at home and that she would really be acting as a kind of supplement to himself. But Stephen's face had at once contracted into the white stare she had first seen in the restaurant the night of her miscarriage.

"So Tyler's taken you over, too."

"Too?"

"First Mother, then he. Between the two of them, they ought to be able to turn you into the Hill they've despaired of making me."

"Would you mind telling me what you're talking about?"

"Oh, they're smart, the pair of them. One's all rosily female and the other all dryly male. But they know just what they're about, and what a crushing team they are! They'd just about given me up. A dreamer, an idler, a half-man who babbled about books and pictures. And who finally went into teaching, the ultimate refuge of those who can't 'do.' And then, to top it all off, he gets himself involved in a stinking scandal and is fired from a school of which his own father is a trustee! It's the end, isn't it? But wait a moment. Hold your horses. Isn't it just possible that something can be salvaged from the bloody mess? Hills don't lightly give up anything. Witness those textile factories you were talking about. So let's have a look. Just who *is* this scarlet woman who seduced our weakling? Could there be anything to her? Well, for heaven's sake, if she doesn't have a brain! And some force of character, to boot. *Considerable* force of character, wouldn't you say? Maybe the Angus Hills have a man in their branch of the family after all."

Natica felt her throat beginning to constrict with an ominous wrath. "Keep it up, Prince Hamlet. It's a fine monologue."

"Is that all you can say? Well, riddle me this. When you start working for Tyler, is there any point my continuing to go to the office? Or shall I stay home and play bridge with Janine and Susan?"

"It's better than going to the movies."

He stared. "The movies?"

"Isn't that where you were today? Grant said you might be."

"You were down in the office?"

"Of course I was. That's where I had my talk with Tyler. I came down to see the lobby of the Standard Oil Building. To see the names of the original partners carved up there in all their glory. With Ezra Hill among them. I was so proud! And then I came over to see if his grandson, my beloved husband, could spare an hour to take me to lunch. And where was he? Off to the Marx Brothers. If it had been to read Karl, that might at least have been worthy of Ezra. The pioneer of one generation can be the rebel of the next. But to chuckle at Groucho!"

Stephen had covered his face. Behind his hands he seemed to be stifling a sob. "Oh, Natica, don't! I didn't know you could be so cruel. Poor Tommy!"

She gasped. "You call *me* cruel! Why, I never . . ." And then she knew she had to stop. Her world was teetering. She had the will and the fury to say irreparable things. She might even have the power to destroy him. She clenched her fists and took several deep breaths. "Look, Stephen. Let's quit this. I'm not going to work for Tyler. We're going on the way we've been going."

"Go ahead," he moaned. "Go ahead and work for him. You might just as well, now."

"Never. The discussion is over."

And she meant it. She refused to say another word on the subject. They ate their dinner in silence, and afterwards, as he sat moodily on the sofa drinking scotch after scotch, she pretended to read a novel as she contemplated their future.

✓ ✓ ✓

The next day at noon she lunched with Aunt Ruth in a corner of the Clinton school cafeteria, as far away as they could get from the chattering girls.

"I thought you should hear the last scene in the melodrama to which I have so long treated you," she concluded to her soberly listening relative. "But it's not just for your entertainment, if indeed, poor Auntie, you find any in it. I've got to have another point of view. I can't afford another mess in my life. At least not yet. I'm only twenty-four. Almost the age when Keats died, already 'among the English poets.'"

"Let's leave Keats out of this. Has this really changed your feelings about Stephen?"

"I don't know. I have an awful sense that those feelings may be somewhere between anger and contempt. How *dare* he be so unhappy with all he's got?"

Aunt Ruth's smile was a bit grim. "Meaning yourself, dear?"

"No! I mean his money, damn it all, his social position, his serried family, his good looks, his *opportunities*. Think of those things, Aunt Ruth. And he has the nerve to mope!"

"God sends manna to those who have no teeth. Maybe it's his way of hinting what those things are really worth."

"Oh, of course I know there's no point in berating him for not having my tastes. The real point is that somehow I've got to pull him through. It's not just a question of moral obligation, though I suppose that may exist."

"I'm glad you admit that."

"Now don't get stuffy with me, please, Auntie. It's too serious for that. My only use for morality is if it makes for the good life. And it certainly isn't the good life to be always making people unhappy. I've failed with one husband, and it's far too soon to fail with another. What am I going to *do* about Stephen?"

"How long do you suppose it will be before he can get the kind of school job he had at Averhill?"

"Who knows? And there's even a question in my mind whether he really wants to teach anywhere *but* Averhill. He seems to have a fixation about the place. It was there he found God and there he lost him. He may imagine it's the only place he can find him again. An Eden he's been kicked out of."

Aunt Ruth reflected. "I suppose the war might take care of the problem. If we get into it, that is."

"Yes, a nice short war where he could be very brave and not be killed might be just the thing. It could make him feel manly and superior to Tyler Bennett, who would be sure to wiggle out of military service. But wars aren't made to order, are they? And even if they were, one wouldn't dare order one, for he just might be killed."

"Which would never do?"

"Oh, Auntie, you really *do* think I'm a fiend. But of course it would never do. I suppose we could travel. South America is still available. But I don't want to strike the note of the honeymoon again."

"How about a farm?"

"Can you see me on one?"

"I think, my dear, I can see you any place you put your mind on. But I have a better idea. Why don't you buy a bookstore? You could run it together."

Natica's first reaction was that it was surprising she hadn't thought of this herself. "Really, Auntie, you're like the Lady from Philadelphia in *The Peterkin Papers*. What can you do when you've put salt instead of sugar in your coffee? Pour another cup of coffee! A bookstore might be just the thing. You don't happen to know of one for sale, do you?"

"As a matter of fact, that's why I thought of it. Lily Warner and her sister want to sell their shop on Madison Avenue and Sixtieth. They're getting on and it's a bit too much for them. And they have a wonderful clientele. I think they dictate what half the social register reads."

"I know that store. It's one of those places that makes you want to read. And they welcome browsers. I wonder what they're asking for it."

"Does it matter?"

"Oh, yes. Stephen, like all people who never think of money, spends all his income and more, and he can't touch the principal unless the bank consents, and it rarely does." And then she suddenly recalled what Tyler had said about the wives of the earlier generation receiving settlements. "But there's always Mrs. Hill, God bless her!"

She went straight from lunch to the pink palazzo and had the luck to find her mother-in-law in. When she came home that evening she not only had Angelica's promise; she had obtained a month's option to buy from the Warner sisters.

Stephen looked at her with astonishment.

"But I thought you wanted to work with stocks and bonds!"

"What I really want is to do something with you."

At this he actually hugged her, something he hadn't done in weeks. "I can't fight you both, darling. You *and* Mother. The bookstore it is!"

18 ....

NATICA LOVED the store from the beginning. Stephen's attitude was less enthusiastic, but he had no objection to her taking the lead in all the arrangements.

"The great thing about your mother's gift," she told him, "is that it will allow us to operate in the red until we've established the character of our shop. Once that's done I have no doubt we can attract a steady clientele. And in the meantime we are spared the agony of Christmas and birthday cards, and those overpriced little papier-mâché boxes, and prints of birds and flowers, and, above all, children's books. We'll provide a small, hospitable center for serious readers."

"What about best sellers?"

"We'll have *all* the best sellers. Only we won't put them in the window with a sign screaming they're that. Popular books will take their chance with the others."

"And detective stories?"

"But they appeal to the most serious readers of all! As a matter of fact I intend to make myself an expert in crime fiction."

And she did. In a few months' time Natica became known among browsers of the upper East Side as the attractive and intellectual young member of a famous clan who could discuss the latest book on the Axis powers and the newest whodunit, and who never showed impatience with a non-purchaser. She had always been a rapid reader, and with the added material of reviews and releases she found it easy enough to keep ahead of the neighborhood ladies who, as she put it to Stephen, "matronized" their tastefully redecorated little store.

Angelica Hill and her daughters were constant customers, and their friends and relations soon followed. Tyler Bennett's mother, Aunt Sally, as round and dimpled and friendly and breathless as her Hill brothers were lean and grim and dry — proof enough, as Natica took it, of the blander effect of inherited wealth on their sex — was a passionate lover of mysteries and came in almost daily.

"Tyler told me you had a head for business, my dear, which I suppose is why you do this so well. Of course, he doesn't consider a bookstore business, and he thinks you're throwing yourself away. Isn't that just like Tyler? But I tell him that his glorious 'downtown' isn't the only place in the universe, and that when he's made all the money in the world, what does he think he's going to do? He doesn't go in for cards or sports like his cousins, so he'll probably end up on a porch rocker reading thrillers like his poor old ma!"

Stephen soon began to feel and, much worse, to show impatience with the less intelligent and more demanding lady customers, and Natica tactfully suggested that he spend more of his time in the little back office, invisible to the public, taking care of ordering new titles. She kept him from interfering with their hard-working and efficient lady bookkeeper, who shared this space, by persuading him that such toil was beneath him and tried to salvage his pride by sending some of the more intellectual customers back to "consult" with him.

They had no need of additional help as yet, but one morning before Stephen had arrived (he rarely appeared before eleven) a young man of no more than nineteen came in to apply for a job as salesman. He immediately interested her. He was short, with thick black hair and bunched-up features rendered almost unnoticeable by cold gray penetrating eyes which stared at her with an impertinence sufficiently surprising in one seeking a position.

"You won't remember me, but I was a prefect last year in your husband's dorm in Averhill."

She glanced at his scanty résumé and then recalled the name: Giles Woodward. "I have certainly heard Stephen speak of you. But shouldn't you be in college?"

"I've been suspended for a year." The stare now seemed to put *her* on the defensive. "It was supposed to be for a drunken prank, but that was the front for a trumped-up morals charge they couldn't prove. They think I won't come back, but they have another think coming."

He waited with an air of near defiance for her to ask what the charge was. She decided that it would be more interesting not to. "And you want a job in the meantime?"

"Well, my old man won't give me a dime."

"I see." It was still early; there were no customers in the shop. She asked him some questions about current books and found him succinct, sharp and astonishingly well informed in his answers. What could she lose?

"Can I talk to my husband and get back to you?"

"Tell him I'd like to work for him. He was one of the decent guys at Averhill. There weren't many."

Stephen was concerned when she related the matter. "A morals charge! That's apt to mean buggery. Some form of inversion, anyway. Poor Giles. How like him to tell you more than he had to."

"Shall I take him on?"

"Why not? I'd like to help him. But imagine my not having heard about his suspension. It shows how careful people are not to discuss Averhill topics when I'm around."

"Did he have that kind of trouble at school?"

"At school it wasn't considered trouble. By the students, anyhow."

"I see. Boys will be boys. Well, it certainly won't be noticed in the book business."

Giles was just as good as she had hoped. He was the first to arrive in the morning and opened the store. He arranged the new books and even decorated the shop window. He rapidly learned the names and tastes of the principal customers, and knew which had charge accounts, so that prices and addresses did not need to be mentioned. A lady walking out of the store with two books under her arm almost felt as if she had been given a present, and complimented on her literary acumen to boot. He was scrupulously polite to Natica, whose orders he executed promptly, but she continued to feel a guarded impertinence in his manner, as if he knew a good deal more about her than he chose to tell. And of course it was impossible that he did not know every detail of her career at Averhill. But did she care? He gave her a curious sense of being an ally.

He was different with Stephen, whom he evidently admired. She supposed that if Stephen's theory of the reason for Giles's college suspension was true, the youth might well have a crush on her handsome husband, even one that had started at school. She had no objection to this, which should simply add to the efficiency of her new employee, but she didn't like Giles's constant volunteering to take jobs off Stephen's hands, which had the result of the latter's taking off more time from the shop to spend in the bar or squash courts of the Racquet Club. However, she could only take care of so many things at once. Her present job was to get the store on its feet.

One afternoon, when she and Stephen were in the back office opening book packages, Giles burst in to announce the approach of a presumably unwelcome visitor.

"It's old lady Knight! She's flying over Madison Avenue and preparing to land here."

"Flying?"

"Well, she's on a broomstick."

Natica found a moment to wonder if he even knew everything about her and Estelle. "What do you suppose she's doing in New York?"

"Maybe she's founding another poetry class. Isn't that what she did at school? Shall we pray for a recklessly speeding bus?"

"Don't be ridiculous, Giles. Stephen, shall we ask her to lunch?"

"In God's name, no! Don't even tell her I'm here."

Natica went towards the door to greet her former friend. The poetess looked even older and more raddled under a large shiny black straw hat. She stretched both hands out to Natica and crooned:

"My my, *my!*"

"My, my, what, Estelle?" Natica rather coolly took one of the offered extremities.

"My, my, *my,* aren't you the clever one?"

"Clever?"

"To have achieved not only a beautiful husband with a thumping bank account, but to have set up the most popular bookstore in town!"

Natica did not mind Stephen overhearing this — it served him right for cowering in the office — but she didn't like the presence of the grinning Giles, whom Estelle of course did not recognize, having had no contact with students. She pointed to a browsing customer, and Giles left. "What happy chance brings you to town, Estelle?"

"Well, you know I have to have my breathing spells, and Wilbur made me sell my Boston flat."

"*Made* you? Wilbur?"

"Oh, he was very stern. Not at all like his usual self. He said that he would never set foot in it again. I decided I'd better humor him. And anyway, I like coming to New York. But he went on like a madman at the idea of my taking another apartment, so I'm staying at the St. Regis. I suppose he doesn't trust me with flats. Dear me, maybe I should be mum about all that." Here she glanced conspiratorially about the little shop.

"I don't see any reason that you and I should not discuss apartments, Estelle."

"Well, you *are* a cool one. Perhaps I'd better buy a book. What do you recommend?"

"You don't have to buy a book. Tell me the news. How are all our friends at Averhill?"

"Friends? I don't know that I number many such in that benighted institution. Do *you?*"

"Well, there's one I may no longer be able to call a friend, but whose welfare I shall always care about. And that, of course, is Tommy Barnes. How is he?"

"You never hear from him?"

"Never. And that's only natural. I don't expect him to write. But have you seen him?"

"I haven't. Wilbur has. Indeed, Wilbur and he have become rather thick. My righteous spouse may be trying to make up for that Boston business. Whoops! There I go again. Mum's the word. Anyway, Barnes is leaving at the end of this school year."

"Oh. Lockwood was ruthless about that?"

"My dear, what did you expect?"

"A miracle. And their day is over. Do you happen to know what Tommy is planning to do next?"

"I think Wilbur said something about his getting a parish in the South. The Deep South, I believe. In a Negro neighborhood."

"Oh, Estelle!"

"Well, they have souls, too, I suppose."

Natica was hardly aware of what either of them said after this. When Estelle took her leave at last, she hurried to the back office where she found Stephen pale and tense.

"I must go up and see Tommy," he announced grimly.

"Oh, my dear, what can you possibly accomplish?"

"That's just what I'm going to have to find out."

19 ···

THE BIG three chambers of the *piano nobile* of the pink palazzo had been cleared for Angelica's spring ball, an annual event for her and her children's friends. The library with its tall tiers of ancient volumes, never read but reputedly valuable, a bibliophile's collection purchased to fit the room, was used for the buffet, the dining hall, with its stately blue and green marble walls and its vast hunting scene tapestry, being more suited to dancing. In the conservatory, by the central fountain of a bathing dryad, under a Tiepolo ceiling, Angelica and her elder daughter received the guests.

Natica sat on the stairway, halfway up, with Edith Bennett, drinking champagne and looking down on the passing show.

"Do you remember the first time I came to your family's house in Smithport? I made the most awful scene."

"But we were awful to you, Natica! You had on some ghastly dress you'd hooked out of your mother's closet. And none of us would even talk to you. Aren't children horrors?"

"They show what we've learned to conceal. But I had it coming to me. I was pushing myself in where I wasn't wanted." She took in Edith's sidelong glance. "And you're thinking I'm still doing it, aren't you?"

Her friend was hardly bothered by the imputation. "But you've arrived, my dear. You're a *succès fou*. Far more than I am, anyway."

"I don't know that I'm so *fou* with Stephen. He hasn't really found his niche."

"Well, maybe that's just as well with a man. Tyler's found his, God knows, and he's the most awful bore about it. His mother's always after me to get him to relax and take an interest in something besides business. She can't get it into her fat head that he's utterly immune to female influence."

"Are you happy, Edith?"

"What a question! I haven't really thought about it. But yes, I suppose I am. Tyler and I are hardly Romeo and Juliet, but I have a lot of things I want."

"Would you ever think of having an affair?"

"Really, Natica, what a funny mood you're in tonight."

"I suddenly feel I can be absolutely frank with you. Maybe it's because you saw me way back. You saw how much I wanted all this." Her gaze took in the floor below.

"And does it make you happy, now you have it?"

"Isn't it odd? Yes, it does."

"I thought those shiny things in the store window always looked a bit shabby when you got them home."

"Oh, they do. But what's happened is that I don't mind their shabbiness. I know, for example, that the Tiepolo above us is a copy, and a bad one at that, but it's successfully decorative. I know the family couldn't read half the books in the library, even if they wanted to. They're in Italian or Latin. And I know that my father-in-law would be just as happy living in some Victorian horror. He wouldn't notice the difference. And I know he dislikes me."

"Oh, Natica!"

"Oh, he despises me, of course. I don't mind. Just so long as he doesn't say so. And I think Stephen's mother is the most beautiful and romantic figure in the world, even when I know she's an amiable, self-indulgent egotist who is beginning to put on too much weight. And his sisters are dears but such sillies."

"Have you a kind word for anyone tonight?"

"But for all of them, of course! Don't you see that I *am* kind? The fact that my eye isn't clouded doesn't make any difference to my heart. I love them all! Even Mr. Hill. It's because, for the first time in my life, I feel I *belong*. You can't imagine what that's like, Edith. You have to have spent your life on the outside looking in."

She had been talking to amuse herself, but she suddenly realized it was true. The feeling that bubbled up so richly inside her, filling her, drowning her, exhilarating her, had to be happiness! She had an impulse to tell Edith about a reissued novel of Trollope she had been reading in the store that morning, but Edith never read anything. Trollope had understood as no other novelist the ecstasy of belonging. No doubt it was why so many intellectuals despised him.

"So now you have everything." Edith looked bemused. "You wouldn't even need an affair."

Natica understood that she wanted to return to that theme. "No! What could an affair with the sexiest man in the world add to the joy I now feel?"

"I should think a good deal. I suppose I'm in a period of suspension. Between the early years of marriage and the time when a girl might like something . . . well, something more exciting."

"And that time might come for you?"

"Mightn't it for anyone? Except for happy you, of course. And even happy you had a thing with Stephen before you married him. Don't try to kid me."

"I shouldn't dream of it. Of course we had an affair. But Tyler might be more tolerant than my 'ex' was. You and he might have some kind of civilized arrangement. The way we're always hearing the French do."

"Not he. He'd lay low until he had the goods on me and then divorce me without a settlement."

"Would you, Tyler?"

He was coming up the stairs towards them.

"Would I what?"

"Edith and I were discussing how husbands behave to wives who take a little fling. I said you'd be civilized about it."

He scowled at Edith. "That depends on how you define 'civilized.'"

"Well, if it means who makes the most money out of it, we'd know how you'd behave," his wife retorted.

"I came to ask my loving spouse to dance, but that changes my mind. Will you dance, Natica?"

On the floor she tried to follow his shuffling lead.

"Where's Stephen?"

"He had to go to Boston. He'll be here later."

"Business?"

"Not what *you'd* call business."

"If *you* call it that, I will. I hear your shop's going great guns. It was smart of you to remember what I said about Aunt Angelica's marriage settlement. You'd never have got the money out of Uncle Angus."

"Oh, I knew *that*."

"He didn't like your going around him, though. Watch your step with him, Natica."

"What can he do to me?"

"There's no telling. My Hill uncles are all three alike. They can never get over the fact that it was their father and not they who made the money. They dole it out to their handsome wives and feckless offspring, but under a strict condition: that Daddy, however small and bald and silent, is always boss. That condition has not been met by a certain daughter-in-law."

"Even if my store is a success?"

"I'm not sure that doesn't make it worse. They're not like me, you know."

"No, with you success is the total answer."

"It's my credo. I've never denied it."

And then she saw Stephen. He was standing by himself in a corner of the conservatory, properly dressed in a tuxedo, watching her. Or rather staring at her. As they danced towards him, she saw that it was a baleful stare. He did not wave or even smile.

She excused herself to Tyler and went over to him.

"Is something wrong?"

"I must talk to you. Shall we go home?"

"What will we tell your mother? Can't we do it here?"

He glanced about the room and shrugged. "I don't care, if we can find a place."

He followed her up to the third floor where they found the family living room vacant. She took a chair by the unlit fire before which, after closing the door, he took a rather ominous stand.

"How did you find Tommy?"

"Unexpected." His tone was grating. "He said he had planned to stand me up, but that curiosity had got the better of him in the end."

"To learn what you proposed to do for him?"

"To learn how much I'd pay to clear my conscience."

She had never seen his eyes so hard. Whatever he had discovered, things were not going to be the same between them again. Very well, then, things would not be the same. She was beginning to be irritated. "What *did* you offer him?"

"I offered him the chance to start his own school."

"And how, pray, were you going to do that? When you couldn't even afford to start one of your own?"

"I was going to beg, borrow or steal the money! I was going to tell my mother if she didn't give it to me, I'd put a bullet through my head!"

"Don't be melodramatic, dear."

"I've never been more serious! I was even willing to sell your sacred store, which you'd have taken much worse. But you needn't worry. Your first husband made it very clear that he would never take a penny from your second. Not if he was starving!"

"I told you he had his pride."

"But there's something else you *didn't* tell me."

It was curious, now that the dreaded crisis was at hand, that she was conscious only of a cold detachment. She simply waited for him to continue.

"I felt I couldn't leave him without giving him some excuse for my conduct towards him. I told him I'd felt obligated to save my child from being aborted."

"I don't suppose that was an argument that carried much weight with a *mari trompé*."

"Don't use French phrases to me, Natica. He threw in my face that it was *his* child!"

"And what gave him that notion?"

"That you'd been sleeping with him all the time that you and I were lovers!"

"It's a lie!"

"He's a minister. A man of God. And I believe him."

She had not expected this argument. She changed her tactic. "Anyway, it was only once. He was horribly jealous of you, and it was the only way to keep him quiet."

"Only once! You expect me to believe that? When you swore he had never touched you after we first came together? Oh, Natica, the truth isn't in you. You *knew* I'd have agreed to an abortion if there was any doubt whose child it was. How could an honest woman not have told me?"

At this she got up and approached him, her fists clenched. She was even angrier than he. "How did I know you'd pay for an abortion if you thought it was Tommy's child? I had no experience with this sort of thing. All I knew was that two men had taken their pleasure with me and that one of them was damn well going to have to pay!"

"And which one did? The one with the money, of course. Oh, you were willing enough to have the abortion. You couldn't wait to get rid of that offending foetus. But when I, sentimental idiot, wanted to save the infant I was naïve enough to believe my own, you saw a rich husband falling right into your lap. Poor Tommy! He was cast off like an old shoe and I was picked up like a new one. Well, I know where I stand from here on."

"You're a fool, Stephen. I'm the best thing that ever came into your life, if you could only see it. And I still could be, if you'd let me. But no, you'd rather stuff your head into the big downy pillow of your own self-pity. Go ahead and enjoy it. But don't expect anything from me until you're ready to offer me a full apology for the outrageous things you've said tonight."

"An apology? You have your nerve. It'll be a month of Sundays before you get anything like that. I'm going home now."

"And I'm staying at the party!"

"I'll be sleeping in the spare bedroom."

She left him without another word and went downstairs where she found her mother-in-law at the buffet.

"How is Stephen? I thought he looked tired."

"He is. He's going home."

"Actually, my dear, I think he often looks tired these days. Has he been working too hard at the store?"

"I think that's it. He's been working too hard at the store."

"Maybe he should take a vacation and go hunting or fishing."

"I think I'll suggest that."

"And you'd go with him, of course."

"I'm afraid I can't leave the store just now. But it won't matter. I think he needs a rest from a lot of things. Perhaps me included."

20 · · ·

STEPHEN LEFT home in the morning without speaking to her. He made no appearance at the store. That evening, when she was having a solitary cocktail, he walked into the apartment and took a seat across the living room from her.

"I'm not coming to work anymore. You can run the shop any way you like. I'll turn the accounts over to you. And I'm moving to the Yale Club."

"You're leaving me, then."

"I don't know what I'm doing. I've got to think things over. I've got to think my whole life over. I just don't know about you and me. We'll have to wait and see."

"Of course you realize that I consider myself completely guiltless in all this."

"All I realize is that I don't know you anymore. And I wonder if I ever did."

His bland, steady stare seemed to put an unbridgeable distance between them. She began to wonder if her own knowledge of him might not be equally limited.

"I hope you won't tell your mother of your doubts about the paternity of the child we didn't have."

"Why? Because you're afraid she might not agree about your guiltlessness?"

"Yes." Her tone was defiant. "She belongs to a stricter generation. Leave me her friendship, Stephen. Don't take everything from me."

"I'm taking nothing from you. And I certainly shan't take that. If I had doubts about that poor little baby it's nobody's business but my wretched own."

When she got up the next morning he had already left, but a note informed her that he had changed his mind about the club and would be staying in the gardener's cottage at Redwood which Angelica had refurbished for their weekends.

Her life in the next two weeks followed the same routine. She spent long days at the store and usually dined with her parents-in-law, who assumed that Stephen was taking the vacation that had been discussed and found it entirely natural that he should go back to his beloved Hudson for fishing and shooting. They weekended at Redwood irregularly and did not happen to go there at this time. But Janine, who also had a cottage on the place, reported privately to Natica that she had gone over to call on her brother and found him very sour and aloof. She had not stayed more than half an hour.

"What's eating him?"

"Oh, it's just a mood, I guess. He'll snap out of it."

"No, Nat, this is different. It's more like one of the depressions he used to have as a boy. If I were you, I'd go up there."

"But I have a business to run!"

"Even so. I'd go. I don't like the look of it."

And then Giles Woodward quit without notice. He simply walked into the back office one morning and told her he was going on a trip. When she protested that he should stay at least until she found a replacement, he curtly refused. At last she lost her temper.

"You might remember that I took you on without a reference and without asking embarrassing questions."

"Oh, you knew what you were doing," he retorted with a brazen laugh. "You were getting a first class man for a serf's wages. I've watched you operate from Averhill days. Don't think you can play the high and mighty with old Giles!"

She gaped at his insolence. "Good day, Mr. Woodward!"

Stephen's other sister, Susan, still unmarried and with little to occupy herself, volunteered to take Giles's place at the store, and though enthusiastic, she was not a great help, sometimes forgetting what books her friends had purchased. But she was cheerful, and Natica was in a mood to appreciate that quality. One morning, a week after Giles's departure, Susan came in, breathless and late as usual, but bearing a message from her mother.

"Mummie's coming to the store at eleven," she announced in the tone of conveying important news that Angelica's daughters were apt to use in her respect. "She said to tell you she had to consult you."

Natica had her eye on the door when Angelica appeared. That her mother-in-law was prompt could only mean that the matter was serious.

"Can we go to your office, my dear?"

The bookkeeper fled as the lady she knew had bought the shop came in with the proprietor. Angelica, seated, leaned across Natica's desk, her lovely features clouded with concern.

"You know that Stephen is still at Redwood?"

"I assumed so. He hasn't written or telephoned."

"And do you know why? Do you know who is with him?"

"Oh." So that was it. She noted the way Angelica's black, skull-fitting hat came down in a triangle over the top of her high brow as if to point to the beauty below. "Is it Giles Woodward?"

"So you *did* know. Then you can hardly be aware of what sort of creature he is."

There was a hint of spark in Angelica's serene blue gaze.

"Well, I believe he was in some sort of trouble in college."

"He's a pervert, Natica! Angus spoke to his dean. He was considered the leader of a small gang of decadents. Have you had any reason to suspect that Stephen was ever inclined that way? No? Then that horrid creature is up there preying on his melancholy. For Janine tells me he *is* melancholy. His father and I hadn't known, of course. The whole thing must be stopped at once!"

Natica was silent. She even found herself wondering why she should care so little. The same thought struck Angelica.

"My dear, don't you *mind?*"

"You may find it odd, but somehow it doesn't seem really to concern me. Men do such funny things. I wonder if they don't basically prefer each other. All those sports and clubs and fishing."

"Well, you're very tolerant, I *must* say. I don't feel that way about it the least tiny bit!"

"If Stephen leaves me, should I much care who he leaves me for?"

"Oh, my child, do you really think he's left you?"

"Hasn't he? And isn't it my fault if he has? Why should I throw the blame on the wretched Giles?"

She suddenly wanted to tell Angelica about the aborted abortion. It was the same impulse that had come over her on their first meeting at the Crillon in Paris. She repressed it, but only with a sigh of something like despair. For the truth would always stand between her and this wonderful woman, whether or not it was known. She did not, after all, "belong" to Angelica's world or to Angelica's family, and the brief moment of euphoria she had experienced at the spring ball while talking to Edith had been only the airiest of bubbles. Angelica continued now:

"Angus and I are going up to Redwood as soon as he returns from Chicago where he and Tyler are inspecting some plant. I wanted to go myself now, but he was very emphatic on the telephone that it was not the kind of thing a woman should undertake alone and that I must certainly wait for him. Will you come with us?"

"Do you really think that would be wise?"

Angelica hesitated. Perhaps she was considering that it might indeed be better if one of such pernicious broad-mindedness should be absent from the disciplinary scene.

"Perhaps you're right. Perhaps you'd better leave it to us. But you can count on our sending your erring husband straight back to you!"

Their meeting was on Thursday. On Friday morning the impudent Giles himself loomed over her desk. He did not even greet her.

"I'm just back from Redwood. You'd better go up there, Natica."

The name startled her. He had always addressed her formally. "Is Stephen ill?"

"He's in the worst sort of depression. A really black one. Those can be dangerous, you know. And his parents are coming up to the big house this weekend. He kicked me out. He can't face them with me there. I'm not sure he can face them without me."

"I take it, then, their suspicions are justified?"

"*They* would think so, anyway. They'd hardly make distinctions in these things. I was trying to console Stephen. To cheer him up. What we did didn't amount to much. I'm not sure he isn't even basically a womanizer. With him it was more like a return to boyhood, a kind of desperate nostalgia, if you like."

"I don't like it at all, thank you very much. How was it with *you?*"

"Well, I was always hot for him at school. He was my hero. I couldn't believe I'd ever have him. And then suddenly there he was, alone and miserable. Anyone could have had him. But he's not really my type. I guess nostalgia may have played a role for me, too."

"I wonder you have the gall to stand there and talk this way to his wife."

"Don't give me that shit, Natica. We both know why you married him. At least I wanted him."

She suppressed a retort. What was the use? Would such a man understand that a woman's motives could be mixed? But at least he respected her intelligence.

"There are things I could say to that. But let's stick to Stephen. I take it you think there's danger of suicide."

"There's always that danger with these things."

"Then, if I'm such a mercenary bitch, why should I care?"

"Because he's worth more to you alive than dead. I read that piece in *Fortune* about the Hill trusts."

She could not restrain a gasp. "I take a lot from you, Woodward."

"Oh, you're a tough girl, all right. Don't think I don't admire it!"

"I'll take your advice, anyway. I'll drive up tomorrow."

✐ ✐ ✐

The first thing that was wrong was the police car at the gate. But the officer made no move to stop her and she drove over the blue gravel down the long winding road through the trees to the white columnar front of the big house which she had to pass to arrive at the cottage. But she did not pass it. She had the shock of seeing some twenty or thirty persons gathered on the lawn of the turn-around. Her heart beat heavily as she pulled up under the porte-cochère to find her parents-in-law standing by the door.

Angus Hill turned away, but his wife went up to the car as Natica got out.

"You've heard already?"

"Oh, my God, what?"

"Stephen hasn't been in his cottage since yesterday at noon. One of the gardeners saw him go out then with his gun, and the maid who cleans there says his bed has not been slept in or the kitchen used."

Natica noticed the trembling of Angelica's upper lip.

"Where do you suppose he's gone?"

"He may have had an accident. We've called in the neighborhood. We're going to search the woods. You had better stay in the house, my dear. There's coffee in the dining room."

"No, no, I'll go with you, of course."

The search, interrupted by her arrival, now started. The women spread out along the bank of the river, leaving the woods, where it was considered more likely that Stephen would have roamed with his gun, to the men. There were little tufts of bushes into which they poked vaguely with sticks. Some wandered to the edge of the water and peered apprehensively down. As they became scattered and diminished to Natica's vision, they seemed listless and pale, like figures in a classical landscape by Puvis de Chavannes. Her sense of unreality became giddying.

She tried to bring the river and the willow trees and the great white house into focus by concentrating on the image of Stephen lying dead, face down on the ground. And then, as it became clear to her mind, she stopped in her tracks and closed her eyes. Dear God, did she *want* it that way? Did she want it to be over at any cost? Was she as much of a horror as Giles supposed?

No, she reassured herself as she beheld the landscape again, she was like others, only she had the capacity of separating her myth, the myth by which man lives and has his civilized being, from the fact, which is always there. If Stephen were dead, his family would assume he had taken his life over shame at what he had done with Giles. Oh, yes, they would find that a quite sufficient motive! And would they not be sympathetic over his double abandonment of her and make her a settlement?

Natica! she whispered hoarsely. Surely one had better hang on to *some* myths.

To get away from her thoughts she turned to look for Angelica, who was nowhere in sight. She went back towards the house and saw her at last entering the box garden with the topiary. She knew it contained a circle of tall hedge with a hollow in the center. Hurrying after her, she saw her suddenly push through the hedge, and she anticipated the scream that would follow so vividly that when it came it seemed to come from her own throat.

Ruth's Memoir . . .

At Stephen's service at Saint James' on Madison Avenue I sat with my sister, Kitty, and Harry in the fourth pew, the first three being reserved for Hills. The church was almost full; the large family connection explained that. The organ played the Chopin funeral march, repeating the sad little melody of the second movement almost unbearably. I tried not to stare when the immediate survivors filed in from a side door just before the service began. There is always something of the cast taking their places on the stage in this, and curiosity as to how they manifest their sorrow is only natural. Angus Hill looked exactly as always, impenetrably correct, and his daughters, their heads bowed in obvious self-consciousness, walked in rather too fast. Angelica's loveliness was concealed by a veil; she clung tightly to the arm of her son-in-law, who looked stout and reddish in the pride of his support. Last came Natica, in black, of course, but with her face unveiled. Calmly, perhaps even a bit defiantly, she surveyed the seated congregation.

"Why must she look so *hard?*" Kitty hissed to me with something like anguish. "Why couldn't she have worn a veil?"

I could think of nothing to say in answer but a silly old adage of our grandmother Felton. But it had a nice touch of Old New

York. "Do you remember what Granny used to tell us?" I whispered back to her. "That the two things people never approved of was the way you spent your money and buried your dead?"

I was grateful for the impersonality of the Episcopalian service and the beautiful words of the King James Version. A statement by a relative or friend would have been objectionable; a eulogy impossible. But I could not help thinking that poor Stephen had little need for the "many mansions" in his Father's house.

When it was over I managed to lose Kitty in the crowded aisle; I could not bear any more of her moralizing. Outside on the avenue I had to pause, as the family were getting into the black limousines that would transport them to the private interment at Redwood.

And then suddenly there was Natica, at my side.

"I want you to walk in the park with me."

"But, Natica, dear, aren't you going to the interment?"

"No. It's all arranged that I don't have to. Come on, before Mother spies us. I saw you were sitting with her."

"Dearie, are you quite sure you know what you're doing?"

"Perfectly. Auntie, you can't argue with me today."

She put her arm under mine, and we walked the two blocks to the Seventy-second Street entrance to the park. Neither of us spoke until we were seated on a bench overlooking the boat pond where serious men soberly sailed their elaborate model craft.

"The first thing I want to tell you is how Stephen's depression started."

For the first time I learned the story of the averted abortion and of Stephen's later discovery of a possible other paternity. In a low and level tone she simply presented the facts, without ascribing motives and without describing emotions, except for Stephen's passionate resentment.

"And do his family know all this?" I asked when she seemed to have finished.

"I told his mother the whole thing. I didn't know whether it would make it better or worse for her to minimize the role Giles had played and magnify my own. But I decided that I had taken enough decisions on my own and that I had better stop playing God. And to be utterly frank, as I am now trying to be, I had come to realize that my withholding the full story from her was motivated by my desire to retain her friendship. And I saw that was gone, in any event."

"Why? I saw her take your hand before coming down the aisle. It seemed to me a most affectionate gesture."

"Oh, she's capable of that, of course. But there's a limit in the long run to how different a stand she can take from her husband's. And he is adamant. It doesn't matter to him whether Stephen killed himself because I tricked him into marriage or because of shame over the thing with Giles. It's all part of the same thing. *I* corrupted him and he went to hell."

"Surely he doesn't tell you that!"

"He doesn't tell me anything. He won't even speak to me."

"But I feel sure Mrs. Hill doesn't judge you so harshly."

"She doesn't judge me at all. She doesn't judge people. She's too wise. I don't think she really likes me very much, or that she ever did. She was nice to me — oh, wonderfully nice — but that was all for Stephen's sake. And then she knows what I've been through. She knows I've tried."

"And surely she knows you loved Stephen!"

Natica's expression was patient. "She knows the facts. She doesn't need deductions or inferences. She was poor herself once. And she made her way. That's a bond."

Even with my sympathy for her I couldn't help a momentary return to my old role of censor. How she pushed one into it! "You mean the bond of getting ahead in the world?"

"More than that, I guess. The bond of being women."

I was taken aback by its seemingly exclusivity. "Don't you and I share that bond?"

"To a lesser extent. You compromise. You tend to believe in the system. Oh, you have your moments of outrage, I grant."

"Well, I suppose one has to be practical. You've never struck me, my dear, as exactly having your head in the clouds."

"I've been what I *thought* was practical. But where has it got me? Two failed marriages, no child, no career and no money."

"No money?"

"Not a penny. I had an instructive talk with Tyler Bennett yesterday. Trust him to give it to you straight. Stephen's been living over his income for years. His estate is insolvent. And his big trust, in default of issue, goes to his two sisters."

"But surely they'll waive that! Two women as rich as they are."

"They couldn't, even assuming they wanted to. And that's a rash assumption in the Hill family. The principal is simply added to their own trusts, which they can't touch."

"You don't surely mean to tell me that Angus Hill will let his daughter-in-law starve!"

"No, Tyler tells me that his uncle is prepared to make me some sort of allowance. Until I die or remarry and so long as I bring no further disgrace to the family. But I have my own pride. Or at least I think it's time I developed some. I can't take money from a man who feels about me the way he feels. And for whose total lack of the smallest trait of anything like imagination I have nothing but contempt!"

"What about his wife, then?"

"Ah, that's different, of course. And that's really what I wanted to talk to you about. I've made up my mind in the last two days that I want a career of my own. Something better than pushing best sellers and whodunits to Park Avenue dowagers. I want to be a lawyer, Auntie."

I almost clapped my hands. "It's what I've always thought you could be!"

"It would be getting on with my life. And putting the past firmly behind. Perhaps there are things I should atone for, but I've always thought atonement smacked of self-pity. It will take time, of course. I'll have to make up for the college credits I gave up when I married Tommy. But I think the whole thing can be done at NYU in something like four years. And I thought I'd ask Mrs. Hill to stake me to it."

"It's the least she can do!"

"And the most I'd ever ask. I shall expect to pay the money back in time."

"She'd never take it."

"No, but I'd like to be able to offer it."

"Well, all I can say is that I admire you." I had a vision of Portia mesmerizing the Venetian court with her silver-toned defense of Antonio. Silly old soppy aunt that I was, with tears in my eyes! "When I think of all that's happened to you! And all that is happening to our poor old world." We were living through the fall of France. Civilization itself seemed to reel.

"I suppose we'll get into the war now," she replied with a shrug. "I can't see it as my affair. Men made the rotten peace that caused this war. Men can win it, as I'm sure they will. But it's time I did something of my very own."

"I wonder if you'd consider letting me pay for your new education," I suggested with some difference now. "I have my savings and something besides. I had planned to leave it to my school's scholarship fund, never dreaming that you'd need it, but now it would give me the greatest pleasure —"

"Oh, I'm sure it would, dearest Auntie!" Natica exclaimed, with her first show of emotion. She leaned over to give me a kiss. "But I really think Mrs. Hill would like to do it. I honestly believe it would be unkind to deprive her of that pleasure."

Part Four

21 ✦ ✦ ✦

SOMEBODY HAD SAID of the renowned constitutional lawyer George Haven that he was the rare case of a great man without the facial features of such, which at once invited the query as to whether he really was one. His long oval countenance was bland, smooth, seemingly incapable of registering any strong emotion. His brow was high and fine; his hair long and thick and quite as silvery as his voice; his eyes small and pink-gray, usually expressing an amused resignation at the follies of the world, qualified by a mild irritation at their inevitability. His tall, trim figure, which Thaddeus Sturges always tended to picture as garbed in a morning coat and striped pants, suggested a constant readiness to appear before some high tribunal, but a lightly loosened tie, an occasional shirt button undone, like the ever relit pipe before his attentively focused eyes, struck a note of indefinite ease under an easily doffed formality, a need to get down to basics, a hint that behind closed doors, or in a pool room, or even out in a village square with pigeons before some columned courthouse, occurred the basic male confidences that were the necessary complement to the clarion oratory. Was George Haven the type of grand old lawyer of the grand old South, or was he playing the part — or was playing the part not precisely what those grand old lawyers did?

Thaddeus knew that these questions were sometimes asked by the more sarcastic clerks of Haven, Tillinghast & Dorr, of 70 Wall Street, but he attributed them to the envy that greatness engenders in small minds. There had been no wavering in his own total dedication to the senior partner ever since his first interview with the latter in 1936.

He had had the good fortune, immediately upon coming to work, to be assigned to the great man's litigating team, and Mr. Haven had asked him to get a certain document from the office safe. When he had returned empty-handed after a frantic search, his new boss had simply inquired if he had looked *under* the safe.

"I see you're new here, Mr. Sturges. Or may I call you Thaddeus? But doesn't that sound too biblical? How about Thad? All right? Well then, Thad, you always have to look on the floor because there's a hole in the back of that safe that some of the papers slip through."

And Thad (for Thad he was to be thenceforth, though he had hitherto been known as Ted) knew at once that this was both the firm and the man for whom he wanted to work.

His background had been a confusing one. His father had been a Boston Sturges, but of an impecunious branch, who had compounded this disadvantage by marrying a dressmaker, and an Irish Catholic, to boot. Thaddeus senior had died young and alcoholic, leaving his only child to be reared by a proud and intrepid mother, who had put him through private school and Harvard College on the earnings of her small but reputable shop. Thad had acknowledged his obligation by his adoration of her and by his passionate embracement of the faith that had sustained her in her lonely and industrious existence. She had hoped he would become a priest, even after he had grown into a rangy, sandy-haired six-footer and played on the Harvard football team. And he had even considered obliging her until his shame over an adulterous affair with one of her clients had convinced him (and her) that he was unfit for holy orders. Thereafter he had thrown all his energies into his courses at Harvard Law and obtained an editorship of the *Review* which had brought him an offer from the Haven firm. He had wanted to turn it down and stay in Boston to be a comfort to his mother, but she had insisted that New York provided the greater opportunity. And thus it was that he had come down to Manhattan, a very serious and literal young man, with a shame of lust doubly inherited from puritans and Irish, whose quizzical and guarded gaze seemed to express the hope, but by no means the expectation, that the world was going to be as straight with him as he certainly intended to be with it. And in George Haven he found the father figure he had always missed.

In a year's time he had succeeded in making himself useful to his leader. In three he had made himself indispensable. Mr. Haven, a former governor of Alabama who had long abandoned his native South for the more lucrative practice of Wall Street and who was nationally known as a legal champion of the conservative cause, was then engaged in his long battle to invalidate what he considered the socialist statutes of the New Deal. Thad threw himself into the fray with all the fervor of a crusader. He had not previously been much involved in economic philosophy, but he now unhesitatingly adopted his leader's credo that the due process clause of the Fourteenth Amendment had been designed to guarantee to corporations the continuation of free enterprise and that freedom of contract was the root of democracy.

The war only cemented the friendship and alliance between the older and younger man. Thad, though strong and seemingly fit, had the humiliation of being barred from combat by a discovered heart murmur which his own physician had deemed innocuous. He had then wanted to serve the government in a civilian capacity, but Mr. Haven had persuaded him that his duty lay elsewhere.

"I'm all for your fighting, my boy, but if you can't fight Huns and Japs and Wops you'd better stay home with me and fight the Hudson River squire. We've seen what he did in peacetime. *Think* what he may do with war powers!"

By 1946, now a full partner in the firm, Thad had become indissolubly associated with Haven in the minds of the downtown bar. The two men were said to complement each other. Thad could be as sober and quiet as his leader was volatile. He could be the person to whom the client might turn when the old man was going too far, to suggest a compromise when Haven wanted to fight to the death. And he knew when discreetly to tug his senior's coattail when an oral argument had gone on long enough.

This latter ability was important, as the oral argument brought out Mr. Haven's particular genius. His capacity to simplify and dramatize the most complicated and dryest facts made him a popular litigant even with liberal judges.

"It's really more than half the battle," he would insist to Thad. "Our briefs are writ on water. They moulder on the back shelves of bar association libraries. All a lawyer really has is that golden moment when the right sentence or even the right phrase wings its way from him to an attentive court, and he senses that it may bring him victory. Did Shakespeare care about printing his plays? Not at all! The passage of his words from actor to pit was all the glory he needed."

Words indeed had become the obsession of George Haven's old age. His constant complaint of the young lawyers of the office was that they couldn't write. "And if they can't do that, how the devil can they think?" he would demand. "Can you have a thought you can't express?" He abandoned his church in Smithport where he spent his summers and weekends when its minister adopted the revised version of the King James Bible. And so it seemed in keeping to Thad, on a winter morning late in 1946, when Haven spoke of a new recruit to their litigating team as "at least someone who can speak the language."

"I didn't know we had a new associate."

"We didn't until this morning. And she's not a new associate. She's been with us for almost three years. She's a transfer from Estates and Trusts. It's Mrs. Hill."

"Natica Hill? Why does she want to be a litigator?"

"She doesn't. Or at least she hasn't asked to be. *I* am the one who wants her. What do you know about her work?"

"Nothing. I hardly know her. I sat next to her at the firm dinner last October. She seems bright enough. And she's certainly attractive."

"Watch out for her, Thad. She's a *femme fatale*."

"Well I certainly wouldn't have guessed *that*. She struck me more as quiet and businesslike."

"Still waters, you know."

Thad perceived that the old man was enjoying himself. There was something he wanted to tell, but he was going to take his own time about it.

"Have you moved her to Litigation to see if I can resist temptation?"

"No. You seem all too resistant to the fair sex. It's high time you thought of getting married, my boy. Thirty-five is half your biblical span."

"But I'm not, I take it, to marry Mrs. Hill."

"Heaven forbid!" Haven raised his hands in dismay. "I guess it's time I explained the mystery. We had an important death over the weekend. Angus Hill."

"Really! I hadn't heard."

"It'll be in the evening papers. I would have called you, but I knew you'd gone to Boston to visit your ma."

"You're an executor, aren't you?"

"I am that. Together with his widow and his nephew Tyler Bennett. It's a very large estate, of course. Bennett came to the house last night to talk about the will. There's one little thing that may give us a bit of trouble. Natica Hill, as you no doubt know, was Angus's daughter-in-law. She was married to the only son, who shot himself six years ago. Because of the way the son's trust was set up, she got nothing from his estate. And now Angus has left her nothing."

"Why was he so hard on the poor girl?"

"She may indeed be poor, but it's for no lack of trying to be rich. She was married to a minister who taught at Averhill School. When young Stephen Hill joined the faculty there she set out to snare him. She got him into bed, claimed she was pregnant and bamboozled him into marrying her after she shed her impecunious clerical spouse. Then she had a convenient miscarriage in Paris, if indeed she was ever pregnant. Angus told me she was quite capable of bribing a Frog doctor to go along with her story. When poor Stephen cottoned on at last to the sort of creature he was hitched to, he blew his brains out. Not that he ever amounted to much. Angus said he was even a fairy."

"Then how did she ever seduce him?"

"Oh, I suppose she flattered him into thinking he was a real man, that he had given her the thrill of her life. And then, when she had him snagged, she probably sneered at his sorry performance."

"I must say, sir, she didn't strike me as that type at all."

"Of course not. They never do."

"And what is she doing working for a firm that represents her husband's family?"

"Good question. Nobody but I, and you now, knows the full extent of Angus Hill's suspicions of her. And his wife did not share his attitude at all. She even put the girl through law school. It was at *her* behest that I hired Natica."

"I see. But what are you and Bennett really afraid of? A daughter-in-law isn't an heir or next of kin. She has no standing in court to contest the will."

"Unless she were mentioned in it. And she *is* mentioned in it. Angus states that he is leaving her nothing because she has been 'otherwise provided for.' Our man who drew the will assumed that this had been done. But it hadn't. Unless you count Angelica Hill's paying for her law school, which is pretty thin."

"Even so, it doesn't sound like much of a case for Natica. I wouldn't care to take it."

"No, but some shyster might, and that's just the point. He'd use it to get his dirty toe in the door and then have a fine old time digging into all the complicated Hill trusts and family corporations. We'd probably end by making some sort of settlement just to get rid of him. Now I don't say that Natica is going to do that. But just in case she has any inclination I've taken her out of Estates and Trusts, at least while Angus's estate is in administration. I don't want her poking her nose into inventories and appraisals."

"Did you tell her that?"

"Do you think I'm a complete dodo? No, when I talked to her earlier this morning, I told her frankly that I knew of divisions of opinion about her in the Hill family, that I took no side and had no opinion of her myself, except that Tom Hilliard in Estates considers her a first class lawyer. I then suggested it might be easier on all if she were to be out of the department while members of the family were going there on estate business."

"And did she buy that?"

"She was too smart not to pretend to, anyway. And I sweetened it a bit by telling her I'd heard about the fine writing style of her memoranda of law and that I'd like her help on one of my briefs. And I capped it all off by telling her she'd be working for the great Mr. Sturges!"

"That must have really done it."

"Anyway, she allowed as she'd be happy to make the switch. So there you are, Thad. She's all yours!"

22 · · ·

THAD WAS soon to reflect that if Haven had been trying to promote something between him and Natica, he could hardly have done better than voice the warning he had. For the contrast between the serious, silent and very efficient young woman who listened attentively to his instructions and then departed to effect her researches in the library, and the lurid seductress of the unhappy Stephen Hill invited constant speculation as to her true character. Sometimes he thought that the late Angus Hill's suspicions of her motives and plots must have been sponsored by paternal possessiveness or even by the actual malice of a money-obsessed old man living in his nasty fantasies. At other times Natica's coolness, her imperturbability, the very plainness and neatness of her business suits, struck him as verging on the sinister, the mask of a nature capable of awe-inspiring crime. But in every role in which his fantasy cast her she was always interesting and at times dramatic. And her very lack of flame aroused erotic thoughts as to what a little fire might do to her.

Haven had been retained by a southern state to argue the constitutionality of "separate but equal" schools for blacks. The argument in the brief that Thad was preparing for him, and in which Natica was assisting him, was that a federal court could not take judicial notice (as urged by the NAACP) of the fact that such legislation invariably resulted in unequal schools. The fact had to be proved.

Natica's supporting memorandum of law went further. She contended that even if inequality was proved, it had to be shown that the state legislature had anticipated it. "We might even argue," she suggested, "that a court has no warrant to interfere with state government unless it be shown that it was actually impossible to achieve equality under the statute. So long as equality *could* be achieved, the statute is valid, and the student who suffers discrimination must be left to his remedy in the state courts."

Thad could not help wondering if she was trying to ingratiate herself with a partner by favoring his known partiality for states' rights. He decided to take her to lunch at the Downtown Association where she might talk more freely than in the office. She accepted his invitation but without the alacrity with which clerks were wont to respond to such bids from members of the firm.

"Do you mind if we wait till one?" she asked. "I'm expecting a call from my landlord about the renewal of my lease."

Thad *did* mind. He was a creature of habit who liked to eat at noon. But he reflected that Natica was not an ordinary clerk. She had, after all, been part of a family which was one of the firm's principal clients.

At their table at the Downtown he suggested that the time had come for them to be on first name terms. Again her assent was polite but casual.

"Which do you prefer? Thad or Thaddeus?"

"The former. And you're Natica, not Nat, is that so?"

"Yes. Though some call me Nat. I've never really thought the name lent itself to abbreviation."

He found, when he directed their discussion to their case and its merits, that she showed no disposition to gratify him by adopting his constitutional principles. Indeed, she was surprisingly outspoken in her more liberal views. When he asked her at last how she would decide their case if she were a justice on the court, she did not hesitate to answer that she would invalidate the statute.

"Your attitude is certainly not reflected in your memos."

"No, why should it be? A job's a job."

"And you don't find it disagreeable to have to argue a position with which you don't agree? Which indeed I suppose you may even find inhumane?"

"Not at all. Time will take care of these matters. The South won't be able to hold out forever. I don't think we should have even fought the Civil War."

Thad did not like this at all. His grandfather had fought in the war at the age of seventeen; the Sturgeses had been ardent abolitionists. He saw no inconsistency between this and his position on states' rights. The Constitution was the Constitution. He voiced his thought.

"You don't have much concern for states' rights, I take it."

"Very little."

"And the Constitution?"

"Oh, the Constitution can always be stretched to fit what the majority really want. What would the founding fathers have said to what we've done to the commerce clause?"

"Then you think the Constitution offers no protection?"

"To whom?"

"Well, to minorities. What about the Bill of Rights?"

"I can't forget that only five years ago a unanimous court permitted thousands of U.S. citizens to be put in prison camps without trial."

"But that was wartime, Natica!"

"And can't wartime come again? Or other emergencies? The only true safeguard of liberty is that the majority values it. If *that* should ever change!"

"I had no idea you were such a cynic."

"I'm not a cynic. I try to be a realist. The Constitution is a very man-made thing. I mean made by men. You tend to believe that things can be tied down with words. Women know better. I doubt we'd even have had a Constitution if women had had the vote. It's a kind of straightjacket you have to keep getting yourself out of every time a major social change is needed."

"So you're a feminist, too."

"Wouldn't you be, if you were a woman?"

"But you have the vote now. Women voters outnumber men. You're a lawyer, a member of the bar. It seems to me you're doing all right."

"Just tell me this, Thad. How many women partners do you have?"

Of course he had none. Decidedly, he was not enjoying the conversation. The lunch was not turning out at all as he had visualized. But he didn't want to get angry at her. He asked her now about the call she had been expecting before lunch, and they turned to the safer topic of rent control. At least they both hated their landlords.

In the office, in the days that followed, she was just as she had been before, impersonal, industrious, possibly a touch more aloof, as if to correct any misunderstanding incurred at their lunch. He invited her again, to prove there had been none, but their conversation was confined to business. What bothered him increasingly now was that in their discussions of the brief she never took any position but the one they would be taking in court. And if he ever ventured a remark to show that "strict construction" was for him as much a matter of personal conviction as of practical advocacy, she would simply be silent. And her silence seemed somehow to give her the edge.

Impatient one morning to the point of anger with himself, he paused on an abrupt impulse when passing the open door of her cubicle of an office. For a moment he simply gazed at the reading figure at the desk. She looked up at last in mild surprise.

"You look as if you'd had a sudden brainstorm."

"I think so," he replied.

"Well, tell me. Let me write it down quickly before it disappears."

"Oh, it's not for the brief. I was wondering if you might have dinner with me tonight."

"What we call a working dinner?"

"No, no. I thought we might explore our different constitutional philosophies."

"Just that?"

"Well, of course, what I really want is the charm of your company."

"Then what you're really proposing is a date?"

Really, she had a way of bringing a man down!

"I suppose you might call it that," he responded lamely.

"Then I'm afraid I must decline."

His lips parted. "Am I so objectionable?"

"Please come in, Thad." She rose and walked with deliberation to the door which she closed behind him. "You must know that I can't be ignorant of what your partners think of me."

"My partners?"

"Well, Mr. Haven, anyway. He's almost the partnership himself. He was my father-in-law's confidant and closest advisor. He had to be aware of Mr. Hill's view of my character. And I am almost certain he counseled him to shut me out of any participation in the family affairs."

"I suppose he did what his client wanted. Isn't that what you said the other day? A job's a job?"

"Yes, but I'm a humble clerk. Mr. Haven can pick and choose his clients."

"Would any lawyer turn down a Hill?"

He had wondered what a little fire would do to her. Now he was finding out. She was almost beautiful in her pale indignation.

"Yes, a gentleman might! Or at least he might tell his client that he was premising his testamentary scheme on a vile and unproven suspicion!"

"How do you know he didn't?"

"I don't *know*. But I've seen enough of how rich clients are treated by members of this firm to make a pretty shrewd guess. Mr. Hill knew nothing whatever of any troubles between his son and myself. All he knew was that poor Stephen blew his brains out. The rest was in his own sordid imagination. And I have little doubt that your sainted Mr. Haven chortled with sympathy while his favorite client voiced his horrid suspicions. Oh, I know. You think I'm just sore about the money. But it's not that."

"I don't think any such thing."

"It would be perfectly natural if you did. But I'm way beyond that. Mrs. Hill actually offered to settle something on me, and I very gratefully declined. My law school was all I would let her pay for. But I *do* care about my character. And that's why I don't want to be the date of a man who's not only the partner but the alter ego of a person who thinks I'm such a prime bitch!"

"I wonder you even want to work for his firm."

"That was Mrs. Hill's idea. She sponsored me. And it was the best offer I had. I wanted the experience of working for a big corporate law firm for a few years. I never had any intention of staying here permanently."

"Even if we made you a partner?"

"Which you never would!"

"Stranger things have happened."

"Stranger things have *not* happened. Stranger things, no doubt, *will* happen one day, but I'm not waiting around for that."

"At least I hope you don't think that *I* hold any of these vile opinions about you."

Her look became searching. "You don't? You really don't? Are you quite sure?"

"I think you're as straight as they come."

Her lips twitched. For a moment he thought she was going to weep. He hoped so, anyway. But she didn't.

"Thank you, Thad. For that I can almost forgive you for being a states' righter."

Her smile was charming! Suddenly elated, he was about to repeat his invitation when a counter-impulse checked him. What the hell was he getting into? If she accepted, after what had just passed between them, it would be a much more serious thing than had she assented in the first place. It was time to pull up. It was even time to recall that in the eyes of his church this woman had a living husband.

"Even a states' righter can recognize defamation of character.

And now, if you will forgive me, Natica, I must let us both get back to work."

But he strode down the corridor to the senior partner's large corner office with its double view of the harbor and the Hudson River. The inside walls were lined with Haven's own set of *Federal Reporters* broken by little alcoves with shelves for his collection of Chinese porcelains. Its occupant was alone, at his desk, smoking his pipe and gazing out one of the great windows. Thad, ignoring his cheerful welcome, went straight to the point.

"Did Angus Hill have any real basis for the things you told me he charged Natica with?"

Haven's reaction to a crisis was always to appear even more relaxed. "Well, my boy, I suppose that depends on what you call a basis."

"Did he have such evidence as would convince a reasonable man?"

"I don't rightly know what evidence he had. But *he* was certainly a reasonable man. I don't suppose a reasonable man would condemn his only son's wife without something to go on."

"But don't millionaires see fortune hunters behind every tree? Haven't you told me that yourself? They think nobody could marry them for anything but their money."

"And maybe there's something in that," Haven retorted with a chuckle.

"In Mr. Hill's case I can well believe it. But Stephen was a very handsome guy. I remember him when he was a student at Yale and used to come down and lunch with you and his old man. I can see that the wife of a stuffy minister cooped up in a stuffy church school might have fallen for him. I'm not defending it, but it's very different from what Mr. Hill was supposing. I repeat: do you know of any proven facts against her?"

"Look, Thad . . ."

"Please, sir, tell me. Do you know of any?"

"All right, no, I don't." Haven now fixed his junior with a stare that seemed to call him to order. "But I do know this. She's a gal who ruined the school careers of two men in order to switch from a poor husband to a rich one. Can you deny that?"

"Why did she ruin the minister's career?"

"The scandal, my boy, the scandal. And Stephen Hill's suicide hardly leads one to suppose that she made him very happy. Everything about her smacks of bad news. I hope you're not getting too involved with her."

"What do you mean by involved?"

"Well, I wouldn't mind a flirtation. I wouldn't mind an affair so long as it didn't get out of hand. But I hope to God you're not thinking of marrying her!"

"How could I marry her? She's a divorced woman."

The eyebrows of the never surprised Haven rose. "But Barnes is dead. He was killed in the war."

"I thought he was a minister!"

"He signed up as an army chaplain and went down on a torpedoed troop ship in the Pacific. I may be a fool to tell you, but you were bound to find out eventually."

"Thank you, sir! Thank you very much."

For the second time that morning Thad now loomed in Natica's doorway.

"I've thought of a reason for you to break your rule of not dating a partner of Mr. Haven's!"

Her smile was quizzical, not unfriendly. "And what is that?"

"I'm the only one of them who can properly ask you."

"Because you're the only unmarried one?"

"Oh, you know."

"Everyone here knows everything about the partners. It's our favorite luncheon topic. But I *will* break the rule. Because you said I was straight. I liked that. Why don't you pick me up at my apartment at 900 Lex at seven? I can give you a drink before we go out."

He reflected that like George Haven she seemed resolved never to show surprise.

23 ✦ ✦ ✦

NATICA HAD never entertained a sentiment for a man such as she now began to feel for Thad. With both Tommy and Stephen there had been a distinct antagonism lurking in a corner of her heart even at times when they had been closest to her, like a mean little dog ready to rush out and snap. With Thad her attitude was much kinder; it was almost as if she were trying to protect him. But protect him from what? Certainly he was by far the strongest of the three men. There was an evenness, almost a serenity in his sustained good nature; he appeared always to expect the best of people, without in any way being unprepared to face the worst. What she supposed she really wanted to protect was not so much him as his vision of the world as a place that could be improved by good will and hard work, and if it couldn't, well, that had to be God's will. He lacked imagination — there was no denying that — but his undoubted intelligence, salted with un-expected irony and a usually gentle sense of humor, came near to making up for it. And his political conservatism was devoid of the smirking malice found in so many right wingers. Indeed he wore it as a kind of sports jacket which in another season he might well doff. Or at least which she could hope he would.

That their relationship excluded other romantic interests for both and would lead, if to anything, to marriage, he took squarely for granted from the night of their first dinner together, after which, at the door of her apartment house, he had planted on her lips a single firm but proprietary kiss. He showed no need to demonstrate his masculinity; his large stillness and easy stance lent assurance that his wife would have nothing to complain about in that department. But she would have to wait, and if she couldn't wait, was she really the girl for him? But she *was* the girl for him, a glint in his eye at once assured her. He had no interest in or concern with the changing sexual mores of the day, and he never referred to her two marriages. He clearly intended to regard himself as her one and only spouse.

They went out together three nights a week; on the others he worked. They saw each other little now in the office, as the school case had been settled, the desegregationists having decided a better factual basis was needed for a Supreme Court argument, and Thad had reassigned her to another partner's case.

"I'd rather our friendship wasn't mixed up with business," he explained. "Do you agree?"

"I don't know that I agree. I certainly don't mind."

But she thought he was going rather far in refusing to take her to his downtown club. If they lunched together, it had to be uptown in a French restaurant. Some men, she reflected, had very compartmented minds.

In the brief time it takes for such things to be recognized, they began to be asked out as a couple by their friends. At a dinner party given by Tyler and Edith Bennett Thad was seated at their hostess's right and Natica at the host's, which she thought was going rather far.

"We're not engaged, you know," she told Tyler.

"Well, here's hoping you will be. You couldn't do better. That firm will be known as *Sturges,* Haven, Tillinghast & Dorr before you know it. And lawyers are making *real* money these days."

"So my poor old ship's come in at last!"

"Don't knock it, Natica. I'd almost given you up. Turning down that settlement offer of Uncle Angus's and then going into law. The big bar has no idea of sharing all that moola with you gals. Not for a good while yet, anyway. All you can expect is to draft wills and separation agreements."

"I thought I'd found that out. But then they switched me to Litigation."

"That was a special deal. I know all about *that*. And anyway, if you marry Thad, you'll have to quit the firm."

"Why?"

"They can't have partners married to clerks. It's against the natural order of things."

"Maybe I could come and work for you."

"You're joking, but the offer's still open. Except Thad would never let his wife work."

"What makes you so sure of that?"

"He's the old-fashioned type. It sticks out all over him. He'll want you to stay home and have eight kids."

"As you did Edith!"

"Did, is right. Now we have two she says she's through. But I wouldn't mind if she worked her ass off. Better than getting up at ten and spending the next two hours on the telephone trying to decide whether to lunch at the Veau d'Or or the Crémaillère!"

Natica thought of asking Thad when he took her home that night if he really objected to working wives, but at the last moment she decided against it. Their friendship had become precious to her. She didn't want anything to cause even a ripple in it — at least not yet.

Aunt Ruth found him delightful; she was clearly holding her breath in fear that so desirable a match might not come off. Estelle Knight, who had fled from Averhill at her husband's demise to settle, with all her Jacobean accouterments, in a large dark apartment on upper Madison Avenue, where it sometimes amused Natica to dine, was also charmed by him. There was a district atmosphere among the family and friends that Natica had done better than could have been anticipated. Her parents found Thad, except for his religion, the model of all they could want in a son-in-law. He talked with genuine interest to her father about fishing, a subject of considerable interest to himself, and condoled with her mother in all her fancied trials and tribulations.

It was different with Thad's mother. Going up to Boston to meet her was as close as Natica had come to announcing an engagement, and even this she had tempered with the excuse of a proposed visit to the Gardner Museum. Mrs. Sturges, tall and large like her son, but ampler of girth, was craggy-featured and plain of garb. Nowhere but in Boston could she have made a living as a dressmaker. Natica could easily divine from the deep reserve of her approach and the intensity of her carefully selected questions how miserably torn she was between her disapproval of a divorced Protestant and her passionate longing to see her only son married and the father of her grandchildren. She must have almost given him up as a confirmed bachelor. Might not the infidel be her last chance?

Flying back to New York on Sunday afternoon Natica and Thad had their first serious talk about religion.

"Would you expect your wife to become a Catholic?"

"Only if she were a genuine convert. Of course I'd be very happy if she were that."

"And would you insist that she promise to raise the children in your faith?"

"I'd tell her it would be very painful to me if they weren't. I'd hope she'd always be open to persuasion. But I wouldn't make it a condition, no."

"Would a priest marry you without the promise?"

"I think so. If I assured him I'd do everything I could to convert you."

"Then if I were to marry you, I would in effect have given you my word. For I could never marry you to give you pain."

"I'd take my chances."

"And while we're on the subject of conditions, would you object to your wife's working?"

"Not if she still could be a good mother. If my wife is the girl I'm thinking of, she'd never neglect her children."

They buckled their seatbelts at the landing announcement. "Oh,

I don't know. Some people say the girl you have in mind is a pretty tough cooky. I'll bet your ma thinks so, anyway."

"Mother thought you were wonderful!"

"That remark isn't even trying to be a good lie!"

She no longer had to see much of Mr. Haven in the office, but Thad talked about him a good deal. She tried to keep an open mind, but she couldn't allow Thad's attempt to portray his partner as a champion of the Bill of Rights.

"Don't you think there are some liberties that he's too little concerned with? Do you remember that conference on the school brief when he remarked that having fought the bloodiest war in our history for the Negroes was enough to have done for them? For a hundred years, anyway?"

Thad's slightly impatient head-shake might have indicated some awareness of this imperfection in his idol. "Yes, I saw your look when he said that. Of course, he was not serious. You must remember he was raised in a far from reconstructed South. I think it's actually remarkable how well he has overcome those ancient prejudices. You can tell by the bantering way he has of speaking of such topics that he doesn't mean to be taken literally. But of course his words have a considerably less innocent look in print, which is why it's one of my jobs to see they never creep into anything he writes."

Haven used to invite Thad down to his rambling shingle country house in Smithport for what he called a working weekend. He always managed to relieve these with a little golf, excellent meals and plentiful liquor. He was a childless widower and his household was run silently and efficiently by a gaunt, grim butler, Thorne, who shared Thad's protective adoration of his master. On one of these weekends, when Natica was making a rare visit to her parents only a mile away, Thad persuaded her to join him and Haven for dinner, promising her the ordeal would be short, as the two men would have to work in the library afterwards. But when she arrived she saw at once from his puckered brow that the evening was not going to be as planned. Her host, more pink-faced than usual, hardly greeted her. He was silent and morose and drinking what was obviously not the first scotch of the evening.

Thad took her aside and murmured the explanation. Haven had received a call from Washington that afternoon informing him that the Supreme Court on Monday would hand down an unfavorable ruling in one of his due process cases involving a state law restricting the rights of labor unions and that the majority opinion had been written by Hugo Black.

The tirade in which Haven now indulged took the form of a monologue which lasted through the cocktail period and well into dinner. At length he became actually abusive.

"What the hell, I ask you, is the point of wasting one's heart and mind on brilliant arguments to a court that's stacked with a bunch of rubber stamps who owe their robes to the late happy-go-lucky cripple who occupied the White House for such an unconscionable number of terms?"

Thad now at last intervened. "Hugo Black, sir, was hardly Roosevelt's rubber stamp. You mustn't forget that when a man's once on the court he's free of any political pressure. Look at the other Roosevelt and his appointee, Holmes. Didn't Teddy get so angry at one of his decisions that he said he could have made a better man out of a turnip?"

"But Holmes, my dear fellow, had been Chief Justice of Massachusetts. This man Black was a police court judge!"

"A man can learn a lot of law in a police court, sir. I've heard you say so yourself."

"As a *part* of his experience, yes. Not as the whole kit and kaboodle! No, Thaddeus, there's no point trying to mitigate it. It's just another example of the dirty role Lady Luck plays in our lives. I toil for decades and fool myself into thinking I may have made myself a niche in the glorious history of our Constitution only to see the highest honor go to a redneck from my own state!"

Natica was interested to learn of such an ambition from the man who professed to value the uttered word as the sole important joy of life. "Would you like to have been on the court, Mr. Haven?"

He looked at her as though he had just been made aware of her presence. "Young lady," he said solemnly, "it was the great ambition of my life. And do you know what the great irony of my life was? I was offered the court once and turned it down."

"You turned it down!"

He nodded gravely. "I did. I thought I was too young at the time and that the chance would surely come again. And I needed the income from my practice, as I had run up debts in the badly paid years of my public life. So there you are. I actually said no to President Harding." Here he grunted. "And he lost the chance to do the one good deed of his administration."

"The appointment may still come," said Thad consolingly.

"Are you out of your mind? Truman would rather put an illiterate Nigra on the court than a Wall Street lawyer. Besides, I'm too old. Much too old. The accent is all on youth today."

"Well, even if the appointment never comes, you'll have played a greater role as a single advocate before the court than you would have as one of nine judges sitting on it. *That* will be your great part in history, sir, the saving of the Constitution!"

Natica regarded with dismay the earnest countenance of the man she was thinking of marrying. Was it possible that he could be such a toady? And wasn't it worse if he was sincere? Deliberately now she hoisted her pennant of dissent.

"In my opinion, Mr. Haven, Hugo Black will go down in history as one of the court's great justices."

Thad gave a little gasp, but it struck her oddly that it might have been feigned. Could it be that her cool defiance of the old boy amused him? Oh, if *that* were only true!

Haven was shocked into a more temperate reaction. "Do you think so? Thad had told me you were of the liberal persuasion. Though he claims it doesn't affect the quality of your work in representing the saner sort."

"A lawyer should be able to step into any client's shoes, isn't that so, sir?" she demanded.

Thad lumbered heavily to her aid. "May I remind you, sir, that you argued in the Sterne case that the death penalty was a cruel and inhuman punishment and, five years later, in an amicus brief you urged it for a kidnapper."

Haven grunted, not much liking the reminder. "It's true that in trial work there are inconsistencies. At the appellate level you will find more uniformity in my briefs. I wouldn't take a case where I had to argue the constitutionality of a New Deal statute."

Natica's indignation had been heightened by Thad's temporizing effort. "Then I take it, Mr. Haven, you're in favor of continued segregation in the South, entirely aside from the question of states' rights?"

"Entirely. It's the only way for the two races to live together in peace and harmony."

"You mean with one on top and one on the bottom? Why isn't that a revival of slavery?"

Haven hit the table with his fist. "We're not Nazis, damn it all! We treat the Negroes differently for their own good. That's something you Northerners can never understand."

Natica paused to consider her answer to this. She glanced at Thad and wondered if his eyes were pleading for restraint. But his eyes were enigmatic. He might have been watching her with as much curiosity as fear. Was she idiotically risking her future? But then a sudden memory tore like a rocket across the murky sky of the past. She was sitting in Dr. Lockwood's study puffing a cigarette in his infinitely disapproving presence. Yes, yes! These hateful old men had to be resisted at any cost! Any at all!

"You say we Northerners cannot understand, Mr. Haven. Perhaps that's because it's so difficult *to* understand. You say you're not Nazis. But I think I'd rather have been a Jew under Hitler than a Negro in the postbellum South."

"Oh, come now, Natica," Thad protested, now genuinely aroused. "Nothing in the South could compare with the gas chambers!"

"I'm not so sure of that. Let me put these alternatives to you. Which of the following two lives would you prefer?" She paused again to arrange her conditions. "Let me see. All right, I think I have it. The first I offer you is that of a black farmer in the South, say in the early nineteen hundreds. I'll be very fair. I'll give you a kind overseer, a pleasant cottage and a loving family. You'll even be surrounded by children and grandchildren when you die in your eighties. But you'll be illiterate. You will have been forcibly kept in a state of ignorance. And now for my other life. You'll be a Jewish doctor in Berlin, at the height of your career just before Hitler. You will have discovered a cure for some kind of cancer and be a candidate for a Nobel Prize. But you will die with your wife and children at the age of forty in a gas chamber. Which life do you choose?"

Haven, intrigued in spite of himself, breathed a bit heavily. "One is deprived of life, the other of books. Is that the gist of it?"

"That's it. Which is the crueler fate?"

"Obviously, you want me to say the Negro's. But his fate would only be cruel if he were a white man. Your choice is not a fair one."

Haven turned now to Thorne, who was removing the dessert plates, to tell him they would have coffee in the library. "Except I won't have any. I'm tired and I'm going straight to bed. No work tonight! I suggest, Thad, that you take my pretty cross-examiner to some night spot. I'll see you in the morning."

At a roadhouse on the Jericho Turnpike, a half hour later, Natica sipped her whiskey and contemplated her companion's enigmatic expression. He had said nothing in the car about her conduct at dinner, yet he did not seem in the least resentful. It had probably never even crossed his mind that there could ever occur such a thing as his having to choose between her and his partner.

"You're a female Daniel, my dear. You entered the lion's den and emerged unscathed."

"But the lion will never forgive me."

"You think he minds your views that much?"

"I don't think he gives a tinker's damn about my views. What he and I were really fighting about was you. Oh, make no mistake about it. You're the indispensable partner, a kind of surrogate son. And he's damned if he's going to let me get my hot little hands on you!"

Thad reached across the table for one of them. "How is he going to stop you?"

"I'm not sure. You *worship* him so, Thad."

"I don't worship him at all. I admire him. I consider him a great man. Is that so wrong?"

"It might be misguided. He's getting old. And he's scared to death of losing you. Oh, yes, he's scared of that and he's scared of me."

"Because you might take me away from him?"

"And I would, too. If I thought I could."

"But, Natica, what would it profit you?"

"It's more of a question of what it would profit *you*. It might make a man of you."

She liked his not resenting this.

"So you don't think I'm even a man?"

"Perhaps not quite such a one as you could be. My standards are very high. Where you're concerned."

"But can't you admit he's a rather wonderful old boy? Aside, that is, from his constitutional opinions?"

"I'm afraid I can't separate him from them."

"You mean you don't even *like* him?"

"I don't like him at all. I thought I'd made that very clear."

"Then how can you like *me*?"

"Well, that's just it. Do I?"

"I'm glad you smile when you say that. Let's forget poor old Haven. Tell me, dearest. When *will* we get married?"

"Oh, Thad, I don't know. Let's give it a little more time. There are so many things to consider."

"What, that we haven't considered?"

"Well, I'm a two-time loser. And you're so fresh and pure, if that's not an insult. God knows I don't mean it as one."

"I only wish I were purer. I have a past, too."

"Oh, but a man's past. That's nothing. It's not like mine. No, dear, don't argue with me about that. I know all too much about that. And then it seems so odd to me — so rather dreadful, really — that you wouldn't have proposed to me if poor Tommy hadn't gone

to the bottom of the ocean. It's as if for the second time I were trying to build my happiness on his defeat."

"In time you may learn to leave those things to God."

"Exactly. That's why I need time." She was shocked by the pain
in his eyes. It was rare that he showed pain or even considerable
discomfort. It was why it was so hard to determine the depth of his
feelings. Yet why in the name of heaven (*his* heaven anyway)
should he want to marry the "likes of her," as his mother would
no doubt have expressed it, in the absence of the deepest feeling?
"Oh, I suppose you think I wouldn't need time if I really loved you.
But that's not true. A woman with my experience learns caution.
It's not only that I don't want to play with my own happiness. I
don't want to play with yours."

"Can't you let me be the judge of my own happiness?"

"I'm perfectly willing to drive to New York right now and spend
the rest of the night in your apartment. Does that shock you? Does
it make me seem very brash and forward? It seems to me the least I
can offer."

He took her hand again across the table. "No, no, I'm only afraid
that I've shocked *you*. A man these days isn't supposed to say no.
But you must try to remember that if you and I did what you suggest we would be committing a sin, at least according to my lights.
And I don't wish ever to associate *you* with the sins I've committed
in the past. Do you mind that terribly?"

She paused to reflect. "No, I don't think I mind it at all. I think
I may even rather like it. It's nice to be special. And now I think
you can take me home. Mr. Haven will probably have woken up
and will want to have a nightcap with you. You see, I'm really not
jealous of him at all!"

24 · · ·

ESTELLE KNIGHT had few friends in New York, having lived away from the city for forty years, and she was so touchingly pleased by Natica's occasionally dining with her that the latter made a point of going to her once every two weeks. Estelle was certainly a foolish woman, but she was animated and gay, and her rhapsodic admiration of poetry and drama, leavened by moments of critical acumen, provided an agreeable recess from the dryer world of law. Then there was also the bond of their Averhill past and the shared memory of the hated headmaster. It was also pleasant to Natica that Estelle, though much liking Thad, who played a little game of seeking to discover how much flattery she could take, still did not regard him, as did everyone else, as the catch of catches, whom Natica was an idiot not to grab while she could.

"He doesn't have your play of mind, my dear. And his cultural education is, well, shall we say porous? The other day, when I was describing how divinely evil the divine Sarah had been in her famous *Sortez!* to the doomed Bajazet, he said he thought Roxane was supposed to be a 'sweetie pie.' He was thinking of Roxane in *Cyrano!* But of course that's a detail in a husband. He's big and strong and rich. He *is* rich, isn't he?"

"Not what the Hills would call rich, by any means. But I imagine he makes a good income."

"Well, after all, we don't need steam yachts. I think on the whole he'll fit the bill."

"Of course, there's always the question of religion."

"Pish! Another detail. So many Catholics one knows today are half agnostic. I don't mean the Irish, naturally."

"But Thad's devout. And his mother's Irish."

"Then let him be as devout as he wants. And if I were you, I'd become a convert. It'll make him so happy he'll buy the world for you. And it won't mean anything to you. My dear, I *know*. I became a Catholic myself once, but I lapsed."

"Estelle! I never knew that."

"Oh, it was long ago. During a summer that Wilbur and I spent in France. It didn't give me half the consolation I'd looked for. But *you* wouldn't be looking for consolation. So that part of it wouldn't matter."

"Was Wilbur a convert, too?"

"Heavens, no. I don't know which he disapproved of more: my embracing the faith or my forsaking it. He was such a puritan, poor dear Wilbur."

When Natica turned to the subject of Thad's political principles, her friend found her objections even more trivial.

"Dear heart, you must recognize that men are always going to have silly views about their government or their church. You mustn't pay attention to that. It's like their golf or fishing. Let them have their head in those things and keep the important decisions for yourself."

"And what are they?"

"Why, everything else. Life! Where you live, how you live, what friends you have, where you go for the summer, what concerts or plays you pick, what parties you give. Really, Natica, one would hardly guess you'd been married *twice*."

"I suppose I *am* being rather a fusspot."

"And last, but not quite least, you do love the man, don't you?"

"I think I must. Because it's really him I worry about. I thought I was thinking of Tommy when I justified my marrying him on the ground that I might be able to give him the impetus to become a headmaster. And I tried to believe I was thinking of Stephen in helping him to save his unborn child. But I wasn't, in either case, and that's why I've got to be sure I can make Thad — and myself, of course, too — happy in a union of such different religious and political views. For if one is unhappy, the other soon will be."

"Oh, you love him, my child, that's clear enough. And you didn't the other two, not really. Stop tilting at windmills."

Estelle had now decided that Europe had sufficiently recovered from the war to permit her to renew her once annual visitations, and she departed to spend some weeks in Paris. Natica did not hear from her until her return, but then she learned of it in an early morning telephone call so high-pitched and hysterical that it made little sense. At last she interrupted, having almost to shout to do so, to tell her excited friend that she would come to her apartment. She called her office to say she would be late and hurried to Madison Avenue where Estelle, amid sobs and moans, managed to inform her that she had been caught smuggling a diamond necklace, arrested and released on bail.

"But, Estelle, it's only a fine."

"No, no, it's a third offense! The brutes caught me back in 'thirty-nine, and then again, coming over the Mexican border, in 'forty-five. My lawyer says I'll surely go to jail! He can only hope for a short term. Oh, Natica, dearest, what am I to *do*?"

Natica resigned herself to spending the morning with her distracted friend. As she slowly put the picture together, it evolved that Estelle had from childhood regarded smuggling jewelry as a kind of fashionable game for great ladies, even one that it might be "pussyfoot" not to play. Besides, as she spent all her spare money on exotic jewels, she had nothing left with which to pay the duty. That she had no feeling of remorse was hardly surprising. She even boasted to Natica of the great number of times she had *not* been caught.

At last her sobs subsided. Her lawyer had told her that her only chance of escaping a jail sentence would be if she could find some venerable attorney of unquestioned integrity and national repute to plead her case. Having heard Thad speak glowingly of Mr. Haven she had mentioned his name, and the lawyer had exclaimed he would be just the man.

"Do you think Thad could possibly persuade him to do it? Oh, Natica, if he only would!"

Natica gazed doubtfully at the raddled features of her friend, trying to see them as Mr. Haven would. It was true that Estelle's long nose, oval chin and densely powdered cheeks gave her something of the air of an English duchess, at least one in a parlor comedy. But the high-piled auburn curls of her massive wig (it had to be a wig, didn't it?), the thick black eyebrows and the too briefly skirted black satin gown suggested an old cocotte in a tale by Colette. Could she possibly have fooled herself that her fortress of cosmetics added up to some impression of beauty? No, it had to be her scheme simply to annihilate the image of old age, and so long as that was accomplished, did it much matter what was put in its place?

"Well?" Estelle demanded, uncomfortable at Natica's prolonged scrutiny. "Is there *any* chance the great man would represent the guilty old party you're staring at?"

"I could ask Thad to ask him, I suppose. It's rather an undertaking."

"Are you afraid of what Thad may ask in return?"

Really! The old girl was keen. "We mustn't let you go to prison, Estelle."

"Before such a degradation they will find that, like the captured Cleopatra, I have my own means of escape!"

Natica reflected that the theatre might always see her through. They were already on the banks of the Nile.

"Perhaps you could add your own powers of persuasion to Thad's."

"How do you mean?"

"You could appeal to him yourself. He's a great one on southern chivalry. A damsel in distress and all that."

"You mean I might vamp him?" At her cackle of laughter the lutes of the Nile faded away. Natica was now riding to Canterbury with the Wife of Bath. "Well, bring the old boy on!"

But Natica saw that this would never do. She left her friend to go to her office where she immediately called Thad. He came in at once and listened carefully while she told him of Estelle's plight. He then simply nodded and promised to call her lawyer and get all the facts.

"You don't think it's a terrible imposition?"

"Estelle is your friend, isn't she? What else do I need to know?"

And the very next day he called her to ask her to step into the senior partner's office. She found him alone with Haven. The latter was looking his foxiest, with a gleam of presumably malicious pleasure in his eye. He tapped Thad's memo on his desk.

"The trouble is, the old girl's guilty as a hound dog. They found the diamonds hidden on her person, under her brassiere. She doesn't need a lawyer. She should throw herself on the mercy of the court."

"And who, sir," Thad asked, "could better help her in that? With counsel of your reputation she might even get a suspended sentence."

"On a third offense? And for a diamond necklace? Not a prayer."

"But if there's even half a prayer, sir?"

She had never seen Thad more in earnest. His way of showing it was to stand even straighter and look even more reserved. But his cheeks were flushed.

"You're always talking about what you call my image. How will it be affected by my appearing for a wealthy old tariff thief who sought to adorn her withered charms at the expense of her country?"

Thad brought his fists together. "I hate to ask it of you, sir!"

"And yet you do." Haven looked now for the first time in Natica's direction. His smile was flecked with something like malice. "Will the fair hand of our abolitionist friend here be your reward? Office rumor has you two on the verge of engagement."

Thad looked away. "In no way, sir!" His face was even redder. He strode to the window and stared out for a minute, trying, apparently, to control his temper. "And may I say, sir, your remark surprises me? Will I be deemed out of order if I ask you to apologize to Mrs. Hill?"

"Really! Well, well! A southern gentleman is never rude to a lady, but if my always honorable friend Thad asks me to apologize, I shall do so regardless of what I consider my innocence. And so, Mrs. Hill, I beg you to forgive me. But I still dare to affirm that if there's any chance of the thing happening that I was apparently so crude as to suggest, I am obligated to take Mrs. Knight's case." Haven's smile was perhaps meant to be benevolent. "But it must be on my own terms and conditions. I shall defend Mrs. Knight according to my lights, consulting no one. Not even thee, my dear Thad. And I shall accept no fee."

Thad nodded and gruffly expressed his thanks. Natica was not sure if they had won or lost the battle.

✓ ✓ ✓

The case of United States v. Knight et al. in the Federal District Court for the Southern District of New York attracted a large crowd because a popular radio comedian was among the other indicted smugglers in the docket, and the newspaper coverage had been extensive. When Mr. Haven, splendid in his morning coat and silver locks, arose, tall and serene, to speak, there was a dramatic hush.

"Your Honor, my client has entered a plea of guilty. There is no dispute about the facts. She brought to our shores an article of personal adornment and deliberately omitted to make it known to the customs authorities. All that I now say in her defense is that she is a foolish and vain old woman who allowed herself to succumb to the illusion that she was acting in a sort of melodrama of cops and robbers. I beg Your Honor to consider her age and frailty and the essential harmlessness of the folly of her second childhood in fixing what otherwise would be a merited punishment."

After a shocked silence came these words from the bench:

"Thank you, Mr. Haven. The court will indeed weigh your sensible counsel in sentencing the defendant."

As Natica sat by the quietly sobbing Estelle during the dreary hearing of the subsequent pleas of guilty of the other defendants, her mind was fixed on the image of the old lawyer who, his spiteful task completed, had left the courtroom. In her fancy it had shrunk to a waxen image that could be pierced with pins. Estelle leaned over to her.

"I'd rather have gone to prison for ten years!" she hissed. "I'd rather have died!"

"Oh, Estelle."

The waxen image had now strangely changed its shape. It portrayed a shorter, stouter male figure. But the lips had the same mean, superior smile. The headmaster and the constitutional lawyer were both made of wax, in which could be pressed the seal of tyranny. And what was poor, battered, sobbing Estelle but the symbol of their victim?

When the hearings were over she guided her stricken friend through the corridor and hall to the street where camera bulbs flashed. One reporter was approaching Estelle with a notebook in hand when a male figure stepped in front of him and handed her firmly into her waiting hired limousine. Thad then turned to Natica before she could get into the car.

"The sentencing won't be for another week. But I've talked to the judge's clerk. He thinks she may get three months but that we ought to be able to fix it so she spends the time in a prison hospital."

"She told me she'd rather have died than be so humiliated in court!"

"I know it was tough. But she could have got a year. Maybe two. The old man pulled a neat trick."

"And did he love it! I've never seen such a hateful performance. I'll promise you one thing. I'm never going to marry a man who's his partner!"

Thad's eyes opened wide in surprise. But his next reaction cast the surprise on her. He threw back his head and laughed. It was a loud, cheerful laugh. "Well, would you marry a man who wasn't?"

"What do you mean?"

"Will you marry me if I'm not a partner of George Haven's?"

She turned hurriedly to get into the car, but he restrained her with a tight grip on her elbow.

"No, please. Answer my question."

"Thad, let me go. Estelle's in no condition to be kept waiting."

"Neither am I. Will you marry me if I'm not a partner of George Haven's?"

She perceived that he was now very serious. And then, suddenly, it was very serious for her, too.

"Will you?" he repeated.

"Yes!" she almost barked at him and jumped into the car.

On the drive up the East River she could only wonder what it all meant. She had a feeling that she had somehow been trapped. But she was also beginning to wonder if she cared if she had been.

Ruth's Memoir ، ، ،

IT WAS AFTER my eightieth birthday party, in the winter
of 1966, that Natica suggested I draw a new will. She es-
corted me to the foyer of her apartment, after the last of her and
Thad's guests had departed, to give me a final hug.

"You should have a new will," she said firmly. "And I fully expect to be around to do the one for your ninetieth. Why don't you
come down to my office tomorrow? I use Saturday mornings for odds
and ends, so we'll have time to chat at our ease, and then I'll take
you out for a very good lunch. Okay? Let me send the car for you at
eleven."

I must say, I loved being pampered by my niece. It was a treat to
be driven smoothly downtown on a cold day in a big black Cadillac
to visit the gleaming new offices of Sturges, Dale, Hickok & Sands
at One Chase Manhattan Plaza. In less than two decades Thad had
developed a partnership of half a dozen young men into a mighty
corporate law firm of more than a hundred attorneys. It was still
not, to be sure, quite on the level of the Cravath firm or Sullivan &
Cromwell, but the average income of its partners was as high. Thad
could have been a federal judge, but he wouldn't leave his practice.
Natica had joined the firm as an estates and trusts partner, a position more compatible than others with the duties of a mother. But

as the boys, Thad junior and Mark, were both now at Andover and Angelica, aged fourteen, was all day at Miss Clinton's Classes (though now stripped of its too ladylike name and redubbed Clinton), their mother had resumed a full day's work schedule at the office. She had even found time to write a best-selling book of biographical essays on women in American history.

Her office reflected her organization and efficiency. Three Whistler Venetian etchings adorned her creamy white walls. The chairs and tables had minimal black iron limbs. The long smooth oblong surface of her light-toned wood table desk was bare except for a spotless blotter, a gold pen stand and two neatly stacked piles of papers. Natica herself, looking a decade less than her fifty years, was dressed in simple black with a necklace of black jade. Just after I was seated Thad hurried in, alerted no doubt by her secretary, all grinning and affable, to give me a quick peck on the cheek before returning to a conference.

Natica came straight to the point. I was not to leave any but token bequests to her or her children. They would be well looked after, and I should feel free to leave my estate to my school.

"Clinton has been your real life, Auntie. And my brothers have done all right. They can take care of their families."

"I'm sure they can. And Clinton is very well endowed. I was considering it in that nice office car coming down here. I think I've decided to let the old will stand. Twenty-five thousand to the school and the rest to you. I really shouldn't be taking your time at all, but your lunch offer tempted me."

"Well, we can go now if that's all it is. But I still think you should reconsider. People are going to find it odd that you should so favor the relative who is best off. And what, when you get right down to it, is the point?"

"It's not just a question of who needs the money most. And there's so little of mine, anyway. It's more like a demonstration. I want to show what a big part of my life you've been."

"But, Auntie dear, you and I *know* what we've been to each other!"

"And I want my will to state it. To whom or just why I don't

really know. What difference does it make? You can give it all away
to your nephews and nieces if your children don't need it. I won't
care. There won't be any me *to* care."

"But Thad will object to my giving it to my brothers' children.
He will want me to use anything I have to make up to our boys for
what Mrs. Hill has done for Angelica. Have you heard about that?"

I knew that Angelica Hill, who had recently died, had be-
queathed some shares of a family corporation to her namesake,
and I had assumed that their value was appropriate to what god-
mothers customarily left their godchildren. Natica now corrected
this misapprehension.

"She's left her a million dollars!"

"Oh, no! How wonderful."

"That's not what Thad thinks. Even if we leave Angelica out of
our wills altogether, she'll be ahead of her brothers."

"Anyway, that settles it. You can give my money to your boys.
Not that that will really even things up, but it may help a bit. Why
do you suppose Angelica Hill did it that way?"

"To make up to me for the way her husband treated me."

"But why just to Angelica and not to all your children?"

"Because Angelica's a woman. Or at least she will be."

"Oh, of course. There always was a bond between you and Stephen's mother in that way of thinking. But tell me something, dear.
Don't you think, when all's said and done, that you've done pretty
well for yourself as a woman?"

"Moderately well. Of course, it was only as Thad's wife that I obtained a partnership in this firm. Natica Chauncey would still be
clerking somewhere. I owe more to my feeble sex appeal than I do
to my perhaps less feeble brain."

"But it was you who got Thad out of his old firm! It was you who
turned him from George Haven's Number One Boy into the cap-
tain of his ship."

"I'm not so sure of that. There's always been something inscruta-
ble about Thad. Do you realize I've never been able to alter even
one of his political principles?"

"But do you really want to? It was only Mr. Haven's meanness that made his Toryism so objectionable. Thad accepts the universe so cheerfully! I find a certain charm in his right wing views. They never affect his humanity."

"That's perfectly true. I only mention his views to show you how hard he is to influence. Perhaps he knew, when he left Haven's firm, that the old man was about through. He died only two years later."

"But he left that old man to get you, my dear!"

"And if he did, wasn't that my poor old sex appeal? Oh, don't look so grave, Auntie. I'm not complaining. I'm very happy things turned out as they did. All I'm saying is that what I am and what I've accomplished is more owing to Thad than to myself."

"Well, I suppose we can only cope with the times and conditions into which we are born. But it seems to me you can call yourself a success quite aside from what I regard as your very considerable sex appeal. You profited by your experience with your first two husbands to make your third a very happy man. You were able to put together a useful professional life and combine it with the successful raising of three fine children. You succeeded in remaining friends with Stephen's wonderful mother under circumstances that would have baffled most women, and look what a great result has come of it!"

"Oh, Auntie, stop! Do you realize what you have just described? A monster!"

I rose at this. "Maybe I should have been more of a monster myself. But enough of this. How about that very good lunch?"

I knew I had to change the subject. I knew I had to get out of that room. I decided that I would, contrary to my usual habit in the middle of the day, have a cocktail with my meal. For I had suddenly realized that I hadn't meant what I had said about being more of a monster. I hadn't meant it at all. Whatever my life had been, however constant its anticlimaxes, I could live without the memory of Tommy Barnes at the bottom of the sea and Stephen Hill lying in a grove with a hole in the middle of his pale brow. Maybe it was worth it to have been an old maid. At least in my time.

C.1

F
AUC
Auchincloss, Louis.

The lady of
situations

$20.95